THE
SPECTACULAR
SEA

7 Sea Stories

GREGORY L. KINNEY

DEDICATED TO:

My father, Daniel Dean Kinney, sailor in the United States Navy, a commodore of Westlake Village, champion sailboat racer, and artist of the sea. He had four sons and many grandchildren. 1933-2007

My father-in-law, James Joseph Chmelik, retired United States Marine, retired business manager of the Smithsonian Institution, and golfer. He had six sons, a daughter, and many, many grandchildren. 1930-2020

THE SPECTACULAR SEA 7 SEA STORIES

Includes:
Seashell Jars (Flash fiction)
Hidden Cove Lighthouse (Short story)
Captain Monty's Submarine (Short story)
Lailamindi the Mermaid (Short story)
Pirate Skull (Short story)
Lost Treasure Island (Novelette)
Dinghy to Supertanker (Novella)

ISBN-10: 1674948166 **ISBN-13 (EAN-13):** 978-1674948164
Paperback ASIN: 1674948166 **Kindle eBook ASIN:** B083S5BJCS

HOT SAND
P U B L I S H I N G

Lake Forest, California

Cover:
Painting by author's mother, Marjorie Kinney. Please visit www.marjoriekinney.com

ORDERING AND CONTACT INFORMATION

Available through amazon.com/books in:
USA, United Kingdom, Germany, France, Spain,
Italy, Japan, Canada, Netherlands, Mexico, Australia, Brazil, and
India.

Order inquiries for those in countries not listed above, please contact HOT SAND PUBLISHING:

hotsandpublishing@gmail.com

Regarding wholesale orders for shops, stores, retail chains, event and convention planners, travel agencies, cruise ships, airlines, etc., please go to the website:

www.hotsandpublishing.net

This book may be purchased in bulk, therefore discounted, for business, conferences, fundraising, educational, or sales/promotional use. For comments or questions regarding ordering any number of books, or any other matters, please email us at:

hotsandpublishing@gmail.com

Please give a review! If you, the reader, would like to give a rating and maybe even a review (that can be a few words or a detailed analysis) then here are three website suggestions:
1. amazon.com/books
2. www.hotsandpublishing.net
3. goodreads.com

Thank you and it's greatly appreciated in advance!

CONTENTS

The Seven Stories Briefly - Shortest to Longest 8

Introduction 9

The Seven Stories:

LOST TREASURE ISLAND

Chapters:
1. Art Matlock's Story of Fred Willow 16
2. Art's Story of *his* Adventures with Fred 31
3. Now it was *My* Turn 33
4. Big Sailing Yacht Encounter 45
5. A Speck in the South Pacific 51
6. Beyond 55

CAPTAIN MONTY'S SUBMARINE 60

HIDDEN COVE LIGHTHOUSE 91

SEASHELL JARS 109

DINGHY TO SUPERTANKER

Chapters:
1. The Escape 112
2. Tranquility 122
3. Whale With Wheels and Then Some 128
4. The Wind is Good to Sails and Kites 138
5. Going Down Under... and Still Under 142
6. Desert Soul 160
7. Out of the Dark, Into the Brilliant 171
8. A Pilgrimage 182
9. Work 192
10. From Within the Heart 201
11. Alone Again 224
12. Beautiful Balance 230
13. One Never Knows What Happens Next 239
14. Peaceful is the Pacific... Not Always 249
15. Rite of Passage? 271

LAILAMINDI THE MERMAID 286

PIRATE SKULL 299

Miscellaneous Section:

Quotes from Favorite Authors 321

Favorite Maritime Music 324

About the Author 327

Food for Thought by the Author 331

Conclusion 333

THE SEVEN STORIES BRIEFLY,
SHORTEST TO LONGEST

Seashell Jars: Family fun going to the tide pools. Time period: Current. (Flash fiction)

Lailamindi the Mermaid: A young man enjoys his adventurous activities and his own secret cove, when on one outing he's stunned to observe from afar what appears to be a lady in a mermaid costume. Time period: Late 1970s and beyond. (Short story)

Hidden Cove Lighthouse: A pretty widow and her engaging young daughter meet a man who's in the process of demolishing a dilapidated and condemned lighthouse. Time period: 1968. (Short story)

Pirate Skull: An old man tells the tale of his pirate adventures in the Caribbean, starting when he was eighteen. Time period: 1722 and beyond. (Short story)

Captain Monty's Submarine: An eccentric inventor along with his engineering friend and business partner, design and manufacture a submarine for the primary purpose of pleasure excursions. Time period: 1862 to 1910. (Short story)

Lost Treasure Island: An old man finds a young man to help him recover gold that was buried on an island decades ago. Time period: 1967 to 2019. (Novelette)

Dinghy to Supertanker: A 12-year old runaway attempts to circumnavigate the world and make it back in time for the release of his parents from prison. Time period: 2013 to 2019. (Novella)

INTRODUCTION

This intro is actually a personal history that mostly reveals my experiences revolving around the ocean--and how I came about writing this book.
--G.L.K.

B efore I was old enough to remember the details, my parents sailed with me and my three brothers along the coast of Southern California and to Catalina Island and back--all in a 26-foot Globemaster trimaran.

After my parents sold our home in Inglewood, California, my place of birth, we then moved to Westlake Village, California, when I was almost five years old. I was their third oldest son and we lived there for about three years. Our house was right on the lake in this newly constructed, idyllic community. And, this is where my parents raced sailboats. My father was elected commodore of the Westlake Yacht Club. My second oldest brother raced in the sailing dinghy division. All three of them regularly got first place. With all this enthusiastic interest, we also went to various regattas at marinas on the California coast. So, during this period in my childhood, I was on and around boats a lot. On a side note, many years later, that same brother won a skateboard marathon contest two years in a row which made it as an entry in the Guinness Book of World Records.

Fast forwarding my life, in high school when my family moved to Dana Point, California, I met some friends that lived on a 46-foot ketch--a fine sailing yacht! We would sail around on it once or twice a month and even go up to Newport Beach and back in a day. Still later, while I attended San Diego State University, studying Journalism and Film, we sailed that same yacht to Coronado Island in San Diego, where we got stuck on a sandbank for a few hours very close to the Coronado bridge. I could still hear their father and all of our collective voices of humor and merriment as we tried to figure out what to do next. It turned out that no matter how hard we tried to put our minds together, we couldn't wiggle the vessel off the sandbank or somehow "trick" the tide into rising for us, even long enough for us to hit the engine!

Still fast forwarding in time, three of my friends and I, on our own custom-made surf trip, hired an old Mexican fisherman to take us in his large metallic rowboat with motor to Islas de Todos Santos in Baja California. We had some good, adventurous experiences on the island. On the way back, we would have gotten lost in the fog and maybe even run over by a ship, but for our "captain" who happened to have his portable Global Positioning System (GPS), which unfortunately was out of batteries. Well, I just so happened to have the needed four double A's in my camera. His GPS came back to life and we got back safely. (I have been on many other adventures with these pals.)

I have been on many other motorboats and sail-boats and the bottom line is this: I have always been very fond of the sea. Body surfing, surfing, snorkeling, scuba diving, swimming, walking or running on its beaches, checking out tide pools, exploring rocky areas and caves—all have been favorite activities of mine my whole life.

I would like to just rattle off a sampling of some random memories that spring to mind, that are not in chronological order; the first four memories were with my one-year younger brother: diving off a twenty-foot rock and swimming while on the island of Capri, Italy; paddling on a surfboard to Isla de Venados from Mazatlan, Mexico; surfing in Waikiki, Hawaii; scuba diving north of there at a small, unpopular beach; surfing big waves at Salt Creek Beach, Dana Point; scuba diving with my wife in the Bahamas on our honeymoon; having crab in Maryland and then driving several days up the coast to have lobster in Maine; taking a tour boat to visit peaceful Orcas Island, Washington, then moving on to energetic and beautiful Victoria, Canada; while in Sweden, seeing the *Vasa*, a warship that sank on the outset of its maiden voyage in 1628 and was raised in 1961; taking outrigger canoeing classes in Dana Point where we eventually headed out to sea; doing many other activities around the Ocean Institute in Dana Point, such as hiking to the sea cave; going on several hiking trips with my kids on Catalina Island--that same brother that was the sailing dinghy champion so many years ago, flew us there in his twin engine plane; staying overnight with my wife on the Queen Mary and doing all of its tours; walking the entire Orange County, California coastline with my wife and our six kids, from south San Clemente to north Long Beach; swimming the Aquathon in Laguna Beach just a few years ago; and countless times of miscellaneous beach outings by myself, with family, and with friends.

Once again fast forwarding, my wife and I had arranged to go on our first cruise ship for our thirtieth wedding anniversary in May 2019. It was time to leave the kids at home, which we seldom ever did unless we were just going out for dinner. How many kids? Five of them still at home! Our firstborn, a girl, got married years ago and, at the time, was expecting a fourth child! Anyway, when you have that many kids it's very easy to get sidetracked with lots of details; so, to steer back on course... back to the cruise-ship plans!

Well, there wasn't too much to planning since we were just going to do the San Pedro, California, to Catalina Island, to Ensenada, Mexico, and back. Three days of luxury and relaxation. Nice! Especially since I was captain of an ice hockey team, I regularly trained hard throughout the year, and found the trip a welcoming excuse to just take a break.

So, what was I going to bring to read on the cruise ship? I had been reading a lot of Louis L'Amour, both his novels and short stories. I always loved his style and I always liked the convenience of short stories;

however, I really didn't want to read westerns on a sea trip--not that *all* his books and stories are westerns. Really, it was time for something oceanic... something with the maritime ingredients.

So, I went to the library and thought about all of my favorite books that had something to do with the sea that I had already read, including, but not limited to: *Billy Budd* and *Moby Dick* by Herman Melville; *Ben-Hur* by Lew Wallace; *Goodbye Darkness* by William Manchester; *Adrift* by Steven Callahan; *Dove* by Derek Gill and Robin Lee Graham; *Jonathan Livingston Seagull* by Richard Bach; *Treasure Island* by Robert Louis Stevenson; *Escape from Rat-Race* by Carl M. Heinz Wiebach, *Dana Point Harbor/Capistrano Bay: Home Port for Romance,* by Doris I. Walker; *The Old Man and the Sea* by Ernest Hemingway; *The Sea Wolf* by Jack London: and these three by Mark Twain: *The Innocents Abroad*, *Roughing It* (his visit to the Sandwich Islands), and *Following the Equator*. There are a few other solid favorites that I mention in my novella, *Dinghy to Supertanker*.

By the way, I would recommend reading the Mark Twain biographical book, *Chasing the Last Laugh* by Richard Zacks, before reading *Following the Equator*. It fully details what was happening behind-the-scenes during what Mark Twain chronicles in his well-detailed travel book, giving it an even richer and deeper perspective. I found it to be more informing, dramatic, and inspirational, than comedic; though, the elements of humor were not lost. It's an amazing study and made me profoundly appreciate all that

Mark Twain went through during this difficult period in his life--while much of it at sea!

As long as I've mentioned books, I might as well mention some of my favorite sea movies (which might also serve as movie ideas to get one further into the sea spirit):

Captain Blood, Jaws, Ben-Hur, The Spy Who Loved Me, Captains Courageous, Swiss Family Robinson, Castaway, Kon-Tiki, Big Wednesday, The Endless Summer, Billy Budd, Midway, Flags of our Fathers, The Poseidon Adventure, Step Into Liquid, Master and Commander, Mutiny on the Bounty, The Guns of Navarone, The Finest Hours, 47 Meters Below, Soul Surfer, King Kong (2005 version), The Perfect Storm, Run Silent Run Deep, Hunt for Red October, The Sea Hawk, and The Caine Mutiny. I'm sure I missed a few, but that list should suffice!

But I've digressed; anyway, I looked high and low in that library and couldn't find the sort of thing I was looking for. Why, for example, couldn't I find a book of short stories that had to do with the sea? I liked variety! I would have liked to find some adventurous or light-hearted, fun stuff. It would have been fine to find something inspirational or suspenseful or historical or dramatic. Actually, I wanted it all!

Eventually I settled on a large non-fiction book that was all about the ocean. It had pictures, photos, history, science and every kind of subject matter on the ocean. So, I have to say that I did very much enjoy that book on the cruise! Here it is: *Oceans: A Visual Guide*, by Stephen Hutchinson and Lawrence E. Hawkins. I had also brought along a book on chess, since our ten-year-old son (at the time) and I are big on that. I taught him since he was *three* and now, he beats *me*!

To wrap things up, the seed had been planted! Sometime in the summer of 2019, I started writing the collection of these stories. I finished them in December after spending hours daily in my garage hideout and after many readings to family members over the months. My wife, Rosemarie, who graduated same year with me at Johns Hopkins University (JHU), was my chief editor in this project--as she had been with all my screenplays. My mother, Marjorie Kinney, also helped a great deal in the reading and editing process of these stories. So, many thanks to the two of them!

Anyway, I hope you enjoy the stories!

--Greg Kinney

LOST TREASURE ISLAND

CHAPTER 1

ART MATLOCK'S STORY OF FRED WILLOW

Going to the library that rainy August day, 2018, I had no idea that a case of boredom would turn into an adventurous endeavor that would last for the next few months. I say this, actually now write this on my laptop, while on my deathbed. Currently, it's one o'clock in the afternoon as I punch out the following story on the keyboard:

It was a whirlwind ride to be sure, when you consider how one thing might lead to another, and then seem to spin out of control. Though, oddly, I always seemed to be in control when I just took the one-day-at-a time, one-moment-at-a time approach. For even in the sketchiest parts of this story, I had an underlying sense that I'd break through to the other side, whatever that other side was. The next step perhaps?

Looking back at my life's experiences, for example, if I found myself skiing on a steep slope, losing control, and suddenly falling and flailing; then, if that inner instinct told me that I was going to come out of it okay, and then I did—well, there it was. I had survived it one more time. The next step would be putting my skis back on, brushing off the snow, and heading back down the mountain like nothing had happened.

I have experienced all sorts of occurrences like this. Indeed, I have had close calls, big falls, and have gotten into all sorts of accidents--be it while backpacking, rock climbing, surfing, mountain biking, etc. What can I say? I just love the outdoors and the groove of feeling good.

I owe this love of adventure to my two older sisters who excelled at outdoor sports. My 27-year-old sister, for example, has summited seven mountains over 10,000 feet in elevation and three over 15,000 feet. My 25-year old sister was with her on half of those and continues to be a competitive surfer and mountain biker. She often wins her events or finds herself in the top three. Speaking of three, I did go up the three highest mountains in Southern California with both of my sisters. On each occasion we pitched a tent somewhere near the top for an overnight stay.

On the first outing with my sisters, when I was 15, I got lost when I wandered away from the tent without a flashlight just past dusk. While lost I then managed to fall off a twenty-five foot cliff onto a ledge! I sprained my ankle, got scraped up bad, and yelled for help for half an hour. To quickly summarize what happened next, my sisters rescued me with one thin nylon rope, flashlights, and a lot of sweat and guts. They will always be my heroines.

So, now on to the story that I aim to tell. Strange as it may be how it all unfolded. One moment I was sitting on my living room couch, a Saturday, no plans, wondering what to do next, the next moment I was off to the library where adventure awaited me. Adventure? At the library!

I was a 23-year-old, two years of community college under my belt and enjoying the last days of summer vacation, standing in the non-fiction section, looking at books on World War II. I've always liked history. And I've always liked war history. I wasn't necessarily in the mood for yet another history lesson, but still, I have always been drawn to the guts and the glory. Especially of days gone by. Wow, did I just say that? Aren't all days gone by? Even yesterday? Indeed... and that's history.

An elderly man in a nice-looking suit and tie, who was also looking at the books on the shelves, gradually made his way over to me. He then just looked at me curiously and said, "Nice rainy weather we're having."

"Yes, I like the smell of the ground as the rain first starts up." Why I said that, I don't know, since it had been raining all night and all morning. Just a spontaneous thought said out loud, which was typical for me.

Before you knew it, we broke into this conversation about how his seventy-fifth birthday was a week ago, how he exercises and takes vitamins and supplements, and why he wears a suit on many regular days--that it doesn't have to be some sort of special day.

"When I die, I want to be remembered as someone who was sharp in both mind and spirit," the old man said.

He invited me to have coffee and a bite to eat with him--a café was next door. So, there we sat in a booth tucked in the farthest corner of the large café and conversed. He slowly ate away at his fruit plate and I was still waiting for my croissant and scrambled eggs.

We got along very well. I told him that I had recently, well, three months ago broke up with a girlfriend and that I was aiming toward traveling around the U.S. and spending the rest of my money just checking out different states and doing my outdoor activities. He wanted to know how I earned my money. I told him that I was a bartender for the last couple of years. I made it a point to keep my tip money to save it for this planned year of travel. He was astounded that I could afford to do it on tip money. I told him I was going to ride my bike and "tent-it" at campgrounds. I am not one to spend a lot of money. "It's not that I'm cheap," I told him, "I just don't have a lot of money to waste."

That's when his eyes bugged out. I never saw anything like it. Then he started to choke on a chunk of honeydew. Without hesitation, I had to give him the Heimlich maneuver. I quickly scooted him over, stood him up, got behind him, and thrust my forearm in an upward motion at his abdomen, which successfully caused him to send that juicy projectile sliding across the white tile floor. When it came to a rest at the foot of the waitress, she picked it up with a fork and tossed it in the trashcan, fork and all. She made that "disgusting" look.

The whole incident caused a small stir in the café followed by applause. I waved it off and the old man, Art Matlock, I learned early in the course of our conversation, regained his composure, straightened his tie, apologized and thanked me in the same breath, and immediately proceeded to tell me a story as if nothing had just happened.

As he commenced, he explained that everything he was about to say, was all true and really happened. He even threw in as a hint, that it involved treasure. Just when he said that, again, his eyes began to bug out, so I started to get up, but he sternly told me to sit down, which I did. It turned out, something stirred him in this manner about the story he was about to tell. The fact that he had a chunk of honeydew in his throat the first time must've been some sort of strange coincidence regarding the bugging out of his eyes. Because at this point, I quickly came to realize that he was embarking on telling quite the tale. He spoke a bit like a pirate as he told it. He even looked like a pirate in his facial expressions, though he was in a suit and tie with a clean-cut beard.

I will refrain from mentioning all my little interjections, but the following was the story that old man Art Matlock proceeded to tell; it really turned out to be the story within my story:

"I was 24. The year was 1967. A friend of mine took a plane to Tahiti, thinking he could make some sort of big splash there with his business. Ah yes, the South Pacific Ocean. Very nice, right? His business was exotic goods and jewelry, but it never really got off the ground whatsoever. Fred Willow was his name. He was two years older than me and divorced.

When he got back after a half-year at sea, he woke me up in the middle of the night. I came to my apartment door after throwing on my pants just past midnight. Surprised, and after a brief exchange of words, I invited him in. Well, Fred, who had left a fairly heavyset man, was now looking skinny. He was all wild eyed and told me about all he had just been through. And he told me that he just got off a cargo ship and had to walk five miles to get to my place. He said he practically got mugged but didn't want to get into the details of that because it was nothing compared to his ordeal at sea. He had no luggage. He looked like hell. And he smelled like rotten fish.

Then Fred tells me, 'Art, it's all there, some 240 bars of solid gold—with no identification on them. They're just plain gold. I saw it with my own eyes, we counted it, we took it to an uninhabited island, buried it, I helped bury it with my bare hands, two feet under, it's there! And nobody knows of its location except me and now you!'"

"Nice," I said with now *my* eyes sort of bugging out and taking a sip of my coffee.

Art continued with the part of his story that was

actually Fred's story: "So, I fixed us some tea and Fred kept rambling on with the details. Fred had taken a plane to Tahiti primarily with the mission to do some selling. After the second day there, he sold ten pieces of amber to a jewelry maker, who then gave Fred what he called a hot lead. He told Fred to charter a boat and to go see a rich man by the name of Howard Witch, who lived on an isolated island, which was one of many that comprised an atoll, less than a hundred miles away. Turned out to be more like two hundred miles away and it cost him the amount he sold his amber for. All he had left was six dollars and his brief-case.

When Fred arrived, he walked across the beach to what looked like a sprawling deluxe hut, with smaller huts around it. At the gated entrance, there were two armed guards and a few nice-looking island women walking around the premises. Fred had been told by the jeweler to give the guards the password, "para-dise." He nervously did just that and they let him through. After a brief exchange of words, Howard Witch just shook Fred's hand, and said, 'Okay, let's see your stinking jewels.' So, Fred opened his cus-tom-made briefcase full of gems and jewelry, many in pouches but others displayed on hooks. But before he could go over the details of each piece, this Mr. Witch abruptly told Fred not to waste his time."

"Rude dude," I said. The waitress put a plate in front of me. My scrambled eggs and jalapeño cheese crois-sant had finally arrived. Then she darted off without saying a word. Not the best service, I thought.

Art continued: "Then Fred explained that while Mr. Witch had no interest in his items, he saw that Fred had an earnest look in his eye and commented on it. The man thought he could trust Fred. So, Mr. Witch asked Fred to transport a cargo box to Honolulu, Hawaii. All he needed to do was to get the box there, not ask any questions, and he would be given three hundred dollars cash. All was to be provided for--a 40-foot sailing yacht and a crew of three--traditional islanders that lived on Tahiti. It was to be supplied with plenty of rations, water, and a revolver, in case there were any run-ins with modern-day pirates.

Right after Fred agreed to do it, Mr. Witch said, 'The boat has orange sails and there will be those with binoculars on you the moment you appear on their horizon as you approach Oahu. Don't even consider *not* delivering the box... or my army of men will hunt you down and kill you.' Fred then told him he had nothing to worry about. So, Mr. Witch walked over to him flashing a hundred dollars in cash before Fred's eyes, and put it in the palm of his hand, saying that *that* was an advance, and that there would be the other three hundred when he delivered the cargo box, making it a total of four hundred.'"

"I bet that was a lot of money back then," I said with a smile, then taking a bite out of my croissant.

Art continued, "Fred wasn't a very experienced sailor and was surprised to see that there wasn't an outboard motor. But he went ahead and set sail for Hawaii with the crew of three skinny, but fit-looking Tahitian islanders. There was no way Fred could have refused the deal. He really needed the cash and not only that, Hawaii was one big step closer to getting back to California."

"I would have been curious about what was in that cargo box," I said.

"You bet," Art said.

Art took a big swig from his cooled-down coffee and continued with Fred's story: "Fred and the Tahitians, who were experienced sailors, were eight days at sea. It was smooth sailing, but the crew was increasingly uneasy, you see. Only one of them appeared to have navigational skills, using a compass, sextant, and one topographical map. His name was Petangowano. He was also the only one who could halfway speak English. The other two only spoke Tahitian and some French. Fred couldn't remember *their* names. Anyway, Fred deciphered from Petangowano after a two-hour conversation that Howard Witch was a wanted criminal for several murders and all sorts of theft.

Petangowano said he himself even witnessed one of the killings, while he spied from behind a rock. A man was fishing all alone on a rocky part of the coast on Tahiti in broad daylight. That's when Mr. Witch struck up a conversation with him, then pulled out his pistol and shot him in the side just as a wave crashed on the rocks. He gently laid the man down, took the wallet out of his back pocket, and walked back to their boat. Petangowano, his boating assistant, joined him shortly after, pretending that everything was normal."

A young couple that had recently sat down at a table next to them in the café looked over. Art glared at them and they got up and walked to another table on the other side of the café. I gave Art an uplifted eyebrow and sort of laughed, partly embarrassed and partly amused by what had just happened.

Art wasn't amused at all and continued with Fred's story: "Petangowano insisted that they break open the cargo box with their knives. He was even curious to see if inside the box was the body of a kidnapped boy! Well, for Fred, being entrusted to do the right thing—like back in his boy scout days--that was the last straw. He had sensed from the beginning that Howard Witch was some sort of con man, while on the other hand, Petangowano spoke with great sincerity and seemed to be good-natured. Well, it took some doing but Fred and the three Tahitians broke into it. There was a wooden chest in it with no lock. They opened it up and saw the gold bars. The Tahitians were impressed but didn't show much amazement. Fred, however, contained all his emotions and felt like he had better hold back his explosion of delight.

A café girl asked if we'd like more coffee. We both said, "Sure," and thanked her.

Art continued with Fred's story: "So, Fred immediately said, let's head for that island right over there. It looked small on the horizon. In the course of the eight days at sea, they had passed several small islands or atolls here and there, some farther off than others. So, the island he pointed to looked like it was less than a day away. Maybe even a half day.

A few hours later, Fred found himself telling the Tahitians exactly what it was, bars of solid gold worth tens of thousands of dollars. It would make them rich and they would split it four ways. Fred was one who despised hearing of how explorers, not all of them, but how many of them, exploited islanders. This was the test for himself, Fred explained to me, to show that he was fair and upright. Petangowano then told Fred that they *knew* what gold was and that it was highly valuable.

Fred got a laugh out of that and then explained to Petangowano that he thought they should bury all of it. Because in the event Howard Witch's men somehow seized their boat, they could explain that the box went overboard in a storm—probably a lame excuse, Fred added, but he couldn't think of anything else, And if they were captured by pirates, they could just give them his briefcase full of gems and jewels. Anyway, after burying the gold, they would sail to the southern point of Oahu, change out the orange sails to white ones, and get back to California. Then they could make plans to get back to the treasure at a later date when nobody was on the lookout for them. Well, Petangowano and the other two liked the idea.

So, Fred and his islander friends approached the beach high tide. They lowered and furled the sails and used two oars to help guide her in. Next, they set anchor about 60 feet out inside the tranquil cove and waded initially chin-high through the water carrying the heavy chest, and buried the treasure, using their bare hands and knives, beneath three palm trees that were clustered together but standing alone on the beach. Many other palm trees, many much taller were lined up and down the beach that curved off sharply about a quarter mile equally on each side."

"Wow, nice. Talk about an island paradise," I said.

"You betcha," Art said, and continued with Fred's story: "After resting on the island for a day, they jumped back in the yacht. The tide was lower and a bit livelier as the wind had picked up to about six knots with sporadic gusts. Getting out in a low tide seemed like an advantage initially but as they got several hundred yards out, they ran into a shallow reef and got stuck for half a day. It turned out to be a big ordeal as there was a lot of effort trying to figure out if the sails were better up or down, constant adjusting of the rigging, using the oars in such a way to reposition the boat, and bailing out water. It was exhausting. Finally, as the tide rose and they were able to break free from the reef, back at sea they discovered a small leak that they had to tend to 'round the clock for the next excruciating thirty days. It was enough to fill up a bucket in about an hour, so they took turns at it. To make matters worse, even after careful rationing, the so-called supply of food ran out after the twenty-fifth day and the water ran out after the twenty-eighth day.

Therefore, the last five days before they made it to Hawaii and their new destination, the southern-most part of Oahu, they went without food. And, the last two days they went without water. They were exhausted, half dead, and dying of starvation and thirst.

Two of the islanders died on the twenty-ninth day. Petangowano and Fred were greatly saddened, but they were also physically and mentally diminished themselves and thought that they were likely next.

They didn't know what to do with the deceased bodies but seemed to think that the going tradition to do in the high seas, was to wrap the bodies up, if possible, and toss them overboard with prayers and good wishes for the afterlife.

So, they grabbed two sheets, carefully rolled the bodies up, said sincere prayers and also thoughtful words about memories they had with them... and then, as hard as it was, pushed them overboard. When they splashed into the salty water and sank, Fred and Petangowano looked at each other sternly, but then for whatever cockeyed reason, couldn't control themselves. They started to laugh... and laugh some more... and still laugh... until they cried... and then they hugged each other... like it was for dear life... because it was! Instinctively, they knew that either one of them, or both, could succumb to the agonizing torture that required an amazing amount of endurance. A torture that no words on paper could describe. One would have to actually be in the moment, a human body living in the actual circumstances, like they were, to understand the suffering.

Petangowano passed out just as Fred, who had a fever and was barely hanging in there himself, docked the yacht at a small fishing village. The friendly locals quickly tended to their needs. However, Petangowano died that evening and was buried the next morning. Fred slept all through the next day. When he woke up and heard of Petangowano's death, he said it was the saddest day of his life. Well, days went by and Fred was befriended by those Hawaiians. He was so grateful that he gave them his briefcase and only kept five of the best gems. About a week later, he managed to get a ride on a cargo ship, using those gems and his hundred-dollar bill as payment, to San Diego, where you and I sit right now."

Old man Art Matlock interrupted the story by going to the restroom, then came back and without small talk or hesitation, told me the conclusion of Fred's story:

"Anyway, Fred explained that on the cargo ship, they were a mean-spirited bunch and had put him in a very small cabin and given him very little to eat and drink. Off the ship, he stumbled into a bar like a bum and passed out. The bouncer gave him some water and two biscuits left on a customer's plate and sent him out. He also gave him a dollar and told him not to come back.

Fred passed out in a park, woke up, didn't know how long he had slept, and walked the five miles to my apartment. Said he just about got mugged but managed to yell for help just as a police car drove around the corner. It scared off his assailants and the cops drove him a mile up the road to my apartment, then dropped him off. It would have been more like six miles, but I always took a mile off for that ride. Anyway! Too many details. Sorry, I get sidetracked!"

Just then, some of the patrons looked over, but then

minded their own business.

"Quite something, Mr. Matlock." I said.

"Quite something? Well that's just the beginning," he said.

"There's more?" I asked.

He then got up and said, "Look, it has stopped raining for some time. Let's take a walk to the town square and I'll tell you the rest." He left a twenty-dollar bill on the table.

"Sure. Why not," I said. After all, it was a very interesting story and I had grown curious about that buried gold.

CHAPTER 2

ART'S STORY OF *HIS* ADVENTURES WITH FRED

A s we walked, the old man, Art, then explained how he and Fred in thirty-five years searched on four different occasions, looking for that island. Each journey was an adventure all its own. Each journey was epic I might add, but they never found the island. The only thing they found was trouble, near-death experiences, a lot of joy in between, but in the end, tragedy. Fred died of dehydration on their last voyage. They had always sailed on a yacht around 40 feet in length, and that was to be the last time. On their last trip in 1995, they ran out of water on their way back and it took four more days to get to California—Marina Del Rey that time. He died on the way to the hospital. "I couldn't believe my best friend left me," Art said as tears welled up in his eyes and he got choked up.

"That was all amazing, and sad, to hear. Truly," I said. "I'm very sorry to hear about Fred… and those poor three Tahitians that died, now so many, many years ago."

"Indeed," Art said as he cleared his throat.

"That's the sort of thing I would like to have done," I said.

"Well," Art said as he put his hand on my shoulder and looked sincerely into my eyes, "I still have enough life in me, my boy."

"It's Mark. Funny, I never told you my name. I'm Mark Hanover." We shook hands.

CHAPTER 3

NOW IT WAS *MY* TURN

So, before we knew it, I was sitting on a 42-foot sailing yacht, a ketch, with my newfound friend, this old man, Art Matlock, except now he wasn't in suit and tie. He was well dressed for nautical life. And so was I. It was late mid-September and we were heading out to sea. By late evening, San Diego's skyline was very distant, and we were entering the dark void of the Pacific Ocean at night. This was a very peaceful moment.

On second thought, it should've been a peaceful moment, but I was scared. We had so quickly gotten everything together in the last two weeks. I studied up on seamanship and navigation. We bought and packed all the necessities. We seemed well prepared and excited. But it suddenly dawned on me that I had only sailed briefly two times in my life before and I had about as little experience as a person could have.

How I suddenly found myself in the middle of the ocean, at night, and moving deeper into all of it... well, it was terrifying for several moments. I was literally having a mild panic attack. I say "mild" only because I kept my cool, all things considered. But a dizzy spell and fear came over me that really had me repeating in my head to stay calm and not to panic. *Stay calm and don't panic. Stay calm and don't panic.* My sisters had instilled that in me for many years. I was glad that I let them know what my trip plan was. That was another thing they had taught me: Always let others know of your trip plans, even if it's for a day.

I started to sing, "What Shall We Do with The Drunken Sailor." That calmed me down especially when Mr. Matlock joined in.

The advantage of this trip, compared to the first three of the four trips that Mr. Matlock had made with Fred, is that we had autopilot, a modern GPS navigational system, an underwater sonar system that would help detect reefs, a ham radio especially for emergencies, and an outboard motor with several extra containers of diesel. We also brought a hundred gallons of water and three-months' worth of a variety of canned and freeze-dried food. The ketch also had a rubber dinghy set back from the bow and strapped down. It had a small outboard motor, oars, and two small shovels. We also brought lots of clothes for every weather occasion, kept in four large pieces of luggage down in some large storage cabinets in the cabin. This sort of packing arguably was overkill, but we were totally okay with that--definitely better with too much, than not enough.

Art bought his sailing yacht, a very nice ketch, nine years ago and kept it well maintained. He said he had a regular boat maintenance man that charged him fifty dollars a month to keep it all in good order, even though it was properly covered and parked on a trailer in a boat storage parking lot. He had a roomy cab, fit to sleep four, small kitchen and sink, and storage space. The deck was wide for a yacht of that length and it had two masts.

Art Matlock was the accountant for the owner of the parking lot, so they swapped parking for accounting needs. He was a retired Certified Public Accountant but still held onto a handful of clients. He also did well with a few properties and stock investments that "kept him comfortable" as he put it, to live out the rest of his life. He was never married and never had kids. Though, he had three girlfriends in his life that all broke his heart one way or the other. The last one lasted for ten years but she dumped him when he decided to go on that fourth voyage with Fred. He never did tell any of his girlfriends that he was looking for the lost treasure. However, he wanted it to be a surprise for his last girlfriend, but it wasn't in her heart to wait for him to get back. She left a note saying that she moved to Montana and that it was nice knowing him. She had no regrets but needed to move on.

Five days out at sea, smooth sailing, Art explained to me that before he had gone on that first trip with Fred, he had hired a private investigator to see who this Howard Witch was and if there were any sort of public records of gold stolen by anyone at any time in that part of the world. After two months of researching, the investigator came up with something like this: First, the man known as Howard Witch, one of many aliases, was captured by Tahitian authorities in 1991, tried, convicted of three murders and several other crimes, and sentenced for life. Second, he said that all sorts of things are stolen on the high seas, like anywhere else. So, of course gold had been stolen. Then he wanted specifications as to what gold Art was referring to, but Art thought it was time to pay him for his services thus far and be done.

As far as Art was concerned, the investigator was fishing for more information for himself to get in on the loot. But Art finally concluded that he had done his due diligence and the gold was officially up for grabs. He figured, likely, since Fred said the bars had no identification or markings, that it was black market gold, which is basically gold acquired any which way and then melted into bars that can't be traced to anything. How could an investigator even know the original source or sources? "Heck," Art summed it up by saying to me, "Howard Witch probably stole it from other thieves and so on and so forth. It was time for that gold to get into the hands of honest folks. Folks like you and me!" We got a good laugh out of *that*.

Ten days out at sea, in the middle of the night, we were bumped by a whale. We mostly kept the engine off and relied on the wind and current. The engine was off every night and had only been used initially getting out of the harbor and two other times when we were in the doldrums. No wind whatsoever. That night the engine indeed was turned off and the sails and the seas were calm. We were doing around eight knots. Suddenly, in our own separate bunks, we felt and heard the big bump as it dumped the two of us onto the floor. The boat nearly capsized as we tried to get to our feet and grab onto anything. I flipped on the light switch. As the boat uprighted itself, half spinning, I could barely make out the body of the leviathan as it plunged downward. I think it was a humpback, but it was so dark, I couldn't tell you for sure.

We inspected the boat with flashlight and lantern and noticed that the bowsprit was somewhat knocked ajar and part of the railing was tweaked. But there didn't appear to be any leaks or serious damage. To think, we had just been grazed by a whale! At dawn I did what I could with our toolkit and after two hours it seemed to be looking decent again. Took some bending, banging, and screwing down. It appeared, fortunately, that the whale only skimmed the bow. Had it been anywhere else, it could have ripped off our rudder or our tiller or just out-and-out sank us.

"Could-a killed us, that whale," I reflected.

"You know, Mark, I live like every time I go to bed at night, it's my deathbed. It helps me to think about what I've done and what I haven't. What I've lost and what I've gained. Then, I wake up in the morning and it feels like I've been given another chance to do all the things I wanted to do. Even if it's as simple as feeding the birds that day or volunteering at the soup kitchen. Not much adventure in *those* activities... but guess what? It works. Life has its own way of balancing it-self out, if you let it."

After he said all that, that really got me reflect-ing. I couldn't get over the message: Being on your deathbed, and then getting that second chance to get out and make the best of your day. Imagine, you're on your deathbed, then you're *not* on your deathbed? And that becomes your daily philosophy? Huh, okay, that's something I could roll with.

And speaking of that, the days continued to roll on by. I had long gotten over my fear of being at sea. Instead, I pondered at the rolling of the waves, enjoyed the dolphins that occasionally swam about, noticed all sorts of fish jumping out of the water--a few big ones. But neither Art nor I cared for fishing. We had nothing against it, it just wasn't our inter-est. We brought plenty of food. We did bring one big fishing pole with a very small tackle box only in case we really needed it. There was the constant handling of the sails and rigging, just trying to maximize the wind and roll of the waves. Occasionally, I took it off auto pilot and manned the helm. Into the third hour of doing it myself, I suddenly felt the great joy, maybe for the first time, of being a sailor. Yes, maybe I was new to it. But it felt like I knew what I was doing. And being at the wheel, I was the helmsman. Nice.

It felt a little bit like surfing, in its own way. Once you get it, you feel like you're a part of the energy—the board, the motion of the waves, the salty air against your body and face, the wind, and how you choose at any given moment to interact with all of it. There are times when you have to duck under a crashing wave or get to it in a nick of time just to quickly pivot around, paddle hard, and take off. Then it's the carving and gliding and embracing that immense volume of sea water as it curls and peels and hurls you forward, either to the right or left of the breaking crest.

Being the sailor on a boat is sorta-kinda the same thing. It's just a totally different sensation and interaction. Once you start to get the hang of it though, there's a new sense of control and confidence that makes it all-the-more a part of your bodily workings —the physical and the mental.

Art thought it a necessity to bring guns and ammunition since on two of his trips, Fred and he ran into high-seas trouble, call it piracy or just bad guys. On the fourth trip, they did bring guns and ammunition, since on their third trip, when they could have really used them, they learned their lesson the hard way and were overtaken by pirates and taken captive for three weeks. They managed a narrow, harrowing escape, but that's another story. Indeed, the guns did come in handy on that fourth trip of theirs and Art swears it absolutely saved their lives.

But I told Art not to worry about it. We had a great hiding spot for the gold--that's if we ever found it. The place to stash it was a hidden storage compartment tucked in a far corner of the cabin under a latched-down cabinet. This was custom built by a handyman Art had hired for the task, since he had hoped to go back to the island many years ago, but just didn't find the right sailing partner or opportunity to go, until he met up with me. With me? A shipmate? Who was I trying to kid.

In the end, I won the argument, two days before our trip. He had the guns and ammunition ready to go —all bought, paid for, and registered--but I wouldn't have it. To me it sounded like a magnet for trouble. I felt like if we were to run into any bad guys, that we could manage to outrun or outsmart them. When I had asked why not first take a plane to the nearest island and then charter a boat, he just snorted back at me, "You, why you... new youth! You just don't get it don't you!"

I dropped the subject and decided that taking a boat was just the right sort of thing for an outdoorsman like me. I was a little worried of the no-turning-back factor, but hey, I had rock climbed a few tough routes on Tahquitz in Idyllwild. Could the old man do *that*?

Twenty-six days into our trip, the wind was whispering along calmly. Art said aloud and reverently, "Our boat is but a tiny twig, oh God, on your mighty ocean."

"Do you believe in God?" I asked.

His eyes pierced into mine and then after a short moment of silence, he said, "Of course." That sent a shiver up my spine and for the first time in a long time I felt the presence of God.

We then saw a seabird for the first time since the day after we parted San Diego. It was a seagull.

"Land," Art said with eyebrows raised. "We must be getting close to an island or islands."

Sure enough, on the GPS, we were starting to head

into the Marquesas Islands. Our coordinates were precisely aimed at a remote island somewhere between those islands and the ones of the Tuamotu Archipelago—two island groups among the ones of the French Polynesia.

Art said that after scouring dozens of islands over the first three trips and then into the fourth one, that Fred Willow continued to think they had at last found the right one. However, each "right one" turned out to not be the right one. Sometimes they had to circle the island or atoll to discover that it didn't match the description. Fred thought if they could just capture the island at the right angle, he could be certain of its identification. For the same island looks a little different depending on which direction you happen to be looking at it. Also, the time of day, position of the sun in the sky, and weather, were all factors that could dramatically change the look of an island. What really burned Fred up was when Art would accidentally utter the phrase every now and then, "It's like finding a needle in a haystack."

After about the fifth time in thirty years with his sailing partner, Art slipped up and uttered that sentence yet again; that's when Fred grabbed him by the collar and flat-out screamed in his face, "Torch that cliché! Or I'll torch you!"

Art *never* used that tired expression again.

"Old Man Art," as I started to call him and he seemed to like it, gradually and sporadically--since we had so many days out at sea--came out with more details of the story. How on their fourth trip Fred swore that they had finally discovered the island. It was lost no more! He had never looked so ecstatic! He feverishly explained that it looked exactly as he described it, since day one. From a distance it looked like an aircraft carrier, mostly flat, but with some smallish hills standing up in the middle of it. There was no way he was wrong this time, because it was the exact angle and everything. There was even the tiny island off the tail end of it, about a mile away from the north end, that made it look like an exclamation point. Fred and Art were some fifteen miles away when he spotted it. It looked exactly as it did when he first pointed it out to the islanders. Even Art found that his heart was beating like a drum. Art's eyes really bulged out when he described this part of the story. I guess the thought of getting your hands on the treasure can do that to a man.

Art continued with the final details, explaining that this was the one trip, again their fourth one, that not only did they have autopilot, but GPS. They quickly jotted down the coordinates in their sailing log. The island, the "lost" island was now officially targeted.

Unfortunately, within two hours they were cut off by a squall and night set in. It was one of the worst storms they had endured during their trips. By morning, their GPS was no longer working as it had taken in too much saltwater—so much for waterproof technology in the 90s. They had lost their bearings and were thankful that they didn't run onto a reef like they had two trips prior. They felt rattled, disheveled, worn out from struggling all night to keep the boat from capsizing, and ironically, they felt seasick, even though they had spent months at sea.

Their rations were low, their water supply was also getting low and Fred, of all adventurous types, had to get back to a big meeting in Los Angeles in two months. He had become a marketing guru for a moderate-sized firm. Anyway, they were forced to head back. They were exhausted. They were disappointed and downtrodden. And 58 days later they sailed into Marina del Rey. Art Matlock was barely hanging in there, but Fred didn't make it. That's when he died on the way to the hospital. Mr. Matlock put his head on his friend's chest and wept. And he wept and wept some more. Two days later he woke up in a hospital bed. He couldn't believe his long-time, sailing-adventure buddy was gone.

And, he pondered for hours in that hospital bed how the mission once again had failed. Maybe the gold would be lost forever.

But, then again, he had the coordinates of the island in the log. The island that Fred Willow absolutely, positively said that it was "it!" "The real it!" "The only it!" Fred had gone on and on and on. In fact, in the middle of the night, in a dream, halfway back to the mainland, without our gold, he suddenly sprang from his bed and cried out, "It's it!"

And that's the very two-word expression that stuck with Art like a light-bulb memory.

So, all these many years later, when Old Man Art and I saw that seagull, and as we saw that we were entering the waters of the Marquesas Islands, we knew that if Art's coordinates were correct, we could be arriving at the lost island within ten days. The GPS, gauging our speed predicted nine days. The excitement was almost unbearable.

CHAPTER 4

BIG SAILING YACHT ENCOUNTER

About a half hour before dusk, we were having a can of chili mixed with tuna fish and green beans. We seemed to like to just mix it altogether. It was a time saver and most of the time we didn't even bother to heat up our random mixtures since each can had pre-cooked or ready-to-eat contents. Occasionally, over the weeks we saw a distant oil tanker or ship. On less occasions we saw a distant sail or two. But on this evening, we saw a distant island and a large sailboat with sails that looked reddish brown.

As the "sailboat" got closer to us, I could see through binoculars, several people on her deck. This was one big sailing yacht, perhaps a hundred feet long. Maybe more. "Wow," I whispered aloud, "what a beauty." I put down the binoculars and looked at Art who was also staring at her.

He said, "Why is it headed our way, is what I'd like to know."

I started to wave my arms and yelled, "Hello! Ahoy there!"

"Put down your arms and be quiet you incredible idiot," he said glaring at me. "Are you mad! They might think we're in distress when you do that!"

"Just trying to be friendly," I said.

"And that's another thing," he said. "We have no idea if they're friends or foes. Besides, the more we mind our own business, the better."

"Sorry, Art."

"And now... here they come, right for us." Art lamented.

Much to our chagrin, they came alongside our boat, despite our efforts to wave it away. Over a megaphone, when they had been approaching some two hundred feet from behind, they demanded that we take down our sails and come to a halt, which reluctantly we did. There was one of them, a very tan white guy, at the helm, in his 40s who looked like some sort of maniac with an assault rifle slung around his shoulder. He had facial hair that made him look like a lion—big hair and big beard. Turns out he was the one with the megaphone. They lowered their sails too and managed to draw in our boat with ropes that had metal grappling hooks--one they threw near our bow and the other one near our stern. These ropes were each managed by a Polynesian man, one in his 20s, the other in his 30s. A beautiful Polynesian girl, 20s, just stood and watched. She stood somewhat close to the maniac with the gun.

Soon after a big, baldheaded, shirtless black man jumped aboard our boat.

The two boats were rolling with the waves and

clunking up against each other. The lapping of the waves and clanking of the rigging of both boats made a lot of noise. Ours looked dwarfed compared to theirs. Art kept complaining and now especially to the black man that his boat's rails were getting damaged and that they were not welcome. The black man then spoke in broken English.

"Stop! You listen me now. They call me Erik. I am from island nation Madagascar. This ship the majesty red sails all mine. We are hijacked. I am here to rob and kill you but is not my real feeling. There is two bullets in this gun. I will shoot under your arms and play you dead, okay?"

The maniac put down the megaphone, starting to lift his assault rifle. With his other hand he held onto the wheel of the yacht. Amidst all the noise of the lapping and clanking, he now yelled out since his position was some sixty or seventy feet away from us. "Hey, what's all the talking over there. I told you to shoot 'em!"

Erik yelled back waving the pistol in the air. "Must I kill boss! They are no harm!"

He raised his assault rifle and aimed it at Erik. "You've got three seconds, dude!"

Erik then aimed his pistol right under my arm pit as I lifted that arm up a little and he fired. I made it like he got me in the heart, covering it with my hands, and fell face down on the deck, motionless. I made sure I wasn't melodramatic about it. In fact, it was the best acting I had ever done. My body and face slammed on the deck. I instinctively knew, that if it looked played out or fake at all, we'd all be dead. Amazingly, Art had enough wherewithal to understand the situation; correction, he knew the situation better than me, and played along with this lifesaving game and fell over near our brass steering wheel, also playing dead.

Then what seemed like an hour but really was probably only fifteen minutes, Erik searched the cabin. He carried and handed over to another black man, in his 20s, who seemed to appear out of nowhere, about 20 gallons of water, which was about one third of our remaining supply, and four out of five of our five-gallon diesel containers. In the middle of this shuffle, while the maniac was eyeing a passing motorboat in the distance, Erik stealthily poured ketchup on Art and then me, telling us each not to move a muscle.

After handing over another gallon of water, Erik yelled, "There is nothing else, boss! Check it yourself! No money, no jewelry, they just traveling for the fun to Tahiti. That's what they say before you kill them for me!"

"Grab his watch!" The maniac yelled. Then Erik took my watch off. I was thankful that it was a cheap one. That further showed that we were not wealthy. The only sad thing about it, is that it was a gift from my best friend in the eighth grade. He died in a car accident two days after attending my birthday party. So, that watch had a lot of sentimental value, but for the moment, all I could think about was somehow surviving the ordeal.

"Did I see him breathing!" yelled the maniac.

Erik whispered loudly to me, "Here coming kick for you." Erik gave me a swift kick in the side. I held it in and didn't flinch but he actual broke a rib. "No boss! He is toast!"

"Well throw them both overboard!"

"They are dead boss!" He lifted me up three feet off the ground revealing my limp body--as I totally loosened up--and blood, the fake blood. But from a distance it must've looked authentic.

The maniac added, "Nice shark food!"

Erik protested, "We need leave before port authority see us, boss! It looking suspicion when two boats are together! You know that! When you set us free for doing your dirty deeds, you give me my boat back you promise me! We need must now go to Argentina! No delay more, man!"

"And leave the evidence behind? That you murdered two innocent men!" The maniac yelled.

"Self-defense. They shooting us! I put gun in his hand!" Erik yelled back, really sweating and starting to bend over to put the gun in my hand. I felt many drops of his sweat on my face just in that instant.

"No! That's my gun!" The maniac cried out. "Okay, let's get outta here!"

And that was that. There we were "left for dead," as they literally sailed off into the horizon. This is one moment in my life that that phrase really and truly took on a meaning. Art insisted that we continue to play dead as one of them would have a telescope or binoculars on us making sure that we didn't make a move. So, we waited and waited, laying very low until they were way off in the distance.

CHAPTER 5

A SPECK IN THE SOUTH PACIFIC

W e hoisted up the sails and were off again. Nine days later, at the crack of dawn, there it was. The so-called lost island! It fit the description! Our GPS and auto pilot had us heading straight for it. We were only ten miles away. It really did look like an aircraft carrier-shaped island. And there was the tiny island to the north of it looking like an exclamation mark.

We kept a sharp eye on the GPS and any indication of reefs. All was looking great. As we got a mile away, I could clearly see the palm trees up and down the beach. As we got closer, I could barely make out the three palms in the middle of the beach clustered together. My heart was dancing. Art's eyes were bulging more and more as we got closer and closer.

I said to Art, "Your eyes are a gold barometer." He smiled and looked on at the approaching island.

There were breakers but they were only a foot high. Conditions couldn't have been better. Blue skies. Very light breeze. The tide was high, and we eased in. We could see reefs about six feet below us. We navigated to a thirty-foot gap in them and sailed cautiously right through. We anchored forty feet from the sand, lowered and furled the sails, and got into our eight-foot rubber dinghy with two oars and very small outboard motor. We rowed it ashore without the motor. We landed!

There wasn't a soul in sight. Just the wonderful nature of the island. A few seabirds flew off in the distance. We grabbed our two small shovels and got onto shore.

"I could just soak this all in for the rest of my life," I said.

"We have no time to lose," Old Man Art said.

"Are you kidding me? We made it! We have nothing but time. Yahooo!" I was so full of energy and life and I don't think I had ever experienced such joy. Then I pointed at the three palm trees only two hundred feet in front of us. "Is that the most beautiful site you've ever seen?"

Art just started walking toward it at a pretty good speed for a guy his age. In moments we were standing at the base of the palm trees, looking straight up. Art, just a little out of breath, then said, "Fred told me they were about thirty feet high. Well, apparently, they've grown."

"Yeah, they look twice that height now," I said.

Art added, "Fred said that they dug the hole in front of the palms—the oceanside being the front. Let's hope we found the right three. They sure fit his story."

"Yeah, right. I guess this is the moment of truth,

hopefully not ugly," I said. Without further hesitation, I started digging. In thirty seconds, I was two feet down and hit what sounded like wood. "Ahh!"

Art started digging too and in about five minutes, mostly from my frantically fast scooping, we had completely uncovered the chest. And there was no lock on it, just the way Fred and his Tahitian friends left it! We opened it up and...

We were blown away. Our eyes widened; our mouths dropped; we screamed; we hugged; we jumped up and down; we ran around the palms; we high-fived; we jumped up and high-fived with both hands; we hugged again; we yelled again; we cried; we laughed; it was the most amazing feeling anyone on the planet had ever experienced. It was beyond amazing, to see all those gold bars; to see them all so neatly stacked, so neatly nestled, so peacefully nestled; it was a masterpiece--the aqua shallows, the white sands, the little sea shells, the swaying palms, our anchored yacht with its sails furled, distant puffs of white clouds, a few dark clouds even farther off, and most of all this old wooden chest! It was fairly-well preserved, quite a bit decayed, quite a bit decomposed, but mostly intact. But upon opening it, oh, those shining bars, those warm bars, those cold bars, those golden, sweet bars. Unbelievable. No, believable. We were there. It was really happening. It was *really* happening. We just discovered a fortune. Especially when you consider how the price of gold had skyrocketed since those times. What times? I did not know and did not care. We found the gold! We got it!

Art insisted that we get the chest on board and not dilly dally. And we did just that. It all went without a hitch.

CHAPTER 6

BEYOND

Now getting back to San Diego? Yeah, oh wow. It was one o'clock in the afternoon when I started writing about my account of all that I'd been through since that day at the library, and now... it's three-thirty in the morning. I've been writing this out as fast as I can with a few short breaks in between. It has taken me longer than I thought it would, because I've gone back and forth, tidying up sentences.

So, since I'm on my "deathbed," referring back to Old Man Art's philosophy, I need to wrap this up! I'm going to write about our sailing trip back to San Diego in one paragraph—sure to be a very condensed, long one:

Old Man Art and I left the island and didn't get stuck on a reef, nice! We did, however, run into another storm. Art said it was the worst one he had ever experienced. For thirteen hours our boat surfed the waves with auto pilot off and me at the helm. These were big, rolling waves. I had to point the boat in the right direction, sort of at an angle like what you would do on a surfboard, or we would capsize for sure. We were deluged with rain non-stop and the wind was wicked at 40-knots with 50-knot gusts. Art accidentally shattered the port cabin window when he tripped, and a ceramic breakfast plate flew out of his hands. A week later, we ran into the red-sailed yacht again, except this time as it pulled beside us, Erik, the very man that cleverly saved our lives, spoke into the megaphone; he said they got rid of the "boss man." We waved back, lowered our sails and spent some time with him and his crew. We were so grateful to him that we gave him five bars of gold; in return, he insisted in giving us a very big pouch of uncut diamonds. We exchanged contact information. I exchanged contact information with the Polynesian young lady. We hit it off, even romantically--held hands and kissed--it was spur of the moment, but we only had about thirty minutes together. It was time to go. Halfway back to San Diego, I decided to jump off the bow into the ocean for a swim when the wind was dead. Art was beside himself and immediately threw the roped life preserver in the water and tied the other end of it onto the stern rail. I grabbed the preserver in the nick of time. Stupidly, I did not account for the current. Art had to assist pulling me in as I swam. Also, when I had jumped in wearing just my bathing suit, my ankle managed to scrape a wing-nut on the rail and really scratched my leg good. I was accustomed to scrapes and bruises over the years and didn't think much of it. However, when I noticed a dorsal fin some twenty feet behind me, that scratch suddenly became a monumental injury in my mind. A bad scratch can make your day... a bad one. I let go of the life preserver and swam with Olympic speed toward the stern of the boat. Just as I got there and lifted myself up, Art assisted and screamed as the shark bit off my three smallest toes on my left foot! He was going for the leg, of course, but that's how fast I was moving. Our first aid kit and rubbing alcohol came in handy but my three toes were gone! From that point forward it was smooth sailing except for a lightning storm that lasted a day which is a bit unusual for the Pacific. It was an exciting, loud, and difficult day. But we slept well that night when it had cleared, though the wind was still up at about 15 knots. Old Man Art accidentally dinged his left eye badly; when he turned around, a wire securing the main mast--the starboard sidestay--had come loose, whipped around in the wind, and got him. We treated it with water and eye ointment. We ran out of water with one and a half days to go. So, we were dying of thirst getting back. One has no idea how bad that feeling is. When you hear about it, it's not at all the same thing as living in the actual situation. When we docked in San Diego, the harbor patrol provided water for us, then proceeded to interrogate us and search our cabin. They even took a dog down there. Art was too weak to bicker. I thought he was going to die, and I got angry at the officers for not getting us to a hospital. I felt like I was barely hanging in there, let alone the old man. The bottom line is, it was a good thing that dog wasn't trained to smell out gold. I think they're generally trained to smell out drugs, gunpowder, and greenbacks. We didn't have any of that. Since we weren't the tidiest of men, the dog must've run into remnants of old dried tuna bits and what not. Also, before we had stashed the chest away in the secret compartment, we had scrubbed it with the same detergent and oils we used to maintain the deck and the cabin on the journey. We then let it dry out for four days on the sunny deck, hidden behind the sidewall, then stowed it away in Art's secret compartment. We did all of this in anticipation for such a search. Fred and Art had been through half a dozen of them on their trips, three with dogs. Wow, it sure paid off to be with a wise old man of the sea.

So, I'm going to leave it at that. It's now four o'clock in the morning and I'm hammering out these last sentences of the story. I'm dead tired--no pun intended. It's almost time to close my laptop on this.

But here are my final thoughts: We've been back for a month now, from our successful treasure hunt, and I've got to give the old man a call first thing in the morning. Sadly, Art did lose his left eye and now wears a patch over it. Aargh, he looks better than ever if you ask me. We're meeting at a dive bar tomorrow night to discuss what our next step is. That chest is in a big safe at his house. He spent a thousand dollars on that safe at the time he bought the boat. It has his guns, ammunition, and will in it. That gold, surely, as agreed, is fifty-fifty ours.

I think I'm going to have to tell Art when I meet with him that I've got to take a break for a while. I'm going to go on that bike ride around America for the next year. I have been in touch with my sisters and they might want to join me. Anyway, when I get back from the bike trip, Art and I can discuss the plans with what to do with our fortune. In the meantime, if he wants to spend any of his share on whatever, he can go for it. I've already told my sisters that they're each getting three of the gold bars from my portion.

I sure wish I had my three toes back, but a therapist has got me doing some balancing exercises and I'm going to consider prosthetic toes or custom shoes or whatever. It's all no worries.

You know, Art's deathbed philosophy ain't bad. In a nutshell, you act as if the next day will be your last and then make the best of it.

On second thought, when it comes right down to it, a deathbed philosophy? Nah, it just sounds too dismal for me. I'm going to go back to my own philosophy, that is, *living life to the fullest.* We've all heard that before, but it's what works best for me. Maybe there's more to understanding God, too, that I have yet to explore.

Anyway, just thinking about that old wooden chest, with all those gold bars, in Art's safe, well, it makes me feel quite pleased. I'm done. I now close my laptop and go to sleep.

CAPTAIN MONTY'S SUBMARINE

The year was 1901. The Gilded Age had blossomed, and American ingenuity had experienced its all-time high. Or, at least it sure seemed like it. Yet one never knew when new inventions would beget new ones.

I now jot down this information in a journal, summarizing events in my past. Currently it's 1910 and I am sixty-six years old, but I want to write about primarily what took place in 1901 and the two and half years thereafter. I just thought it was about time to put together my thoughts on the matter. My name is Maxtor Star. I sit in a lounge on a pleasure-excursion steamer heading for the countries surrounding the Mediterranean Sea and then finally the Holy Land. I'm retired and thought it would be interesting to try to somewhat follow Mark Twain's journey that he describes in his book, *The Innocents Abroad*. I also thoroughly enjoyed his book, *Following the Equator*, but I just didn't want to go on *that* big of a trip.

So, back to 1901, I was a self-taught engineer, with many years of experience under my belt working for an inventor. His name was Alfred Monty. The two of us both came from Connecticut. I met him when we were fighting for the Union in the Civil War.

So, I suppose I've got to go even further back in time. Both Alfred and I enlisted April 1862 and stuck it out through the end of the war in April 1865. Young men we were, indeed, in our late teens. We were privates fighting under the directives of the various officers under General Grant.

We ran alongside our fellow troops and shot at the enemy, but then would run slower, hang back, and hide behind whatever we could find. We carefully aimed and almost always hit our mark, so we definitely contributed to the effort. After all, it was a matter of "kill or be killed." Anyway, when all the raucous commotion settled, we would mingle back in with our surviving comrades and assist with the injured, which was always a sad and difficult experience.

One time a sergeant had apparently spied on us from behind a large boulder during a bloody and nasty melee. Alfred and I had been caught in the crossfire and both hit the dirt and played dead. There were killed and maimed soldiers every which way you could imagine on both sides like we had never seen before.

During this conflict, a solo confederate soldier charging full speed on foot, with bayonet projecting straight out, got blasted by a cannon ball. It was difficult to make out what happened because it looked like his head was a cloud of smoke, but amazingly he kept running another six strides when the bayonet stuck into a tree--which is where it left him standing. It was the most eerie and horrible sight especially as the cacophony died down and the smoke cleared.

By the looks of it our side won that battle, confused as it was, once again, and when we eventually stood up, the sergeant also stood up on the boulder twenty feet behind us and told us in no uncertain terms that we were to be court martialed for our cowardice. Apparently, he figured out that Alfred and I had been playing dead. Then three shots rang out from off to the side. The sergeant standing on the boulder grabbed with both hands at his peppered torso and fell head over heels, landing with a big thud flat on his back.

A dozen of our fellow Yankees quickly chased down the three confederates, who had shot the sergeant, and killed them. In the meantime, Alfred and I went to the aid of the sergeant. We started to apply pressure to his wounds, but to no avail, and he passed away.

In the days to come, from that point forward, Alfred and I found ourselves advancing upon the rebels on the front line. If they started to retreat, we wouldn't hesitate to lead the charge with wild-eyed, do-or-die madness.

Several weeks later, when the war came to an end, Alfred Monty and I, best friends, found an apartment in New London, Connecticut, and soon realized that one thing we had in common was having a great and sensational time, attending as many celebration parties as we could. During the calm hours of the week we also realized we had another common interest, that of the subject of scientific study, particularly in the areas of mechanical engineering and invention. My interest was weighted more on the former, his on the latter.

Now, before I move on to what had happened next, I should mention that Alfred, before the war, had an increasingly depressed and lonely uncle, Uncle Matt, who lived in Hartford, Connecticut, and who had made a fortune in stocks. His wife had died of a mysterious disease in 1859. That same year, Alfred's parents died in a disastrous river boat accident. So, that was definitely a sad and tragic year for not only his uncle, but also for both Alfred and his older sister, Alice.

But that wasn't the end of it; near the beginning of the war, March of 1862, Uncle Matt's three sons—Alfred's cousins—were killed in battle fighting for the Union!

That's when Alfred and Alice moved in with Uncle Matt in December of 1862. They did what they could to make the best of things and actually had cheered up their uncle so much, that it turned out to be Alfred's most memorable Christmas.

Four months later, Alfred enlisted to fight for the Union. And that's when I met him. We were assigned to the same company and we hit it off when he bit off the end of a cigar and, instead of spitting it out, he chewed on it and accidentally swallowed it, which I found hilarious. I never laughed so hard in my life.

So, now getting back to the end of the war, Alfred got the news that his uncle died of bad lung complications just days after the war had ended. He and his sister, Alice, were greatly saddened to hear of his death. They attended his funeral and, afterward, both agreed that he was now in a better place in heaven with his wife.

As for Alfred and his sister, Alice, according to their good uncle's will, they were given the inheritance!

After it took two years for Alfred and Alice to fairly split up the fortune—in a very cooperative and loving way--Alice sold the mansion and moved to Maine. They kept in touch by mail two or three times a year. Indeed, they always continued to love each other very much.

Anyway, it's clear to see that Alfred didn't need to get a job--not for the next three hundred years. He was very nice just to give me enough money "to stay out of work and out of trouble," as he would put it. "Best friends," he stated on several occasions, "should always look out for each other."

We went to many libraries and just studied and studied. We enjoyed it. We studied all week and enjoyed the Union celebration parties on the weekend. They did go on and on in our particular district and when they finally petered out some months later, we continued to find parties to go to through our network of friends. Birthday parties, holidays, weddings, christening of ships, championship contests, you name it--even funerals could get festive.

Anyway, after six years of this lifestyle, we founded a new company, Monty's Firefly Company. The reason for the name was this: Alfred Monty had the bigger ego of the two of us; in fact, I had none. Alfred wanted the company to be all about inventions. He thought the firefly was God's greatest invention so that's where that part of the name came from.

Alfred finally had completed his first invention, a mechanical cricket. I assisted in the drawings, the mechanics, the development of the parts, and a bunch of other technicalities. Alfred paid me a good salary for this. He wanted me to keep all his inventions top secret, the only exception is if he were to die. Then, I could go ahead and do what I wanted with them or go public, because I would own all the rights. I made the same deal with him in the event I were to die. We put this in writing because we just wanted to make sure that a will and a trust would be properly handled. It wasn't at all because we didn't trust each other. His sister, Alice, and I were to get ninety percent of his assets and monetary wealth and the church would get the remaining ten percent. I put in my will the same thing except substituted my name for his name. I didn't really have much of anything since it all came from Alfred, but anyway, it was just a formality.

As I jot all of this down as notes for a biography of my best friend, I cannot help but to see ahead of the chronology of events, which I presently refrain from mentioning. When I went out on deck to get a breath of fresh air, I puffed on my pipe, enjoyed looking at a passing ship with three masts and full sails, some two miles away, and went back to the lounge to resume writing.

I want to keep this simple for now. I, Max Star, want

to reveal to the world this most unusually fascinating and terrific person that I have been writing of, none other than Alfred Monty. He was a great man of kindness, invention, and knowing how to have a good time—to be shared by all. If one ever had the chance to meet him, one would immediately know what I'm describing. He had an infectious optimism, friendliness, quick wit, and just a general overall savviness like no other. He also had a mustache that he kept slick with an oil and his hair was combed straight back and was shoulder length—all shiny black that made his intense dark brown eyes stand out more. When he got into his fifties, the color of his hair and mustache changed to silver.

Our next invention, the mechanical cricket, was a success in terms of form and function. It had all the gears in it not unlike a fine-tuned watch. The tricky part that took us two years to complete was getting the cricket sound just right. The completed project was amazing. The mechanical cricket looked and sounded just like a cricket, and, amazingly, it jumped like a cricket!

Only Alfred and I knew of this invention. We celebrated for a month on this invention alone. We invited friends to our apartment hall. They had no idea what they were celebrating other than we just told all of them to come over for a good time.

Oh, yes, I almost forgot to mention it; when Alfred had secured his inheritance, we had moved to the fifth floor of a narrow six-story brick building. Alfred lived on the south end; I lived on the north end. Our doors were almost across from each other. This was an unusual layout in terms of architecture. Each floor had only two apartments, so it really felt like you had the floor to yourself; though, the floor was shared by one other tenant, who in this case happened to be my best friend, Alfred.

We invited all sorts of friends: friends from our battlefront days, friends we met at the library, friends we met at celebration parties, friends we met at the town square, friends we met in the stairwell, friends we met at the zoo, the grocery store, the pond, the docks, the ice cream shop, the bar, you name it, we met new friends. Our parties were the liveliest ones to be sure.

And women, oh you bet--the loveliest and most vivacious and sophisticated on the planet. Some were untouchable in terms of their talent or intelligence or creativity or gracefulness or beauty inside and out. These were the women that were going to have a great influence on the world—in ways we couldn't even imagine!

So, while some of these fine ladies were untouchable, Alfred and I did occasionally have courtship with them, but somehow the relationships never got too far. For example, one of Alfred's lady friends must have been the finest flautist on the planet. She didn't work out, though, because Alfred refused to shave off his mustache as she fervently requested. And an example of one of my lady friends is that she literally wouldn't even hold my hand unless I proposed to her. Indeed, that was very proper; however, I moved on.

Fun girl though. She sounded like a seal when she laughed.

The real matter was, frankly, that we told each one of these fine ladies that we had no time for a serious relationship and that we were too busy to ever consider the married or family life. Alfred and I agreed with each other that it might take an act of Congress if we were to ever leave this scientific and bachelor lifestyle. We had a nice balance. And speaking of that, we also went to church once or twice a month.

We also enjoyed musicians coming over to our parties. Every kind of ensemble you can imagine frequented them. We only had one rule regarding music: if anyone sang or played out of tune, that was it for that person.

We even designated an "intellectual" bouncer just to remove these individuals from any given ensemble. Musicians and singers, therefore, knew that they had to be well-rehearsed or skilled enough to do it on the fly, because they were only granted one second chance. Beyond that, they were out. They could still attend a party, but just not sing or play an instrument.

We also had a regular bouncer that would get rid of the unwanted, such as those not invited or those who became troublemakers.

But I digress, so what did we do with that mechanical cricket? Nothing. The idea was to come up with six mechanical insects and then sell them by mass volume as a grouping. They could be bought as gifts or curiosities or whatever. The next insect Alfred wanted to develop was the ladybug. We got quite far with it and Alfred really enjoyed painting the thin brass wings red with little black polka dots. The biggest problem we had was getting the wings to flap quick enough to get it off the ground.

Alfred had a mind that wouldn't stop and we went on to many other inventions, which included: an ant trap, where a million or so ants would be lured into a box with an ointment--then the kindhearted person could release them into the wild; a thin, metallic toy disc for throwing that had a protective, hardened rubber edge—unfortunately it would only last for a couple dozen throws before the rubber started to break off; and, a ball that rolled around by itself and bounced at unpredictable intervals.

More importantly we felt we made improvements on underwater diving suits, and we made them in a wide variety of sizes, even for teenagers. What made it a diving *outfit* was that every suit came with the standard copper helmet, with four circular windows and an exhaust valve. The main oxygen supply came from the customary hoses connected to our particularly large, modified, and loud "diving air compressor" that we bolted down on a large dock that we had built. The suits were purposely made with large pockets to create some buoyancy so that when the belt of weights were removed, the diver could potentially rise to the surface and float on his back or swim.

However, because the diver did wear the weights in order to sink, we also developed a terrific adjustable buoyancy valve unlike anything we were aware of. A separate, smaller hose veered off the hose to the helmet and filled a pocket in the suit at the waist. Another valve, at the waist, released the air when turned. It required our team of brilliant engineers dozens of trials and errors to make it work just right. Now, if that design concept was already out there, again, we weren't aware of it.

Anyway, regarding our inventions, the list went on and on. But Alfred, strangely, did not want us to take the time to sell them or mass produce them. He wanted a good bundle of inventions completely developed before he would display them to the world. That way, if any of them failed in the eyes of the public, the other successful ones would more than make up for the deficit. Our company would be assured success with this strategy. Well, that sounded good to me. I wasn't one to question such a mastermind. Anyway, while we tinkered around with our inventions, for nearly three decades, we assisted a variety of manufacturing facilities with engineering and design. Indeed, we were endlessly distracted and sidetracked!

But let us now finally advance to 1901, the Civil War had ended thirty-six years ago, and Alfred Monty and I were now in our mid-fifties. Our greatest project, our biggest project, our costliest project, our most time-consuming twenty-years-in-the-making project was about to get craned into the bay. Our submarine. Eighty feet long! She was a submarine not designated for war, not designated merely for transportation, not one necessarily for scientific research, no, she was specifically designated for enjoyment. Her whole purpose was for us to invite ten of our favorite guests on any given outing and to explore the depths and mysteries of the sea.

We didn't invent the submarine, for there were many predecessors, and even new ones in the making. But what we "invented" was the first *pleasure excursion* submarine. Even Mark Twain had written about being among those on the first pleasure excursion ship. One can read all about it in his book that I've already mentioned before, *The Innocents Abroad*. Well, that struck a chord with us. How about the first pleasure excursion submarine?

The only controversial aspect of our submarine was this: Alfred had hired a spy, nicknamed "Rat," to get all the information on submarines he could. This was the same spy used by our various lieutenants and other officers in the span of our three years in the war. He had gathered so much information on the approaching enemy dozens of times that he may have singlehandedly been the reason why our army companies kept winning.

Anyway, a few submarines came into the public eye within ten years of our own submarine. Some of the "borrowed" technology we used, some we didn't, some we greatly improved upon. Those improvements, in the end, those great and brilliant improvements, never saw the light of day to anybody but us. We were the sole benefactors--in all its complexities--the sole benefactors of its secrets; namely, Alfred Monty, me, and only two other engineers that knew everything we did. We trusted their secrecy;

and frankly, they needed to know every component of the vessel for it to be "bombproof" as they would put it.

Also, all the guests that were to be invited onboard needed to be of the highly trustworthy sort... and agree to secrecy. When it came down to it, in the end, they, the guests, were the only ones that completely enjoyed the sea vessel. We had to do all the years of work to get her to sea, only then to enjoy the fruits of our labor.

I will add this just for the sake of the engineering aspects of the sub: that we did indeed use electricity, primarily utilizing batteries. We also utilized a diesel engine and came up with all sorts of ways of storing its fuel.

One more controversial aspect is that our spy, Rat, had acquired three torpedoes. These were new technology--U.S. Navy torpedoes that he said he paid for with Captain Monty's spy funds. Rat had signed a contract, paid a big sum, and swore that it was a top-secret deal with a certain Lieutenant whose duties included stocking naval ammunition. Anyway, Rat delivered them in cargo boxes on a flatbed truck. He said he burned the contract since it was top secret. We chuckled at that. Captain Monty didn't know what to do with them. Rat said to just modify the sub plans to include torpedo tubes. He had managed to acquire engineering drawings and specifications for such tubes and operating panels. He said they needed some sort of defense against modern-day pirates.

Captain Monty and I were too far into the sub's

manufacturing to even consider such a change. We didn't know what to do with them, the torpedoes, figuring that this "top secret" transaction was likely an illegitimate one. Our spy talked us into just stashing those cargo boxes, torpedoes and all, in the forward compartment area which was located near the head and made for a miscellaneous storage area. We wrapped several blankets around them to keep them hidden. Rat said he would eventually find a use for them but needed time to think about it. Well, those boxes were pretty much forgotten and were left there.

Anyway, Captain Monty dismissed Rat saying kindly to him that he was no longer needed. So, with one last payment, he went on his way. In the days and weeks to come, Captain Monty and I occasionally swayed into pangs of guilt, realizing that using a spy made our submarine one that could never be shared with the world, lest we were to be found out. It all just seemed like merry old fun at the time of hiring a spy, but when the reality of it set in later, it wasn't so fun. So, we decided that this submarine was to be strictly used for our own pleasure and for the pleasure of the guests we would invite.

Alfred Monty had gotten down to his last million. He sold his inventions—not worth much—and sold his two small factories. He held onto the submarine factory and the items inside of it such as a desk, some furniture, a kitchen, and an open area for guests. Indeed, he could now retire. *We* could now retire, except for the running and managing of our submarine. Guests were not to be charged, but instead could donate to help cover operational expenses. We kept a large spittoon near the ladder that served as both the entry and exit. In our tours that would precede each trip, we briefly mentioned that donations could go in there at any time, either anonymously or with a note. As a side note, in the end, we didn't receive funds from that spittoon to cover a hundredth of the expenses, but Captain Monty didn't seem to be bothered by it, so I wasn't either. Well, maybe just a little.

If there were to be any scientific research with the use of our submarine, we felt that it should be of the observation aspect only. We had six large portholes on each side of the sub and a periscope. The latest development of the periscope, for example, was something our spy had acquired. It was so good, that we didn't bother to make a single specification change.

During the lengthy submarine development and manufacturing process, on the side, Alfred Monty continued to work on his underwater diving suit, which of course I assisted on in the technical aspects. We had tested the suits in lake waters for three years. We, Alfred and I, didn't get in the suits; instead, we hired college kids, on summer break, to try them out. Amazingly, the suits were watertight and there were not too many problems with them, except for the aspect of controlled buoyancy. But, we went back to the factory again and again and worked on it. On the last lake outing of this sort, we took a photograph of these students floating on their backs. Finally, we had worked out the kinks!

We ended up manufacturing fifty of these diving

suits and brought just enough of them along on our submarine trips in case of an emergency evacuation. Each passenger would find his or her right size of both suit and helmet. They were then stored in a low-profile bin, located on the deck, secured and latched. The day before every trip, we required that all guests take our course in training for all submarine matters including a tour of the watercraft and the use of these diving outfits. Alfred had me design a system where as many as ten of the diving suits' air hoses could at any time, with the flick of an electric switch, be rolled out from hidden compartments from either or both the port and starboard sides of the deck. Each selected one could be deployed and then manually attached to the diver. Each hose was eighty feet long.

When we had tested all twenty hoses in the sub's semi-dark factory, a week before her being craned into the bay, she looked like a hairy beast. In the test, our fellow engineers and their team of laborers donned the diving outfits, copper helmets and all; then, the air supply, now inside the submarine, but operated by a lever on her thirty-foot long railed deck, was turned on, which created a low rumble. That's when these unearthly, monstrous "bugs" came to life as they walked all around the submarine that rested on heavy braces. It was a creepy sight that gave me nightmares years later.

As a side note, we had considered storing an emergency inflatable rubber boat, but quickly determined that they were prone to leak and fail. Anyway, we chose to focus on improving the development of our underwater diving suits that could even be detached from the oxygen hose and *still* be made buoyant.

Alfred insisted that we paint the sea craft orange with yellow and red highlights. Once it was painted, he named her *Miss Tangerine*, and had the name carefully and professionally painted along her belly. He didn't have to insist to paint her in those colors because I always agreed with him, unless it had to do with a mechanical technicality. Then, he didn't even bother to argue. He completely trusted me and respected my talents in that department.

Well, taking a half step back in time, regarding creating that submarine, it had more technicalities than I could ever have imagined. We had to hire a staff of ten engineers, thirty laborers, and sixteen manufacturing facilities for every little and big item that comprised the submarine.

Anyway, the moment of truth had finally arrived, and our mostly orange-colored submarine was about to be submerged for the first time. Everyone at this point called Alfred "Captain Monty," since he was going to be the one always in charge of that magnificent underwater vessel. Also, everyone involved with the project, signed a document agreeing to keep it all top secret. Though, how we had expected to keep something like that secret when there were so many people involved, and... that it was such a big bright object, was beyond my comprehension.

Amazingly though, during a nearly freezing dawn, a Wednesday in November, 1901, the submarine was hauled by a dozen mules pulling a huge, custom-made wagon. Then a large crane, another custom-made contraption, lifted *Miss Tangerine* and slipped her into an unpopular location of an undisclosed smallish inlet or bay in Connecticut. She was carefully then steered and maneuvered to her designated secret dock. During the two years of her operation, there wasn't a single news item that revealed her. Indeed, she remained a secret, for even the many guests that traveled the depths with her had to sign a document of secrecy. I had no idea so many people could stay mum for so long.

Who knows, maybe going into the next century gave people much more a sense of decency and privacy and honor. Regardless, everyone loved Captain Monty. Nobody would ever consider the thought of betraying such a man. They loved his personality, his hospitality, his genius, and his cordial manner, though, at times, it could be somewhat wild mannered, but that's when celebratory moments would peak and even then, he knew how to maintain his dignity and not step beyond social boundaries.

Miss Tangerine's maiden voyage was to go up to Maine, where Captain Monty and I would visit his sister. We had a crew of six and ten additional seats. However, on this first "test" voyage, we brought along no additional guests. Now, how this submarine managed to go so far is to remain top secret. Even I, who assisted so much in the engineering, have no desire to divulge in her secrets. How she held in so much oxygen, how she propelled us on such a vast, but neatly packaged, volume of fuel, was an engineering wonder. If I had to brag about one accomplishment in my life, this was it, not by a mile, but by a hundred miles.

On that first murky trip, averaging seven knots per hour, we did come across two shipwrecks, saw two humpback whales, and were just mesmerized by all the sights. Those Atlantic waters, oftentimes, were dark and murky and we would go on for many, many miles and just see open water, seaweed, and a variety of fish, usually in schools. The sub's two headlights, which operated off of large-sized batteries, did a fairly decent job. Regardless, at night we always surfaced and then turned down our speed to three knots.

On one night it was so stormy when we surfaced, to our shock we rolled completely over on an enormous wave but managed to stay completely intact. We simply dove and chose to submerge about a hundred feet down to wait out the storm. Indeed, we suffered some bumps and bruises but moments later we—Captain Monty, the crew, and I--had the biggest laugh in our lives. We just found the whole incident hilarious, but one would have had to experience it to understand where I'm coming from.

The next day the weather cleared, and we continued. The submarine had stayed intact from the big roll probably because we had used the finest manufactured materials, the smartest engineers, and insisted on triple-strength measures. The last thing we wanted was to have to deal with leaks.

The visit with Alice was most interesting indeed. She lived in a very small house close to the harbor where we docked. The crew stayed behind.

She was a sweet lady now in her late fifties. Her husband came home at dusk when we had been there for less than an hour. He was tall and handsome and had an abrasive scar that covered the whole left side of his face. Alfred, nor I, had no idea what he had looked like. They had gotten married late in life, five years ago. And Alice wasn't much for words in her letters other than, for example, to say that she had married a wonderful man named, Thomas Cottonwood, which would make her now Alice Cottonwood. Anyway, Alfred and I completely saw past the scar since we were already so used to battle wounds and scars of every kind. We figured out, too, that he had a wooden leg from the knee down.

Alice and Thomas were very conversational while we enjoyed a delicious dinner that Alice had made. Alice's friend, Betsy, was also there and she was a real match for Captain Monty's wit.

Later that evening, Alice confided with her brother, Alfred, and asked that he send her money. He was apoplectic. He couldn't believe that she had already burned through ten million dollars! But that wasn't the case at all, she had given ninety percent of it to her parish and the other ten percent paid for the house, general living expenses, and oh, yes, an "investor" swindled the rest out of her and fled, she thought probably to France, but wasn't sure. Her husband made a decent living as a shoemaker. In fact, they both had very nice shoes on.

Anyway, Alfred her good brother, understood and told her he would send her money, even though his own bank account balance had been greatly reduced-- but he didn't tell her that. Instead, he told her that their mother and father, who had always lived like saints, would be very proud of her. Before departing, they hugged, and cried a little, too.

So, after visiting Captain Monty's sister, refueling, and getting back out to sea, we couldn't help but to think how lucky we were, to feel the crisp salty air, then to go below in *Miss Tangerine* where it was all nice and cozy. The trip back to the secret dock in the unpopular bay in Connecticut went without a problem. Our sub was still as good as new and of course it called for a big celebration back at our primary workshop and factory.

On the second voyage we did invite ten guests. We each brought along a girlfriend and we each picked four more guests. I picked a husband and wife that were real estate tycoons and a nun and a retired English teacher who had recently lost her husband in a train accident. Captain Monty picked a recently married couple who worked together—he the surgeon, she the nurse. The other two were his sister's best friend, Betsy, who took a train down to Connecticut, and his favorite plumber, also a friend, that "could fix a leak by just touching it," as Alfred would put it.

For that trip we went down to Florida and back. On both trips, north and south, we stopped at secretly arranged refueling facilities in Edenton, North Carolina, and Savanna, Georgia. The waters had gotten a bit clearer the farther south we got. We saw the most amazingly graceful octopus, some manta rays, sea turtles, a large eel, dolphins, a shipwreck of an English warship of the seventeenth century—a splendid discovery that was mesmerizing to say the least--and millions of fish as always. Strangely, we still hadn't seen a single shark. Everyone loved the journey. It was full of liveliness, conversation, song, and just good times. Back in Connecticut, we celebrated.

On that trip, Betsy had informed us that Alice's husband, Thomas, had lost his leg and had gotten his facial scar when he ran into a burning gunpowder factory down the street from his shoe shop. A lady and a man were yelling for help from the window on the third floor of a three-story brick building. There were multiple blasts, smoke, and fire, all coming from the first two floors. The firefighters were focused on three other locations of the building when Thomas ran up to the scene and saw the two yelling for help.

He somehow managed to get the two out of the building by breaking down doors, dodging flames, leading them to the rooftop, and going down a ladder bolted to the side of the building. Thomas began his descent when the other two had reached the ground safely. Moments later, an explosion blasted through the brick wall and sent Thomas flying from two-stories up. As Alice said this part of the story, Alfred Monty put his hand over his heart, got all choked up, and said, "A most noble gentleman. My brother-in-law."

When Thomas woke up in the hospital two days later, he was hailed as a hero in the local newspaper. Twenty-seven others had perished that day including six firefighters. Alice met Thomas for the first time at his shoe shop two years after the tragic event. She had a broken heel that needed to be repaired. Three months later they were married.

Moving on to the third voyage, I picked three cousins of mine that had fought for the Confederacy. We had all just decided to move on from the war days. I also picked our top engineer, who was instrumental with our engine components, and his eighteen-year-old daughter, who dreamed about traveling around the world. Captain Monty picked: his dentist; the new bartender next to our factory who was a very witty and upbeat young lad; a wealthy man who owned a steel mill that cranked out the specifications needed for our submarine; and a newlywed couple that he noticed walking out of the church that we usually attended monthly.

Indeed, Captain Monty loved anything random. That's why his guests were always of the most unusual variety and well, that's why my guests were somewhat of a mixed bag, too. New people, new scenery, new explorations. It kept it all very interesting and the guests always greatly appreciated being a part of it all. That third voyage was no exception. We went all the way down to the Bahamas, with the stops along the way and adding one more stop at the recently dredged Port of Miami—there, we almost got stuck on a shoal but managed to pull away from it. Anyway, the shallow waters of the Bahamas had the most spectacular colors and shapes of fish. And sharks, indeed. We saw dozens of them and dozens of varieties. We had to jot down in our journals to make sure that if we ever visited the islands of the Bahamas, that we would *never* swim in those waters.

We also found ourselves in shipwreck heaven. We counted four shipwrecks within eighty nautical miles. At one point the bartender insisted on getting into one of the diving suits, copper helmet and all, connecting it to the oxygen hose, and getting pulled along at about one to two knots. Well, Captain Monty was all for it and we dragged him along underwater for ten of those nautical miles. As we were all amused watching him through the portholes, we eventually noticed a big shark starting to creep up on him. So, without further ado, we reeled him in and got him back onboard.

He was quite dizzy but said it was the most fascinating and adventurous activity beyond his wildest dreams. He was thankful that we got him in quickly when he signaled by tugging three times on the hose, because at that point he described how a large white shark was closing in on him. In return, we said collectively, "We know."

One day I will have to break into my daily journal and relay all the details and conversations and good times of these trips. But for now, I shall jump far ahead in the chronology of events.

Now, to spring ahead, after many wondrous trips in our sub, I'd like to move onto what was our fifteenth pleasure trip in two years and our longest journey without stops along the way. This was to put our greatest secret engineering aspects of the underwater vessel to test. Our chosen guests simply called it an underwater expedition of epic proportions. To make it possible, we had to keep multiple large tanks of auxiliary diesel fuel in the forward compartment. We had decided to go all the way to the Bermuda Islands and back!

There, we explored several of the islands and surrounding waters, discovered a sunken Spanish galleon, but just gazed at it as we had done with other sunken ships on other trips, and headed back. It seemed like a long trip back home even though we sang songs and did whatever we could to keep up the good cheer. As the journey back wore on, however, everyone just got contemplative. It had become a place for quiet and introspection. And peace. Everyone was patiently looking forward to just getting back home and getting back to land.

Except for one thing--we just didn't quite make it.

We got into the middle of our secret harbor, with the shore on each side several hundred yards away. All of us were exhausted but also exhilarated to be back home. We were moving along at six knots, only fifty feet submerged, when we suddenly felt what sounded like our sub's belly getting scratched. And indeed, it was. Not only had we hit a sandbank, but we ran into a discarded anchor that was snagged up against rocks —a fact that was discovered and assessed at a later date. We surfaced and engines were powered off. Upon inspection, in the forward compartment inside the sub, we could see an eight-foot long indentation that was only an inch high. There were no signs of water leakage; however, three vein-like fuel lines ruptured, and diesel was spraying and spurting all over the entire area of the forward compartment. The intense fumes seemed worse than the leakage.

We threw some blankets on the leaks--the blankets that had kept the torpedo cargo boxes hidden--while we yelled for our two chief engineers. Then a guest of Captain Monty's, a banker, stepped out of the head with cigar in mouth, despite that smoking was strictly forbidden on the vessel at any time. Just as we snapped at him to put out the cigar, he tossed it on the ground and lifted his foot to stamp it out--then, boom! There was a big explosion of flames. Captain Monty and I got blown out the open door. The banker must have instantly perished. The bow of the sub was on fire. Then there was another much larger explosion. Emergency measures immediately went underway. We surfaced *Miss Tangerine.* Smoke, fire, pandemonium, and panic from the guests all made for one big chaotic scene.

Captain Monty and I assisted in getting everyone up the ladder and onto the thirty-foot long railed deck. It was late afternoon, but there was still plenty of light outside. Nobody liked the idea of swimming to the distant shore, so we quickly unlatched the low-lying bin containing all of the diving suits and helmets designated specifically for the current passengers and crew. We helped everyone get into their diving outfits, quickly attached the hoses, and then turned on the air supply, which added a rumble to the noise. As everyone jumped into the water and sank below surface, Alfred then helped me with my own diving suit and helmet. There was another explosion that shot the periscope straight up; then, it came straight back down as we covered our heads and it made a big clank sound just two feet behind me. The fire was making the deck hot and as soon as my outfit was ready with helmet secured and hose attached, I wanted to help Captain Monty get into *his* diving suit. But that's when he gave me a swift kick and I hit the water with a big splash.

Immediately, I adjusted the buoyancy valves, floating on my back to observe the burning submarine. My good friend, that I had known for so many years, was jumping up and down yelling for help at a passing fishing boat less than two hundred yards away. It started to come around. At that point, some drifting and burning debris were coming my way, so I adjusted the valves and sank into the water as we had trained everyone to do. The weight belt worked like a charm—sinking was no problem.

Through the glass of my diving helmet, I could see my fellow divers and I could see that the sub started to sink. After several minutes, the oxygen got sporadic, probably due to the system being damaged from the disaster that we were still in the middle of. Therefore, I turned my shut-off valve, detached my hose, and released my belt of weights. I could see the others starting to do the same.

As we cautiously surfaced, a technique we had learned with the training, I got one last look at the submarine underwater; the six portholes revealed the conflagration inside her. It started to tilt away from me and I could read *Miss Tangerine* on her belly that now had a hole near the bow. It was a sight I will never forget. It was surreal to say the least, seeing my fellow sub passengers, in their diving outfits, rise to the surface while the sub was in distress and sinking. And yet, it all happened so quickly. We got to the surface and floated on our backs, mostly since, again, the suits were made to be buoyant when you spread out your body. Breathing with the helmet on was a bit difficult though.

So, with focused effort, I took off my helmet, discarded it, and several times yelled out for my friend, Alfred Monty, but he was nowhere in sight.

When the fishing boat arrived to rescue us, we witnessed the last part of the submarine, the stern, come up at an angle and completely sink. The suits had started to lose some buoyancy and it became more and more difficult to stay afloat, but we were successfully plucked out of the water. Everyone had been saved except for the cigar-smoking banker and... Captain Alfred Monty. We called out for him and looked around, but he was gone. He must've gone down with her. Nobody knew if it was the last blast that killed him or if he had been trapped or if he just chose to go down with the ship in that nautical tradition of the captain going down with her.

Divers the next morning found his body up against the mangled deck rail of the sunken and badly damaged sub. The news of recovering his body saddened me greatly. I couldn't stop thinking how he had drowned and stayed down in the dark cold waters throughout the night, all alone, somehow clinging to our *Miss Tangerine*, once a shared joyous masterpiece, but now wrecked and resting in her watery grave. The whole tragic event was a great sadness indeed.

So, anyway, she was a secret no more as the news of her and her many voyages, full of details and adventurous anecdotes spread like wildfire.

Three days later at Alfred Monty's and the banker's funeral, for the divers had recovered his remains too, there must have been two thousand attendees. It was a solemn event and there wasn't a dry eye. I was stoic all the way through until a little girl violinist, Mary Sweet, who was a passenger on the seventh voyage, played an original song on the violin. That's when I broke down in tears and even now my heart still weeps when I recall the softness and the beauty of the melody.

After the funeral, though, there was much celebrating, because that's the way Alfred would have wanted it.

As for me, Maxtor Star, his best friend, yes, I celebrated, too. A celebration for the memory, the life, and the spirit of Captain Monty.

In his will and trust, as mentioned before, ninety percent of his estate, which had greatly dwindled, went to Alice and her husband, and me. The remaining ten percent went to the church we had attended on quite a regular basis.

That was very generous. We couldn't have been more grateful. Many things happened within the next several years. I bought a rundown one-room cottage on a blufftop overlooking our once-secret bay and fixed it up. I got to know Betsy quite a bit more when she came down to visit her mother who lived in a small town twenty miles away. We fell in love with each other and got married. We invested what little was left of my inheritance--now *our* inheritance--because I shared everything equally with Betsy. We invested in coal mining, oil, and steel stocks. We volunteered for various church needs, fortunately did well in our investments, and now we take this pleasure-excursion ship heading toward those countries that have shores on the Mediterranean Sea.

As I have written this story on and off in the course of three days, indeed, my dear wife now sits next to me on our folding-style deck chairs, while I smoke my pipe and jot down the last words of this story. I can fill it in with all the details later—mostly of all those wonderous underwater journeys--or maybe I can just leave it like it is, where one can fill in the blanks with one's wild imaginations.

We did see for an example what looked like a treasure chest on the sea floor next to that Spanish galleon. For those interested in a clue, it was about a quarter nautical mile northeast off the coast on the northern-most tip of the Bermuda Islands.

I could dish out a dozen more clues regarding a dozen other sightings on our various explorations, but one clue for now should suffice. Besides, I've been trying to figure out if there's any way I could organize an expedition. At my old age, though, it seems a bit too much to ponder... at least for now.

HIDDEN COVE
LIGHTHOUSE

A seven-year-old girl, Lilly, and her mother, Anna Smith, drove down a dirt road in the Fall of '68. Lilly practically begged her mom on this Saturday afternoon to not drive straight home, coming back from Gramma's house, but to take one of several dirt roads that headed toward the Atlantic Ocean. There were no signs in this part of Maine. These dirt roads were not on the map. They were just "question marks," as Lilly would put it.

Lilly was already an artist. She liked to do pencil drawings in her blank tablet daily. She drew sea gulls, beach scenes, flowers, pretty much anything that was in front of her. Indeed, she mostly liked to draw what she could see right before her eyes. This could be an object like a toy or a tree or a building or the entire landscape or seascape. And it could be with or without people and animals in it. She also had an eraser handy to edit her pictures as and when she desired.

This delighted Mrs. Smith to no end. Lilly was her only child and her husband had died in a car accident two years ago. He was driving home from work, swerved around a deer that lunged out in front of his '65 Pontiac GTO--according to a witness—then slid off the road, hit a stout tree, and went through the windshield. Meantime, his wife and daughter had dinner all prepared for him.

As time had passed, Lilly and her mother, moved on with life. They knew that her father would have wanted them to be happy, not sad. So, they made the best of it, though, many times they found themselves in a mood of melancholy and reflection, thinking of all those wonderful years while he was alive.

Driving down that dirt road, Lilly was excited to see what was ahead. What discovery would they make. Her mother was in good spirits, too, and enjoyed the moment for what it was.

"Nothing like a little adventure, eh Lilly?"

"Yeah! Now this is my kind of fun, fun, fun!"

When she drove over some high and low spots in the road, it felt like a roller coaster, especially since neither were wearing seat belts, and it put smiles on their faces. When they each rolled down their windows at the same time, suddenly their hair fluttered wildly around. They "Yahooed," and made other sounds of joy.

After about four miles of driving they saw a lighthouse in the distance. A lighthouse, a bulldozer, and a wrecking ball. The wrecking ball was on the ocean side of the lighthouse and apparently had just made a swing at it, as debris from the upper portion tumbled down.

"What are they doing to that lighthouse!" Lilly

yelled out.

"We'll just have to take a look," her mom said angrily, as she stepped on the accelerator.

She sped up to the scene and slammed on the brakes, dust flying, as her '63 Impala slid sideways to a halt just twenty feet away from the non-moving bulldozer. There was a hefty old man in overalls driving it. Lilly and her mother quickly got out of the car.

"Leave that lighthouse alone!" Mrs. Smith yelled at the bulldozer driver.

"Tell that to him!" He pointed toward the wrecking ball—a crane-like vehicle with the steel ball that swung around in its destructive mission.

The operator of the wrecking ball got out and walked over to Lilly and her mother. He was tall and in his early 30s, like Anna. He was without a doubt very good looking, slim, rugged, a bit disheveled, but only because it looked like he was in the work mode. He wore a somewhat dirty white t-shirt and blue jeans that had some dry grease marks on it.

"Ma'am..." he looked at Anna earnestly.

"What are you doing?" she demanded.

"My job," he said neutrally.

Anna put her foot down, "You're destroying what looks like a historic building. A lighthouse of all things!"

"Ma'am, the county has deemed it hazardous and out of use. Last week, a few teenagers were goofing around and one of them fell from the top and broke both his legs and quite nearly his back. His back will be in a brace for months, the doctors said. And, being the star football player for his high school team, he lost his full scholarship to Yale. So, now his parents are suing the county."

"Well that's ridiculous. The whole thing," Anna protested.

He continued to say, "There's nothing but tragedy and ghost stories that surround it. Six months ago, a man was poking around the place, exploring, and got bitten by a bat with rabies. He died a few weeks later. Five years ago, police chased a convict, who got out of his stolen car and ran into the lighthouse. Apparently, he picked up a discarded gas can and set the wooden staircase on fire, maybe thinking it would be a distraction, but instead he was too afraid to jump from the upper window and burned to death."

"Oh, that's horrible," Lilly said.

"Oh, sorry, ma'am, I shouldn't be scaring her like that."

"I'm not scared," Lilly said. "Mommy has told me other bad stories that happen in history."

"I was a history major in college," Anna said.

Rick continued, "Oh, okay. Fine, well there are multiple other stories of this sordid nature that have occurred here over the years, even decades. One newspaper writer after the latest teenager incident, coined it, 'The Dead Lighthouse,' and it really stuck with the public. So, the county council voted to condemn it. Demolish it. Well, I'm the owner of this wrecking operation. That's my wrecking ball and this is my bulldozer. This is how I make a living."

Then Anna replied, "Well, it's not right."

"Yeah, it's not right!" Lilly added. "I haven't even had a chance to draw it!"

"Draw it?" he asked curiously.

"She likes to draw things," Anna said. "Maybe you can postpone your wrecking operation until you give her a chance to draw it."

"By the way, ma'am, I'm Rick. Rick Rockford," offering his hand to be shaken.

She accepted the handshake. "I'm Anna Smith. My daughter, Lilly. And you don't need to call me, *ma'am,* just Anna will do."

"Pleased to meet the two of you. How old are you, Lilly?"

"Seven. I'll be eight in three months."

"That's nice. Well, I'll tell you what," Rick said. "I can postpone this for two days. I have been given four weeks to get that lighthouse out of here, but I figure I can do the whole thing in three. It'll give me some time to go back to my shop and work on my dump truck. Needs new brake pads, an oil change, and a couple other minor details. I can't haul the debris to the dump without a properly working dump truck, now can I?"

"Do you hear that, honey, he's going to give you two days to draw the lighthouse."

"Oh, thank you," Lilly smiled. "You're nice."

"We can come back here for the next two days. We only live twenty or so miles away," Anna said with a smile.

"Wonderful," Rick said. "Bring your husband out, too, it's an amazing view from the blufftop. You can see the hidden cove."

"My daddy died," Lilly said with a saddened look. "But it's okay. He's in heaven and someday we'll be together again."

Rick then got on a knee and put his hand on her shoulder looking into her eyes earnestly, "I'm sure he's smiling at you from up there even right now." He then looked up at Anna, who had tears in her eyes.

"Sorry to hear that, Anna."

"Thank you," she said softly. "But we're getting by fine now. It was over two years ago."

He then stood up and looked at her beautiful face and her long plain brown dress swaying in the wind. "I guess I ought to wrap it up here and get back to the shop. But it was sure good to meet you two."

"Likewise," Anna said, still with some tears in her eyes.

"You can hug her," Lilly said. "It's okay. I like you."

"Lilly!" Anna looked at her daughter sharply.

Rick looked down, humbly, stepping on a dirt clod. Then, he looked up with a sincere look in his eyes. There wasn't a doubt, that there was magnetism between the two, Anna and Rick. He wasn't sure if it was the right thing to do, but he stepped forward and very slowly put both his arms around her and gave her a good hug. She cried as she looked down at Lilly. Then Lilly joined in and hugged both of them.

The next morning Anna and Lilly were driving down the dirt road again.

"It's too bad he has to go to his shop," Lilly said.

"Well, he's got a job to do. And, you've got a job to

do. Draw that lighthouse."

"I know," Lilly said. "And I want to draw it from different spots. "

"That will give the same subject matter different perspectives," her mother said.

"Well you can call it perspections and I'll call it spots."

"Perspectives," her mother corrected her.

It wasn't long before they pulled right up next to the lighthouse and parked. They got out and stretched. The lighthouse was some four stories tall, wide at the base, and had some squared off sections or rooms at the base of it. The structure overlooked the ocean atop a hundred-foot cliff, set back about twenty feet and fortified with a concrete base and four-foot high walls.

Lilly and her mother stood behind the part of the wall that overlooked the void between themselves and the crashing sea. Sea gulls flew about. Several cormorants sat on a rock outcropping. Three pelicans skimmed the water surface, gracefully gliding over the subtleties of the waves.

"Wow, this is a hidden cove!" Lilly exclaimed.

"A fascinating puzzle piece of our majestic world," her mother added.

It was a bit breezy and Lilly's little drawing pad fluttered until she grabbed it firmly with both hands.

"Maybe we can sit behind that rusty old car over there." Lilly pointed at a completely rusted out car of a bygone era. "It will block the wind, so that I can draw."

"Good idea," her mother agreed.

They walked up to the rusty car and sat down on a big long log perhaps from a tree cut down years ago. There seemed to be a lot of flies around. Taking a look around, Lilly soon discovered that that there was a rat that looked like it had been dead for quite some time in the old rusty car. They decided to move to the other side of the lighthouse. There they just sat on a bare spot in the field of long grass, that waved in the wind. There were some broken shards of glass that they were able to scoot aside with their shoes.

"The place sure is run down, but all in all, it's so pleasant here," Anna said.

"It's such a shame that that lighthouse has to be destroyed," Lilly said.

"I agree with you, Lilly. I certainly agree."

"Well maybe they'll change their minds once they see my drawings," Lilly said.

"How would that change their minds, sweetie?"

"Mommy, I've always told you. That my drawings make people see the beauty in everything," she stated with confidence. Lilly then proceeded to draw.

Later, they found themselves taking a nap in the car. That's when Rick pulled up in his dump truck. The rumbling sound of the diesel engine woke them up. He jumped out of the truck and walked up to the driver's window. "Howdy, Anna," he said with a smile. He wore a clean and ironed button-down shirt, and slacks to match. His black belt matched his black shoes. Altogether, he was one sharp looking young man. Anna looked prettier than ever with a tan-colored plain dress and her hair tied back with a red cloth ribbon. She also wore some makeup this day, unlike yesterday. Not caked on but just right.

"Your dump truck, you fixed it," Anna said.

"Yes. Once I knew I needed to get back to you, I got it all fixed up in a hurry. Normally would have taken me two days."

"That's nice but why did you need to get back to me? Is something wrong?"

He just stood there and smiled. "Nothing's wrong." Lilly sort of crawled over next to her mother and looked through the window.

"Don't you know, mommy, he likes you! And you like him! It's so obvious."

"Now, Lilly," her mother's eyes darted toward her. "Stop that. It's...oh, it's..." She sloppily took her keys out of the ignition and found a place to put them in her purse.

"It's... it's *true*?" Rick smiled. "Is there anything wrong with just simple truth?"

She blushed and just shook her head, then laughed.

Rick laughed. Then Lilly laughed. And they all got a good laugh out of it.

He opened her door like a gentleman and gave her a hand to help her out. He then offered his elbow, which she accepted by putting her arm through it.

"Come on, let's go for a walk," Rick said. "Come on, Lilly."

About two hundred feet north of the lighthouse the dirt trail led them to an old bench atop the bluff. The bench was set back only ten feet and overlooked the rocky, hidden cove with crashing sea waters and a small beach.

"It's beautiful," Anna said. "And you can see the beach from this angle, unlike from the base of the lighthouse."

"I'm going to draw it," Lilly added.

They sat down on the bench and Anna scooted up next to Rick. It was nothing less than natural attraction. Neither one had to say anything. Each knew that they felt good with the other. There was an instinctive trust there. Each one knew that the other was a good person. A warm person. A kind person.

"You know," Rick said. "I don't want to take down that lighthouse. Downstairs, the building part, well, it has an office, two bedrooms, a living room, a bathroom, and a kitchen. It just all needs to be fixed up and taken care of."

Lilly then added, "Sounds like a family could live there. For sure."

"Absolutely sweetheart," Rick said.

"Why don't we go take a peek inside," Anna said.

Rick replied, "You mean to tell me you've been here almost all day and still haven't taken a look inside?"

"Well," Anna said, "maybe we didn't want to become another statistic of bad happenings."

"And so *now* you want to look? Now that I'm here? To protect you perhaps?" Rick asked.

"Well I had no idea it was made to be lived in. Sounds like it could be a good fixer upper. We could hang up Lilly's pictures to ward off any bad spirits—"

"We?" Rick asked.

"We, oh, right, yes, we... me and Lilly, you know—"

Rick giggled, then Lilly, too.

"Of course, the two of you would need to get married first," Lilly suggested.

"Married!" Anna practically screamed. "Now wait a second."

"Come on!" Rick grabbed her hand and they were off walking toward the lighthouse, practically skipping.

When they got close to the entrance, which was now a broken-down door, they tiptoed around some rubbish—broken furniture, trash, and a lot of burnt wood.

Once inside, it had a very big open room with doors to other rooms. There was rubbish, burnt wood, broken glass, broken windows, a few holes in the doors, and the wooden staircase, half burnt, but still intact.

"Well, what do you think?" Rick asked.

"I like it," Anna said.

"Me, too," said Lilly.

Then Rick said, "Hey, you know what I'm in the mood for tonight?"

"What?" Lilly asked with a twinkle in her eye.

"I think it would be fun to make a firepit outside this lighthouse, make a campfire, and roast some hotdogs and marshmallows."

"Yippee, that sounds like fun, fun, fun!" Lilly exclaimed jumping up and down.

And so nighttime came and they found themselves now roasting marshmallows on the end of stiff wires.

"So," Anna started. "Were you ever married, Rick?"

"I thought you'd never ask. But, yes, my wife died shortly after we were married."

"I'm so sorry to hear that," Anna said.

"Sorry to hear that," Lilly repeated.

"Oh, well, thank you. It was about five years ago now," Rick said.

"Can you tell us about it?" Lilly asked.

"Lilly," her mother mildly reprimanded her.

"Yeah, I can tell you about her," Rick said.

"I met her in Las Vegas. You know, that place for gambling. I was on vacation with two buddies. She was a cocktail waitress that kept bringing me luck while I was on the roulette table. I watched my thirty dollars in chips grow to three hundred dollars' worth in thirty minutes. She was a pretty and wild little thing, her name was Emily, and told me if I placed some money on one number, 23, in the next spin, that I would have to marry her. She said she was 23 years old. Well, I was game for it. I figured it was a very small chance but if it landed that could only mean it was meant to be. So, I placed the whole stack of three hundred dollars on that one spot, and when 23 came up, it had to have been the happiest moment in my life. After cashing in that small fortune, I grabbed her by the hand and marched her over to one of those small chapels where they have instant weddings. And it was a splendid and lovely occasion."

Lilly looked a little confused and said, "I don't really understand a lot of that, but it sounded like you got married to a 23-year-old lady the same day you met her?"

"That's right!" Rick smiled.

Lilly then said, "Mommy married her college sweetheart. My daddy. They got married after college."

"She has a good memory," Anna said.

"Well it sounds like your daddy was a fine gentleman and did everything the right way," Rick said sincerely. "Me? I suppose I can make up my mind on things real quick."

"That's okay too. If it's the right decision," Lilly said.

"Wow, you sure are smart for a girl your age. Any age really," Rick said. "Do you mind if I take a look at your drawings?"

She handed him her 50-sheets drawing pad which, as he flipped it, he could see a dozen pencil sketches of the lighthouse. Then he started to look at one more closely. He drew the pad up closer to his eyes, studying the artwork. "Very nice."

"Really?" Lilly asked.

Rick's eyes started to well up. "Your attention to details is amazing. But... it's not just in the details. You have added an element of love to your drawing. There's something magical about it, my sweet little dear." He then put his arm around her and squeezed her shoulder. "You're a brilliant artist. I can see that for sure."

"Thank you," Lilly said. Her eyes welled up, too.

He then turned to the next page and immediately uttered, "Ah, now that just gives a whole new fascinating look to the lighthouse! Your artwork suggests that you have a very intelligent mind."

Her mom then chimed in, "She gets it from her dad. His name was William Tell Franklin Smith. The one and only. He was very logical and word smart. Lilly was three when he died, but she was already talking up a conversation even back then."

"How did your wife, Emily, die?" Lilly asked.

Her mom jumped in, "Sorry Rick—"

"It's okay, Anna. I'm okay with that. It's good to know about one another as we're getting to know one another. I like that. I like it a lot."

"I do too... I really do too," Anna said with her eyes tearing up a little, then she grasped onto his hand and held it.

Rick looked into the bonfire and then, all sitting there, he brought Lilly in closer and kept his arm around her.

"Well," Rick started, "I can't just tell you how she died in a sentence. You see, I'm a long-winded fellow when it comes to explaining things. And there's always a story behind anything.... So, with Emily, we decided to go for a honeymoon cruise to Jamaica. The first day, we were already partying it up at dusk with other honeymooners and guests of the cruise ship. Emily drank too much, you know, got drunk, got stupid drunk, and got me chasing her around the upper deck. Apparently, I was the cat, she was the mouse. It was all good fun, but then when I almost caught up to her, she jumped up as if to sit on the rail. Well, she achieved that but with too much momentum and not enough judgement and flew into a backward summersault down to the sea water some thirty feet below. The ship was cruising at about eight knots and I immediately cried out, 'Woman overboard!' I ran toward the stern of the ship, keeping an eye on her little head bobbing in the water. I kept screaming for help--and noticed that I indeed had caught several passengers' attention--all while stripping down to my underwear, grabbing a life preserver with rope attached, and then jumping in after her. Fortunately, I had played quite a bit of water polo in high school and we even got third place in the state. But now, here I was struggling for dear life to catch up to my drowning newlywed, but the ship just kept cruising on! I had finally caught up to her just as she was sinking. I had to dive five feet under which doesn't sound like a lot, but when you are plum out of breath, it felt like I couldn't have gone any deeper. At surface, while I was gasping for air, she was unconscious. With some struggle, I managed to get her arms, then her head through the hole of the life preserver. Then I positioned her life preserver at her armpits and steadied her. It was all a lot easier said than done. It was exhausting. The cruise ship came to a stop a few hundred yards away. There seemed to be a lot of commotion on board, but it was dark and hard to make out what was going on. Just a few minutes later, a boat was lowered. All the while I was clearing her mouth with my finger, pumping her stomach a few times, then pumping her chest, and giving her mouth-to-mouth resuscitation. It was pretty sloppy since I had to struggle just to stay afloat myself, and again, I can't tell you how exhausting it was. A few minutes later, the boat headed our way. I yelled for help and waved an arm. Even with a spot-light and flashlights, they were having a hard time finding us; they even started heading off at the wrong angle.

"It's all so dreadful," Anna uttered.

"Keep going," Lilly said with sincere intensity but also with a marshmallow in her mouth. "Sorry," she added.

"It's okay," he said as his eyes started to well up just a little. "The life preserver was keeping Emily afloat just fine, but I was practically in a panic just trying to stay afloat myself. And I know the last thing you want to do is panic. I hadn't swum at all in five or six years, and even though I kept in shape by other means, I just didn't have enough swimming strength and en-ergy to deal with the situation. Yet, I *did* deal with it. I was barely hanging in there, barely keeping both of us afloat. Anyway, the cruise-ship emergency boat did find us after about twenty minutes had passed since it had first been lowered. But when they got us on board, the ship's medics tried to revive Emily, but soon after she was pronounced dead." Suddenly, Rick got all choked up and stood up. "I harshly realized at that moment that I didn't save her."

He then picked up a small log and placed it in the fire, just staring. It was quiet for a moment, then he repeated, "I didn't save her." Then, after another mo-ment of silence, except for the subtle crackling of the fire, he yelled up to the stars, "I couldn't save her!"

Anna stood up and grabbed him by the arm with

both her hands, "There wasn't anything else you could do!"

He looked sternly into Anna's eyes, with both their eyes welling up. "I couldn't save her." Then he just sat back down with his head in his knees and his hands on his head and cried. He wept and he cried.

Anna and Lilly continued to sit on each side of him and after a short while, put their arms around him.

After several minutes, when he calmed down and the smoky fire continued to crackle, and... the silhouette of the almighty lighthouse towered over them... little Lilly, with her precious, twinkling eyes, looked into Rick's eyes and said, "It's okay, Mr. Rockford. I love you."

Rick just looked at her with tears in his eyes. Then he looked at Anna. They all had tears in their eyes.

"Well, I told you that I'm a quick-minded individual. And frankly, this is one of those moments in life, when there's no time left to hesitate. And I know what I want... and I think I know what we all want... and that is... I'd like to marry your mother in a church setting where all our friends are invited. And I'm going to tell the county that I aim to buy that lighthouse, fix it up, not destroy it, and make it our home!"

Anna began to pout, but in joyous agreement, nodding her head.

Rick continued, "Are we okay with that plan?"

"Yes!" Lilly cried out. "We love that plan!"

Anna smiled through her tears and they hugged each other—a long, endearing one.

"And save the kiss for the wedding day, okay?" Lilly

added.

"Of course, sweetheart. Of course," Rick said with dignity. "Your mother deserves all things proper. And that's what I aim to provide for her... and for you, too, my sweet little angel."

Lilly then lunged into his arms and the three of them found themselves in that tender, heartfelt, happy, and... adventurous moment... tucked away forever in its own time capsule.

SEASHELL JARS

My sister and I like to collect seashells. I am eleven and she is nine. We love each other a lot. Our mom is very nice to us. She lets us go down to the cove and look around. The tide pools are very interesting.

I almost stepped on a sea urchin. They have long purple spines. Some people say that they sting if you step on them. Some people say they can make your foot swell up or even just kill you. So, I avoid stepping on them. My sister was the one that actually pulled me away and called me stupid right before my foot was about to come down on it. I don't think sea urchins would kill you or else you would see warning signs about it. Maybe I'm wrong, who knows.

But, anyway, our dad always says to use caution and be careful. Not too cautious and not too careful, because you have to enjoy adventures. Adventures now, adventures later in life, and the great adventure of the life hereafter. Not sure about that last part. Not disagreeing, but it's just hard for me to understand. But that's okay.

My sister and I each have two jars of different types of seashells. They are large jam jars, so they are not too big. We just wanted to collect one more jar's worth, each. That would be enough.

We spread our shells, most of them quite small, on an old rug in the garage. Then we marvel at them, and trade them, and tell stories about each one of them. It's all for fun and learning. Mom says we must observe every little thing of nature. God made it all.

We show our friends these shells, too. Sometimes we hide them around the house and make a treasure hunt out of it. We make one shell worth the big prize; the big prize being that my sister and I will go over to their house and do a chore for them, or, that we will invite that friend to the cove with us the next time we go. So far, we have done this game three times and each time we had to go over and do a chore. It was fun though because each mom gave us some sort of nice treat, like a slice of pie with whipped cream on it or a donut.

As we explore the beach, the rocks, and the tide pools at our favorite cove, a cove with dozens of mini tide pools within bigger tide pools, and a gritty beach, and lots of rocks, and a big rocky cliff behind all of it, well, it's all very... very, what's the word... oceanography. Or something like that. We love it all.

When we have filled up our jars with seashells it's time to head back home. I stick my big toe in a sea anemone, not to hurt it, but it's strange when it closes up. Sort of tickles. A big wave crashes up against a nearby rock and I run away getting wet especially when I trip into a deep pool. My sister chases off thirty seagulls on the beach, mom folds up the umbrella, dad closes his book and stands up looking half asleep but happy. It's time to go home.

We always enjoy the walk back, it's only less than a mile. And we will go to our favorite fish 'n chips place. Then to the old-fashioned ice cream shoppe. What great days! Nothing like collecting seashells and putting them in those jam jars. You clean them up under hot soapy water, dry them out, put them back in the jar, spill them on the rug, and when there's nothing else to do, you just gaze at each one of them. They are each marvelous as my sister says. Then, after several months go by, we empty the jars back at the tide pools and start all over.

We also like gazing and talking about our fish in our fish tank, but that's something else.

DINGHY TO SUPERTANKER

CHAPTER 1

THE ESCAPE

I, Philip James Wilburton, had just turned twelve years old and I was a resident of the coastal town of Ventura, California. And... I was making my escape to San Nicolas Island. I was moving along with a breeze at my back in an eight-foot sailing dinghy under partially cloudy skies. The horizon was a blur. This little sailboat was made for kids, like me. Except I wasn't a kid anymore. Not by my estimation at least.

Going back, I was adopted when I was a four-year-old. My biological parents left me. They were drug addicts. That's what I was told by a social worker when I was eight.

So, the ones who I have always considered my parents, were the ones who adopted me. They were nice and all, and very loving to me, and I loved them, but they turned out to be criminals. When I was twelve, just three months before my escape, another social worker told me they were *white-collar* criminals. White-collar criminals, I soon found out, had to do with those who cheated in their business dealings. So, I guess the court and jury determined, through a lengthy trial, that my parents were big-time cheaters and apparently ripped off a lot of people. I guess I was greatly disappointed to find this out--and saddened.

For whatever reason, though, I was a thick-skinned kid. At least that's how my friends described me. Thick skinned like an alligator. I could take bullying; I could take bad news; I could take a hard tumble playing whatever sport or outdoor activity; I could punch back; I could, well, it all doesn't matter, except to say, the thick-skinned description of me really stuck. And, it turned out, I really liked it. So, the bottom line--no pun intended since my dad always spoke about money and the bottom line--I was ready to move on!

I was going to be tough. I was going to be rough. I was going to take on the world. But I was going to do it with a good heart. A good heart? A good *heart*? Really?

Yes, really. A nun had befriended me since I was five. Her name was Sister Nelly. She believed in the Holy Trinity like no one in the history of the world— at least as far as I could ever tell. She instilled in me to always be good. Even if I had to eventually punch back at a bully, even if somebody made fun of my cleft lip, even if I witnessed somebody stealing something, she always advised me how I should handle the situation properly. She emphasized that a true man does all that is right and is not swayed by bad behavior of others. Regarding my cleft lip, also known as a "harelip," it wasn't all that bad since I had a few surgeries to fix it when I was younger.

Anyway, I learned how to sail because of my white-collar criminal parents. I hate to say that because they were always good to me, in all things. So, I will just refer to them as *my parents* as I normally had. They paid for all my sailing-dinghy lessons and dropped me off at the marina regularly. This had gone on for the last three years and there were no plans to stop the routine; however, it did all come to a stop when my parents were busted.

My parents even attended my races. Of the ones I entered, I won two in a row, got third place in four, and didn't place in the other seven. In other words, I became pretty good at sailing and thoroughly enjoyed it. The two wins were two of the best moments of my life.

Even my parents totally enjoyed the evening dinners and celebrations associated with these competitive events. These parties were held at the Yacht Club or a local pizza place or somebody's big house with a big back yard. They enjoyed music, dancing, swapping stories, smoking cigarettes, drinking, gossiping, but most of all laughing. Apparently, they also enjoyed pickpocketing and purse-snatching—just kidding. Their crimes mostly concerned contractual and accounting matters. Anyway, there was always good cheer in the air. Those were amazing late afternoons and nights! Sailing buddies, great eats, trophy ceremonies, games, I can't say enough. If I could only relive those days, I would.

When it comes down to it, there's nothing quite like winning in a big competition. Those moments are pure gold. It's no wonder why in the Olympics, the winners get the gold. And speaking of that, my parents really thought I had exceptional swimming ability and told me repeatedly I could someday win the gold in swimming. I had taken swimming lessons since the moment they adopted me. And, I'd have to admit, I did pretty good at the swim meets. Anyway, I didn't particularly enjoy swimming. To me, it was a lot of hard work and pretty boring... that's when you compare it to sailing. When it came to sport or competition, sailing was my first love. Very kick back, but very intense, too, when you were trying to beat everyone else.

So, why was I making this escape? At such a young age on such a small boat? Well, for starters, my parents were going to prison. I told them I loved them and appreciated all they had done for me. I forgave them and asked that they forgive me for any wrong I had done to them.

I couldn't believe I said that, because I wasn't one to focus on sin. I was one to just focus on being a good kid. Anyway, they hugged me, they cried, and told me that they couldn't wait to hug me again in seven years when they were free again. I cried a lot, too. I never cried so much in my life.

Anyway, my parents were going to prison. During their trial, having a lot of time on my hands, I had managed to read the books, *Two Years Before the Mast*, by Richard Henry Dana; *Robinson Crusoe*, by Daniel Defoe; and *Island of the Blue Dolphins*, by Scott O'Dell. Wow, these books were my cup of tea, and I just wanted to be set free—at sea! And my mom always told me to find my cup of tea in life—whatever it turned out to be. I knew I didn't have the boat or the experience to sail around the world, but I wanted to just "Go for it," anyway.

I had no real complete plan except to first sail to San Nicolas Island. Why San Nicolas? Because that's where the book, *Island of the Blue Dolphins*, took place--on that very island, many, many moons ago. Eventually, that native islander made it to Santa Barbara, which is a beach city just north of Ventura. If she could live on that island, a girl, why couldn't I!

I really wanted to sail off to a much more distant island, than nearby San Nicholas. I wanted to find myself in the tropics, like Robinson Crusoe, or even sail around the world. I even thought about how I just wanted to learn all about boats and about ships, big and small.

Anyway, it was time to take a step in the right direction. Destination: San Nicolas Island, in my 8-foot sailing dinghy--the same one that I had competed in. The little boat was like a buddy to me. So, I set sail and started my escape in the middle of March 2012. I wondered when the social workers or police or coast guard or whoever would figure out that I had left. But anyway, I didn't care. I just needed to be free.

I was thoroughly enjoying the wind at the sail. The sea swelled up and down and the strong breeze wisped through my medium-length brown hair. But the aspect that hit me like one of those lightbulb moments that get impressed permanently in your memory was this: the sensation of the salty water that kept on misting me with the sun on my face as I watched it slowly disappear on the horizon. *That* was such a great pleasure, but I'm sure it partly had to do with the sense of my newfound freedom.

Whenever I have reflected back at that exact moment of time, it always reminds me of a thought I came up with: *Some of the best things in life are just the little things you soak in.*

I was having the time of my life. Porpoises or dolphins, I'm not sure which, started revealing themselves by coming up and ducking down, only showing their dorsal fins. It amazed me that these creatures lived out in the middle of the ocean, and were always there, just doing their thing. *Such a different lifestyle than what I am accustomed to*, I thought. A silly thought to most, I figured, but I was always a deep thinker. And friends or people in general often didn't understand where I was coming from. And that was fine by me. Maybe when it came to thinking, I was like one of those deep-sea divers of a century or so ago with the big underwater suit and copper helmet.

But getting back to my escape, I was out at sea for two days. On the second day there was a marine layer that prevented me from finding San Nicolas Island. I couldn't find *any* island and was getting extremely thirsty and hungry. I started to seriously wonder if I had made a big mistake. It gradually crept up on me that this was no longer a fun-filled adventure, but a scary reality check. I had no navigational knowledge and no instruments whatsoever—not even a compass. If I didn't find an island or get rescued, I would be dead within a day or two—or, however long a skinny kid can survive, now completely without food or water for a day.

Reflecting at the start of my journey: Like a complete and inspired idiot, I brought in a daypack only a camping-style canteen full of tap water, a bag of tortilla chips, and an apple. So, from the moment I had left the dock, I was already close to empty, except that I had had a tuna fish sandwich and glass of orange juice for lunch. But even then, I had left the marina just before dusk. I was so excited about my whole escape plan, that I cared little about bringing much of anything. At the last second, I brought: my passport in a tight-fitting ziplock plastic bag, a coat, and long pants--thinking at the time that I was probably worrying too much. Really, though, I had barely worried at all, and... that was the problem. So, good thing I had that ounce of concern, because in the first half hour into my journey, I put those extra layers of clothes on right away. And yes, I put my long pants over my shorts. Had I not brought those items--I was so, so cold--I would have turned back. Hmm, thinking back, maybe that wouldn't have been a bad thing! But that would have been a different story altogether. And probably, one not of the adventurous sort.

On a side note, I had gotten my passport as a birthday present when I turned 10. My parents and I went to England for a week! And, those were some of the best days of my life!

Anyway, next thing I knew, a thirty-foot sailboat was banging up against my dinghy and a young man was handing me over to another young man. I had passed out for all the obvious reasons. If I were to say *dehydration* was one of the reasons, it would sound so patently obvious, that one would wonder why I would even mention it. But I guess I just did.

These two men, one of them, Steve, 21, the other Mac, 23, brought me back to life within a few hours. Indeed, it didn't take me long to snap out of it. Once I knew I was rescued and out of trouble, I just snapped into shape. I didn't want to come across as a whiner or a wimpy kid or someone who couldn't take an illness--no, that wasn't going to be me. I just accepted that I was rescued, thanked them, and enjoyed learning the new ropes.

New ropes? Of course! This was the biggest boat I had ever sailed on. It was at least three times longer than my dinghy. I was overjoyed with the size of it. The tall sails, two of them, and the solid feeling of the deck and hull were a whole new concept to me, even though I had walked on boats of this size or even bigger while they were docked many times. Docked is one thing… being on the ocean with no land in sight is a whole other sensation. It was also nice to see that they had my dinghy in tow with the sail down of course.

Steve and Mac, best friends, were from Oxnard, California, and kept their boat, that they went in on 50-50, docked at Port Hueneme. Their plan was to sail around Santa Barbara Island and back but finding me changed their plans, which was okay by them, because they said that more than anything, they loved random adventure.

I had told them, sometime after my first hour coming out of my delirium, that I was an escapee. They got a kick out of it and for whatever reason decided not to turn me in. I think they accepted the fact that I would go straight back to some sort of home while my parents were in prison. That didn't sit well with them. They just lived for sailing and taking it to their limits.

An hour after they had picked me up, Steve said to me, "We can take you to San Nicolas, Philip, if you'd like. From where we are now, it's about seven to nine hours away. But, the other islands, Santa Cruz, Santa Barbara, and Anacapa are closer to the mainland. Why go to San Nicolas?"

Mac added, "Besides, there's really nothing there at

San Nicolas. We'd love to explore that island with you, but we didn't come prepared."

I then replied, "Well, that island girl that I told you about, and actually, the two of you said you read the book, too--anyway, *she* sure lived a long time on San Nicolas without anything."

Mac replied, "Again, we can drop you off if that's what you really want. However, after all that you've explained to us, your life story, and particularly about your escape, well, what I think is that you just want to explore the world and to become an accomplished sailor. Isn't that what you really want?"

Steve then added, "And not just rot away on an island with such a sparse population."

"And... you're no island girl," Mac said with a half-smile. We all got a giggle out of that one.

Well, that made me think. And they both just did their thing while I sat there quietly. Steve was at the helm and Mac trimmed the sail while he finessed the thin rope.

Indeed, I thought, they were right; even though, it was hard to stop thinking about how living on an isolated island with a very small population such as San Nicolas really entranced me. Furthermore, I always thought it would be great to have a whole island to yourself—that's if I found a piece of the backside where there was absolutely no one around. It would be magnificent. And peaceful. And beautiful.

But now, faced with Steve's and Mac's comments, it really did make me think. And, as if it were a higher calling, I came to the following conclusion: *I must see the world and become an expert sailor.*

Those exact words, or thoughts, somehow got im-
printed into my skull for I found myself repeating
that sentence in my mind for many years to come.

CHAPTER 2

TRANQUILITY

M y two new-found friends—or I should say, they found *me*, ha-ha--took me to Two Harbors, the small town on Catalina Island. It was called "Two Harbors" because there are indeed two harbors separated only by a narrow passage of land. Nice setup! We came in around the back side, docked, and got out to explore. We walked around the place for a day and spoke with locals and other visitors. I found this little town to be quite cozy and a place like no other. It was so peaceful with the tall trees lining the dirt roads and swaying in the breeze. We were told none of the trees were indigenous. I remember many of them being a variety of palm trees and eucalyptus. I found the latter particularly interesting. They had a tall, grand stature, and were multi-limbed. Their branches and twigs really danced around when there were gusts of wind.

After a second and mostly relaxing day of visiting —at night we slept in the cabin of the boat—it was time for Steve and Mac to head back to Oxnard, California. They offered to take me back to the mainland, but I had made friends with a very old lady, Mrs. Ruthy, who offered me a room if I decided to stay. I had met her when we walked by her house on our first day there at Two Harbors. I commented on her nice rose garden. She was standing by her front door, smiled at me, and waved me over. She was holding a little rusty trowel in one hand and a big weed in the other. Well, it turned out, she needed help pruning her roses and weeding her garden. So, I spent a few hours helping her, and to my delight, she paid me sixty dollars! Wow, I couldn't refuse it because, after all, I had brought no money on my hasty, ill-planned escape!

So, when I saw Steve and Mac off at the dock, I thanked them profusely again for everything, especially for saving my life. They left my dinghy tied at the dock and I went straightway to Mrs. Ruthy's house. She was so happy to see me and invited me in. And what a nice little cottage it was. She had it decorated with trinkets and plates and carvings and paintings that she had collected in her travels around the world. And my small little room was a pure delight. It was decorated with articles of the sea. An old, but well-built window opened to a flagstone patio, a pine tree, and a view of the hills. She also had a middle-aged calico cat named Friskers, which liked to be petted. At bedtime it cuddled up next to me and purred.

Ms. Ruthy said she understood my story and told me *her* education was seeing the world. Both her mother and father were in the U.S. Navy and, as a family, they traveled the seven seas. Her mother also taught her from books and enrolled her in classes whenever she could.

She then went on to explain for about an hour, at least, that she met her husband, Thomas Frank Ruthy, in London. She was 23 and he, a dealer in exotic goods, was 34. "Strapping handsome with the manliest smile," she said.

For whatever reason, they couldn't have children, but they pretty much traveled throughout Europe and the countries of North Africa. "It was part business and part adventure," as she put it. Then, in Morocco, he went driving off toward the hills--saying he'd be back in a week--with some associates who lived there, and he never came back. She said they were on a mission to trade off some pearls for diamonds and furs for tusks.

When her husband didn't come back, she hired a private investigator with what little money she had, to go looking for him. "Well," she said, poking me pretty hard in the chest, "that investigator found out that my husband went on an elephant hunt, and it ended up that he and his party, four in all, got trampled to death. They were buried and I couldn't afford to visit the site. Eventually, I just accepted his passing away." Then she waved her hand and concluded her story by saying, "That was a long, long time ago, and I don't want to bore you any further with ancient history."

After a few weeks, one morning I got up early and hiked to Little Harbor, on the back side of the island, and back. It was a total of about 13 miles, and just a spectacular view of the sea. When I got back late that afternoon, I made friends with a Hawaiian fishing outfit that consisted of five men on an eighty-five foot motor yacht. They helped me carry my dinghy to Mrs. Ruthy's back yard. She was fine with that, because she knew I didn't want to pay another docking fee.

It wasn't before long, they invited me to go along with them to Hawaii! Regarding my story, they only got a laugh out of it while drinking their beer as they were busy gutting a few dozen fish that they had caught that day. One of them, nicknamed, Oahu Jimmy, said, "After the sixth grade, I never went back to school again."

The biggest one of them, who also went by a nickname, Tikimon, replied, "And it's no wonder you're such a stupid goof-off." That got a big laugh out of everyone. Oahu Jimmy just smiled as he held a two-foot long fish and chopped its head off with a sharp machete. It was all good spirits and they continued to joke around while they worked.

Anyway, after living with Mrs. Ruthy for about a month or so, all the while helping her out with landscape and horticulture matters, about a half-acre that surrounded her house, I had made six hundred dollars! And all that with free room and board!

And every day and every night we shared memories and kidded around and conversed and read from books that she kept on a bookshelf. She prepared world-class dishes—breakfast, lunch, and dinner--of the tastiest food. Her pies, cakes, and cookies were the best deserts I ever had. And her gentle gestures and politeness were ever so sweet. I even remember the way her eyebrows perfectly expressed her emotions at any time she spoke... or even didn't speak.

When I said "goodbye" to my dinghy, that was upside down on the left side of the back patio, I sort of played a mellow drumbeat with my hands on its hull. The overhanging eucalyptus leaves swayed with my percussive music.

Then it was time to say "goodbye" to Mrs. Ruthy. At the time of parting, when we both stepped out of her front door, we turned toward each other and hugged, both getting choked up. She then grabbed me by both shoulders, looked me in the eyes, and said, "Now listen here, Philip..."

She paused and gasped for a breath. When she regained her composure, both of us teary, she continued saying in her soft, tender voice, "Go see the world and don't forget to leave a smile everywhere you go."

But... she gave that bit of advice... without a smile. It saddened me to think as I flashbacked how not long ago, she was standing in the same spot with the little rusty trowel in one hand and a big weed in the other, smiling. She was smiling! And now that it was time to leave her, she wasn't smiling anymore. That just broke me up inside.

We hugged one more time, a good long one, both holding back tears, and then I walked away. After every twenty paces or so, I turned and we both kept waving at each other even as I went down the last bend in the dirt road. Seeing her for that last little moment in time was one of the saddest moments in my life.

CHAPTER 3

WHALE WITH WHEELS
AND THEN SOME

However, life did continue to move on, the clock just kept ticking. After leaving Mrs. Ruthy, about a half hour later, I found myself walking up to the docked boat, *Pacific Majesty*. The Hawaiian crew was firing up the engine and starting to untie her. Oahu Jimmy looked at his watch, smiled at me, and gave me a hand aboard—it was a brawny one! That was a lightbulb memory to me. His big, warm hand—and one just chockfull of good vibes. The other men looked at me with thumbs up and smiles, too. "Aloha Catalina!" Tikimon yelled from the bow, adding, "We're off to Hawaii!" Then, there was a sharp and loud "Ding, Ding, Ding" sound from a bell.

Hearing him bellow that out, quickly followed by the sound of the bell, sent a tremendous shiver up my spine. I think it even made the hairs on the top of my head stand up. I knew... yes indeed I knew, adventure was calling.

In the three weeks heading to Hawaii, I learned so much about fishing and navigating and understanding that type of boat. In fact, I was such a quick study, that the Hawaiians put me at the helm at least half the time. They found me to be a reliable "shipmate" as they put it, and indeed I felt like I was. It was a great joy steering that boat up and over the nuances of the ocean swell. I paid attention to all the details they gave me, and I never goofed around—they, on the other hand, were not so serious. But their goofing around was not of a reckless variety. They just liked to have fun while they were "hard at work" as they phrased it, always with a big white-toothed smile, fishing all day.

They also taught me about the boat's instrument panel and how to read it all. They even showed me how to use a hand-held compass and sextant. These centuries-old navigational tools would only be useful in some sort of emergency since the boat already had modern, up-to-date technologies including its own compass and global positioning system that communicated with satellites.

As for the fish they caught, wow, a little bit of everything. Big fish, little fish, and everything in between. They did not use nets, only hooks or lures and bait. When I say small, I mean they threw back anything that was less than two feet long. When I say big, they caught ones as big as swordfish, marlin, a few different kinds of sharks, sea bass, and a whole bunch of other ones. My favorite fish to eat were ahi, yellowfin tuna, mahi mahi, ono, and opakapaka. We also caught two pacific mackerel on the first day and made great fish tacos with them. Anyway, they would cut and chop these fish up this way or that way and pack them in ice down below. I found it all fascinating, but if I had to admit anything about fishing, is that I don't think it would be an interest that I, myself, would pursue. Maybe there was a side of me that felt sorry for those sea creatures when they found themselves on the hook. I don't know. However, the other side of me liked the thrill of the catch, and... I sure did enjoy the fish portions we ate!

The Hawaiians brought along a propane barbeque that was firmly chained down and secured. They were also well supplied with fruits and vegetables, that they also grilled. Of course, I would have to mention that they had plenty of beer. Turns out that they had brought five kegs of it that they had brewed themselves in Hawaii. They called it Tikimon's Pineapple Ale, and all agreed that it was the best for travel at sea. The recipe not only included real pineapple, but also other fruit juices—all grown on their own farm. When I took a sip of it, I thought it was pretty okay.

The hours after dinner were always a lot a fun. Those Hawaiians were outstanding storytellers and they sang all sorts of traditional sea songs. Two of them played ukuleles and the other three played on different island-style drums.

They would give me a basket of other percussive instruments and they taught me that as long as I stayed on the beat, I could pretty much bang or click or jingle to whatever degree. But they also told me that I should always feel out the music—that I should utilize those instruments in a manner that would add character to the overall sound. Well, all this delighted me to no end, because I had never played any sort of musical instrument in my whole life. For the first time, I felt like a real musician--like I truly was a part of the ensemble. Maybe beating with the palms of my hands on the hull of my upside-down dinghy was some sort of sign as to what was ahead of me. Not sure. Anyway, I was very thankful that those Hawaiians almost unceasingly complimented me on my "natural ability" as they would put it. As I learned the melodies, I also started to chime in with the singing. I did have choir experience in the third and fourth grades, so that part wasn't completely foreign to me.

When we got to Waikiki, they sold off their very successful catch of fishes to a fish-market wholesaler. Then, we immediately headed off toward their island home in a gutted-out school bus that was painted gray with these three neat and big letters on the sides of it, "WWW." When I asked if that stood for something, they laughed and Oahu Jimmy, patting his hand on my back, said, "That, young Philip, is the "Whale With Wheels." I found that silly and totally cool! Then I noticed it had other whale features painted on it, eyes, fins, mouth that slightly smiled, etc. When the door opened and we walked up the steps, I could see that it was rather nice because they had left a few padded benches for seating still bolted down, but the rest of the bus was all open for cargo, ice chests, packs, supplies, you name it. Plus, it was all pretty tidy and it looked like it had children's paintings throughout the interior walls. Paintings like rainbows and ships and waves and surfers and pots of gold. So pleasant. So very pleasant it all was.

Arriving at their home, we were greeted by five ladies and ten children of various ages. These were the wives of the five men, that is, of my five Hawaiian friends, and we were greeted with flower leis and smiles. The "home" was an island mansion, but all old-fashioned and just exceptionally nice. It looked like it was part plantation, part tropical hut, part pirate-like, and part 1800's. Now that's a lot of parts but I only describe it that way because I don't know a whole lot about architectural styles. Whatever this was, though, it was pretty much the best. This was all secluded too in the back country.

The ladies and children were both shocked and delighted to see me. But to make a long story short, I spent the next nine months there being home schooled. I loved every minute of it too. They really became family to me, and everyone got along terrifically. I had also become well acquainted with their family friends that lived down the road. The Kims were a husband, wife, and five kids. They had moved from Japan twenty years ago to start a farm on Oahu.

The man of the house, husband and father, Joseph Kim, explained that his father was Japanese, but his mother was Italian, and she came from a family that had one of the largest vineyards in Sicily before her father died of a heart attack. After that, the vineyard was sold off. Anyway, Mr. Kim liked the idea of starting a vineyard in honor of his grandfather; however, it turned out to be a farm of fruits and vegetables since grapes didn't grow well on Oahu. Perhaps a bigger reason for the move was that Mr. Kim fell in love with surfing the waves of Waikiki on his honeymoon. He was literally hooked on surfing at Waikiki, his wife said. And to think, they only had paid twenty dollars for a two-hour surf lesson. Well, they laughed, how that twenty-dollar investment changed their lives. To think, they had lived in Japan their whole lives, then they up and moved to Hawaii—wow!

So, we spent a lot of days on the beach, which was only a half-hour drive away, and it was always with the Kims, too. We just all jumped into the Whale With Wheels, with surfboards, food, towels, and good cheer. I felt like a got pretty good at surfing, especially since Mr. Kim and his 23-year-old son, Francis, were my instructors. And at Waikiki, it was all about the long board. The waves broke very far out and were slow and powerful. But, compared to other waves in other locations, they were a slow-moving powerful force. The waves didn't abruptly break or crash aggressively. When they got big on some days, however, they could get pretty fast and scary looking. And the whitewash was so big that it could keep you under for a pretty long time. I wasn't quite ready for that, but I watched Mr. Kim and Francis have awesome sessions on those days. I watched them through a pair of binoculars since the break was so far out.

Oftentimes, after I had gotten the hang of it, Mr. Kim let me surf on my own, when there would be a dozen or so people on one wave. It was all great fun and exercise. Since then, when I surfed on occasion at other spots, the other surfers weren't quite as friendly. And sometimes, they were just out and out rude and thought it was all about one wave, one rider, and one "me." I eventually learned that I can't stand self-centered, unfriendly people. But I also eventually reminded myself that Sister Nelly taught me that we can pray for them... the very people that rub us the wrong way.

Fourth of July, Thanksgiving, Christmas, and New Year's were very festive holidays during my stay, but when I turned 13 on February 8, my Hawaiian "family" and The Kims threw the biggest, most unforgettable, luau for me! And they invited many, many neighbors and friends. This was the most amazingly authentic event in my life. If there was ever such a thing as an island party that wasn't just a part of your wild imagination, this was it! And it was beyond my wildest dreams.

If I were to summarize it quickly as all the aspects sprung to my mind, it had: tiki torches, drums, ukuleles, singing, chanting, dancing, hula dancing, hula skirts, a roasted hog on a big open flame (it was a hog that the men had hunted down in the forest the previous day, killing it in the traditional manner, with a spear), games of the traditional sort, even tug-o-war, all kinds of good eats and drinks, and people wearing Hawaiian shirts or old-time Hawaiian costumes. There was also swimming in their big pool that had custom-built lava walls, tunnels, a rock to jump off of, and a lava tube slide. I mean, the place was going off. The island was rocking. The island ghosts were awakened and joined the party. There was a timely meteor shower in the starry heavens. It was all just the most dreamlike, adventurous, booming, liveliest birthday party ever. And there wasn't a microphone or an amplifier or anything artificial. It felt like I was living in the old world with some of the modern-day luxuries, such as the swimming pool.

It even had romance! One of the Kims was a 13-year-old girl named, Naomi. She brought her friend along, named, "Bella Sue," who was also 13. Anyway, she looked so pretty in her Hawaiian dress and long, dark brown hair, all in braids. We somehow caught each other's twinkle in the eye and found ourselves on the dance floor together quite a bit. Sadly, she had to leave with her family before midnight and that's when we found ourselves behind a big, pink-flowered hibiscus bush. She said this to me, "Happy birthday, Philip. You're the best dancer I ever danced with."

I nervously giggled and told her, "That was only the second time I had ever danced in my life. The first time was at a barn dance we had in the second grade. But everyone made fun of me, so I never danced after that. Besides, I'm just a bad dancer, let's face it."

"Didn't you have fun dancing with me?" she asked

with just a little alarm.

"Of course, for once I understood why dancing was so much fun," I said.

"Well you're real cute, Philip," she said as she then kissed me on... on the lips!

Then she just stood there for a couple seconds looking into my eyes.

"Aren't you going to say anything?" she asked.

"Thank you... Thank you from the bottom of my heart... and from the top of my heart, too," I said.

She smiled at that, "Good night," she said.

I stood there for about five minutes, mesmerized. Then I touched my lips suddenly realizing that my cleft lip was a birth defect that she looked right through. She never mentioned it or anything. I never thought a beautiful girl would ever up and kiss me like that. I figured only the good-looking boys would always have the girlfriends of choice. But, in that moment, well, let's just say, I was in love.

Anyway, that party gradually died down by 2 o'clock in the morning. But before the night was over, my Hawaiian "family" gathered around me and said that I had officially become a part of their family. Not by state documents, but by the heart. It didn't need any explaining either. I understood what they meant... I was a *family* member—no quotations around the word needed! And that was just a wonderful and blessed moment in my life. They knew that I wanted to be back in California for my parents when they got out of prison, now just six years away, but they also wanted me to know that I would always be welcome in their magnificent island home-- their family paradise.

Shortly after a big bonfire powwow, I hit the sack. But even in that final instant of falling asleep, I was still thinking about that kiss. I didn't wake up until noon the next day... and in my mind, it was a whole new world!

CHAPTER 4

THE WIND IS GOOD TO
SAILS AND KITES

F rancis Kim, again, who helped me learn how to surf, and was a totally cool dude with his long black hair and muscular build, wanted to set sail for Japan. Indeed, he was a sailor, too. He, along with nine of his college friends, five of them with much experience sailing yachts, had recently leased a eighty-five foot, two-masted wooden schooner. The sails were light blue and when I first set my eyes on them, the sun was shining through the mainsail and hit my soul with a warmth that I can vividly remember in this instant. Penetrating, refreshing, radiant. One ecstatic feeling.

Francis knew about my dream of seeing the world and becoming a sailor, so he readily agreed when I asked him to join the expedition. He had to make several calls, though, to a Japanese cousin that was a higher up that worked in port customs. Francis explained to him who I was, and that I had a valid passport. Fortunately, that part was ironed out and I was given the green light.

Next thing I knew, I was on that schooner, *Misty Heaven*, waving goodbye to my Hawaiian family and the Kims, as we were preparing to launch off from the dock with Francis and his buddies. So, it was ten college friends: eight men, two ladies--and me. Dozens of family members and friends were seeing all of us off. Yes, once again, there had been a little bit of hugs and some teary eyes, so I almost hate to mention it again; but, what can I say, I guess I was an emotional kid, even when I tried to be stoic, especially since it was an overcast day and everyone seemed to be in a somber mood. I was very tough and all, but I still had my moments of tenderness. Then, out of the blue, Bella Sue, came running down the boardwalk and came up to our boat, right up to where I stood--she on the dock and I on the deck of the boat looking down at her.

"Weren't you going to say goodbye to me, Philip?"

When she asked that so earnestly, looking stunningly beautiful in her Hawaiian shirt and plumeria flower behind her ear, I quickly got off the boat and gave her a hug. Then she kissed me on the lips, and I looked over at everyone who just stood there quietly, totally stunned. Then, Francis Kim sent up a warwhoop-like cheer and then *everyone* cheered and applauded. And then in a spontaneous grand moment of love, everyone was hugging one another and crying and kissing and... well, the emotional dam had been broken. No one held back, no one was stoic. Everyone wept and everyone hugged everyone else.

Bella Sue and I just held hands and watched it all unfold.

Before I knew it, I was sailing away with the crew. We sailed and we ate and we managed the sails and the rigging and we swapped stories and we laughed a lot and we slept and we repeated this every day, and... to make a long journey short, along with some memorable island hopping, about two months later, we landed at Japan. It was a great trip. I'd have to admit that toward the end it was a bit tiring but, all in all, I learned a tremendous amount about sailing a yacht of that nature, I loved all the comaraderie, and I'd have to emphasize that this voyage was a complete joy to me.

We saw much of Tokyo, but we also explored much of the countryside, going on hikes and camping. These college friends were a bunch of nature lovers and I thought that was great. I really enjoyed the outdoors and it was unbelievable to me that I was going into regions of Japan that no one ever talked about. This island nation had a whole world of natural beauty all its own.

My most memorable part of visiting Japan was meeting a kite maker named, Hideo. He was 68 years old. He lived in a mountain hut. It was very tranquil. It was very plain. It was very neat. And while his hut was nestled in the woods, about a hundred yards away from it, there was an enormous field that was trimmed down by his flock of sheep. The shepherd was his one and only son, Koji.

His kites were ordinary looking in terms of shape. They all had that one Benjamin Franklin-style shape to them--just the top-heavy diamond shape. But he used stout, thin twigs for its crossbeams and a very thin fabric for the kite material. He stuck to only two colors for the fabric, a natural white, or red. He also made a brighter-white kite with the red ball to make it look like the Japanese flag. He explained that one must always be loyal to his country. When he said that, it sent a shiver up my spine, because I could definitely see how he would love his country... as I did mine. Patriotism, the whole element of it, was something I could always relate to. I loved my country, and I could appreciate how everyone could love their own.

CHAPTER 5

GOING DOWN UNDER...
AND STILL UNDER

W hen we were about to jump on our blue-sailed boat and head back to Hawaii, I decided that I was going to instead jump on a relatively small 210-foot long cruise ship headed back to Australia. This was primarily a cruise ship that catered to the Australian citizenry. Essentially, the itinerary was to hit several islands on the way to Japan, the final destination, but then, turn around and head straight back to Sydney, as everyone, usually had had their fill of island hopping and sightseeing. So, from Japan to Australia, I felt like I would be taking an express, which suited me just fine. Covering the most distance in the shortest amount of time seemed like an overall good plan for getting around the world.

I still had four hundred of my six hundred dollars and I was able to take advantage of a promotional discount that I saw posted for the cruise line. Francis Kim wasn't surprised, but the rest of his friends didn't know what to make of it. I insisted, however, that I was on a mission to see the world, become and expert sailor, and get back to my parents just as they were getting out of prison.

Unfortunately, a few of the college crew protested and thought it was a bad idea.

So, Francis decided to go with me! His plan was to go on the cruise ship with me to Australia, and then from Sydney, he would take a plane back to Hawaii and I would be on my own again. It was as simple as that. We worried about getting through customs since Francis wasn't really an official guardian. The plan was that I would just have to tell the truth if they started asking me questions.

Well, when it was our turn, we just showed them our passports with confidence and a smile. Francis simply said, "He's with me." The Japanese officer started to compare the passports.

I quickly added, "I'm on a journey around the world and he's assisting me on this next stretch."

Just then, there was some commotion between what looked like two Australian men near the end of the line. They were angrily talking right into each other's faces. Our custom's officer was distracted as another officer walked quickly toward the scene.

Anyway, he stamped our passports and let us through! As we went on our way, our officer secured the line gate and rushed to the scene himself. Right before we turned a corner, I could see fists of the two men starting to fly as the officers attempted to break it up.

Next thing we knew, we were heading for the land down under! After a few days, Francis and I befriended the crew and eventually the captain of the ship. He was half Australian and half Japanese. "It's no wonder," he joked; "I was destined to be captain of a cruise ship between both countries."

While Francis hit it off with an Australian lady his age, the captain, Captain Stencil was his name, showed me the ropes of this big boat. He showed me the instruments and everything. He showed me the architectural rendering of the ship. He taught me every aspect as he and the pilot managed the wheel. Then after a couple days of his one-on-one lectures, he just handed the wheel to me. *What!* I thought. *Me? Steer a two-hundred-foot ocean vessel! With passengers on board! This was unheard of! I was only 13!*

But he stood right behind me. He didn't even put his hand on my shoulder. He just stood and watched, and this lasted for about fifteen minutes. A few of the officers and navigators were looking increasingly nervous. The captain then said, "Good job, mate. That concludes your lessons on this ship." I thanked him, very sincerely, for everything, and went on my way.

For the rest of the voyage: I had lively conversations with some of the guests and crew, sat with Francis and his new girlfriend during meals, exercised in the gym, and read up on all sorts of subjects from an encyclopedia that I discovered in the ship's lounge. After several weeks at sea, we were finally pulling into

Sydney, Australia. Francis and I got off the boat, ate at a café with his girlfriend, and said our goodbyes. It was a touching moment, but we agreed that we would meet sometime after my return to California, even though it looked like years away. But that would give us something to look forward to. The funny thing is, he looked so enamored with this Australian beauty, that in some ways it seemed like he was happy to get rid of me! *No worries*, I thought. *That's what the land down under is all about.*

Thus, we parted, and I walked into the city with one hundred twenty dollars and my passport in the ziplock bag in my pants pocket. I also had my daypack with just some extra clothes in it. I bought a sleeping bag in a thrift shop for five dollars. That night I slept on the beach. There were some bums around, but I found a spot about a hundred yards away from them. When I woke up, a police officer was looking down at me.

"What's up, mate?" he asked. "Where are your parents? Lost your way?"

I just stared at him and said nothing.

"Okay, well I'm going to take you to a safe place until we can figure out what's going on."

Soon after, he put me in the back seat of his police car. He put my sleeping bag and daypack right next to me and headed south. At least that's what I figured since some of the time I could make out that the coast was to the left of us. But the way coasts can curve in and out to whatever degree and since most of the time

I could only see land and buildings and residential areas, frankly at that point, I didn't know north from south or east from west.

Since I had had a poor sleep on the beach, I took a nap in the back seat of that pretty comfortable police car. I don't know how much time had passed, but the officer opened the back door, walked me about one-hundred feet in my drowsy state, and checked me into a two-story brick building, a juvenile detention center —specifically known as a "juvenile justice centre." There I stood looking like a lost pup with my sleeping bag and daypack. As I was escorted down a hall and into a large room with a dozen bunkbeds, the kids, I observed, were rough around the edges and had poor manners—typical delinquent types.

The next day, the juvenile justice people asked me a lot of questions, but I just said that I was abandoned. I felt bad that they were just trying to do their job and that I wasn't being very cooperative, but the last thing I wanted was to have my story revealed and to be shipped back to California. The truth of the matter was... I *was* abandoned. But I kept it as simple as that.

After a few days there, three boys my age picked a fight with me, but I just walked away. One of them then pushed me from behind and I fell to the ground. But I got up and walked away again. Then another one of them came up from behind but I quickly turned around. "We could become friends, you know," I said. "Don't make me hit you."

"I'd like to see you try," the tattooed kid said with an

added profanity. His friends chuckled, standing behind him.

Then, I turned and walked away yet again.

The three of them then ran up from behind and, collectively, shoved me. Instead of falling down though, I just ran with the push and remained standing. Then I turned around and stared them down.

"Okay," I said, "Who's first?"

The tallest one of them who had a few inches on me, walked up to me and swung his fist at my face. I ducked and he missed.

"Do you want to try again?" I asked coolly. And I just have to add, that I got that line from one of my Hawaiian friends' tales. It was Tikimon who said it. He had avoided a fight when he uttered that at a bar. He wanted to give the drunk, who had swung his fist and missed him, a chance. The drunk swang again, though, and sadly had to pay the consequences. Tikimon grabbed him by the back of his shirt and seat of his pants, picked him up, and with the help of a friend, ran him through the exit. It didn't really hurt the drunk at all except that it must've been humiliating.

Anyway, the tall bully did try again with his fast-swinging fist and managed to graze my cheek as I tried to dodge it. Then, in reply, I stomped with my heel as hard as I could on the upward arch of his foot. Well, that got him to scream in pain and the fight was over. The juvenile centre authorities, in their all-white work suits, came after me, but I ran.

I ran out of that institution, zipping past the security guard, as fast as I could and headed for the open Australian land. It was dusk and I could see city lights down the hill about a mile away. The smell of the natural earth as I was running away, made me give a freedom yell of, "Now this is Aussie land!"

I ran down the gradual slope, which was an expansive area of field and native bushes, toward the sea. It seemed like the easiest escape route. There were no roads and there was no way to find me unless they came a-runnin' with dogs. Then, I'd have to really pick up the pace. Even then, I was young, skinny, and a fast runner. *So, bring 'em on...* I thought. The dogs would likely be on leashes and I could outrun any officer in his full uniform with... *no worries!*

I knew it was the sea I was running toward because I could barely make out the horizon. Also, I could see faint silhouettes of boats with some of their lights on. There also appeared to be many lights coming on revealing what appeared to be a small town. The open land with these bushes, I estimated, to be about three miles long. As I got about halfway there to the coastal community and dark set in, I saw a helicopter coming from the north with a downward spotlight. Now, that was something I never even considered. But, I figured, I was a needle in the haystack. There were multiple dozens of square miles of vegetated open land and hills all around—and night was setting in. Where were they going to look? It was too bad that I had to leave my daypack and sleeping bag behind, but I had had no time to grab them.

Well, that helicopter did head right for the juvenile justice centre and then directed its course as a line from the centre toward the sea. Of course, it then occurred to me that any kid would instinctively run downhill and run toward civilization. So, at that moment of thought, I just hid inside a nearby big bush. It was about twelve feet tall and twelve feet wide. And it was one of many. There were small, medium, and big bushes all over the place. There were also smallish trees peppered around. Looking up through the bush that I had chosen, it was too thick with vegetation to see the stars, that were starting to shine in the sky. I must've been about a mile and a half away from the centre as the helicopter slowly made its way downward.

After about an hour passed, indeed, the helicopter, had gradually and methodically made its way down the slope. The spotlight was approaching. And it was approaching slowly. As if it were sweeping every square foot of the terrain! It hovered a lot and swept two hundred yards to the left and two hundred yards to the right. So, cold sweat started to roll down from my armpits, but I was convinced that the bush that I had chosen to hide in, had a pretty solid canopy.

A few minutes more passed and now the helicopter crept up right over my bush! Light spilled into my hideout. But it was just tiny slivers of light. I slowly pressed up against the trunk of the bush and looked down. I kicked myself for looking up at all. Could they have observed my slightest bit of movement or seen the whites of my eyes? But then I quickly rationalized. I had played hide-and-seek so many times in my youth that I had long learned that light casts shadows, and moving light such as from a car's headlights, moves shadows. So, you can actually move with the light of headlights if you're well-hidden and not be noticed one single bit. So, remembering this, I just didn't budge now that I was pressed up against the trunk. And, sure enough, the helicopter just kept moving on. I could see it continuing to make a large sweep of the landscape. I could see it hovering over larger bushes, not unlike mine, with its spotlight.

Three hours of this went on. I just observed from the edge of my bush as the helicopter kept looking around, getting farther and farther away. Finally, it gave up, turning off its spotlight, and headed back North.

I decided to sleep on the ground right there. The night had been fairly warm, but it was also starting the transition of getting a little chilly. I dug a very shallow trench with my hands and put the thick layer of dry, fallen leaves over me. Now this was the life. Nice scent in the air. Fresh air with the hint of salty ocean accents. Nature. Crickets. Awe, this was good living. This was adventure.

I woke up at the crack of dawn to birds chirping and a pretty big centipede crawling across my chin. I swept it off with my hand and watched it crawl away. Nasty little creature. Actually, I took that back, *not* nasty. It was just minding its own business, and I always appreciated all of nature--the animal kingdom, the plant kingdom, and the mineral kingdom. Animals, of course, included the tiny insects, fish, birds, mammals, etc. However, Sister Nelly taught me that humans are not animals. They are a unique and special creation of God. And, after she spent much time explaining it to me, even referring to my biology textbook, I believed her. She also referred to the Bible, especially the first chapter in Genesis.

Anyway, without hesitation, I headed for the coastal community. Again, at the crack of dawn, it was still semi-dark. I had to find a boat to get out of there. Whatever it took.

I was so determined that I literally just dove into the water, after taking off my shoes, and swam about a half mile to a 300-foot cargo ship that appeared to be standing still. I don't know if it was anchored or just floating. As I got closer, I saw a rope dangling from its side at the stern; it had a knot every foot or so, as if to be climbed up, so I swam to it, and climbed right up it. I got to the rail and threw my legs over, totally exhausted and panting. And there stood an old man, a salty old man, that spit out his pipe in surprise. He grabbed my arm.

"Hell's bells, mate! What do you think you're doin'?" He looked at me with his eyes wide open as his long white beard tossed about in the gusty wind.

I put out my hand confidently to shake his hand.

He took it and we shook hands.

Gasping for a breath, I said, "Well, sir, I'm a run-away." I took a big chance just speaking frankly. "I am running away from the state authorities who want to put an abandoned child in an insane asylum. Is it my fault that my parents went to prison?"

He just looked at me, and looked at me, and then looked again.

Then he muttered slowly in an Australian accent, "Our ship has been sittin' here, ya li'l mate, for the last two hours. The capt'n has finally been assured that we do indeed have our entire cargo of used cars. Apparently, someone falsely reported that one car wasn't accounted for. Do we now have to report the addition of an uninvited passenger, that being *you*?"

"No sir. Let's just keep it mum. Please just help me out," I said, and then shook his hand again with a nervous smile. I was still just beginning to get over panting from the long swim and climbing up the rope.

The old man looked at me very seriously and said, "It's a good thing the capt'n leaves that climbin' rope danglin' over the rail. He's got one on the other side, too. Last year, two men fell overboard on two different occasions and each time the crew watched them attempt to swim to the side of the boat, but there was nothin' to grab onto as the ship moved on. By the time the capt'n turned the ship around, those men were nowhere to be found."

A voice called from an upper deck, "Old man,

Henry! Where are you!" The old man quickly turned around and didn't see anyone.

"Hurry!" the old man said. "You must hide."

So, I just darted to a nearby enormous pile of used car tires and hid behind it.

To cut to the chase, as it was described to me the next morning by the old man, Henry McHenry, I was on a "small" cargo ship. It was carrying a load of 250 used cars, a third of them destined to Tasmania, that big Australian island to the south, and two thirds of them destined to Perth, on the western coast of Australia.

This was one big ship and I made no attempt to walk around and make friends with the crew. I decided to stay hidden. Indeed, stealth was the order of the day. When night set in, the full moon aided my efforts as I quietly made a cave out of the tire mountain. It was easier said than done. I had to move the tires one by one about thirty feet over and rebuild the mountain in a brick-like fashion. Then in the end, I put tires around it in a sloppy way to make it look like the original pile. It took me practically until dawn to get it just right. Then, I just flat-out fell asleep inside my rubber igloo.

After the third day, Mr. McHenry, who had continued to sneak food and water to me, decided to completely crawl inside. There was just enough room for the two of us. He was impressed and lit up his pipe. The smoke went out an air vent that I had made. Even then, it got quite smoky in there, but it smelled good and provided warmth. After a few minutes, we exchanged words, had a few laughs, and he crawled back out.

After a week had passed, the boat docked at Tasmania's capital, Hobart. Henry McHenry told me that I ought to wait it out and not reveal myself until they got to Perth, since that would be one small step closer to getting me around the world. But when he said that we would be docked at Hobart for four days, I snuck off the ship even without him knowing about it, and sort of bummed around the city for three days.

First, I found some flip flops discarded or left behind near a harbor trashcan that fit me pretty good. Maybe they were a size too big and maybe they looked a bit dirty, but they seemed to do the trick for footwear just fine. Second, after meandering around for half a day, I up and decided to do some begging. I was hungry and was starting to feel desperate.

So, "Why not give it a try," I blurted out. At that moment I realized why you sometimes see bums talking to themselves. When you're hungry... when you're all alone... when you start to feel like a homeless person without a direction, well, you start to get a little kooky. I didn't want to find myself in that sort of mindset, whatsoever; however, all things considered, begging seemed to be the answer for the next few days.

And so, I started to do it. I would just walk up to a person or couple and give them my pitch. After all, I quickly discovered that begging is no different than a sales pitch. I used to knock on neighborhood doors, for example, with a friend, and we'd ask if they'd like us to wash their car for five dollars. Well, that was great summer pocket change and we learned how to sell and have a lot of fun doing it.

Anyway, as my begging efforts got underway, I was always on the lookout for police officers or other authorities. A few times I had to slip into an alley or walk into a store, always acting as if nothing was wrong. How was anyone to know, for example, that my parents weren't in the store shopping.

My begging strategy was to tell the passersby the truth, that my parents were imprisoned in California and that I was trying to get back to them. It wasn't the easiest sales pitch and many people ignored me or frowned upon me. On five separate occasions, a person I was telling my story to would try to lure or grab me to turn me in, at least that's what I instinctively figured. But the moment I sensed that intention, I just quickly skipped off saying that I had to get back to the ship. That was also the truth, even if it was in a day or two that I needed to get back.

As it got late into the first day, once again, I bought a sleeping bag at a thrift store for only three dollars this time. Nice! Then, I began my mission to find a place to sleep and not be caught like the time on the open Sydney beach.

I found a ravine on the outskirts, about a mile or so, outside the harbor, and found huge layers of dry brush that I literally carved a path through with my hands, just breaking off branches and twigs. Then, after doing that for about a hundred feet, I made a little pad for my sleeping bag, with the tall dry brush enclosing me in like a room with no roof. It was quite nice, and I enjoyed watching the clouds pass through the twinkling stars in my own private peek-a-boo space. And that's where I slept for three nights. There wasn't even a single incident. I slept like a baby.

So, to sum up my begging efforts—again, which I had never done before--somehow after three days, I "earned" one-hundred and twenty-two dollars! The currency, that also was the dollar, sure looked different than the United States version, but a dollar gotten was a dollar earned—so long as it wasn't stolen. Stealing was a definite no-no. Not right by Sister Nelly's standards, nor the Holy Trinity's.

Before I headed back to the ship, I popped into a Catholic church and put twenty dollars into the poor box. Tithing was another thing Sister Nelly taught me. In fact, when I suddenly realized that I hadn't tithed on my six-hundred-dollar earnings at Two Harbors, I ran back to the church and put another sixty dollars in the poor box. "There, now I was square with God," I thought.

When I snuck back on the ship in the middle of the night, I actually just walked right up the main gangplank. Well, to my delight, the two guards were sleeping, believe it or not. I was prepared to tell them "Uncle" McHenry was waiting for me, but I didn't need to say that after all. Instead, I went straight to my rubber igloo and fell asleep.

Mr. McHenry woke me up in the morning with a sausage biscuit and hot chocolate. He was such an old salt of the sea--he acted like I was never even gone. Instead, he just gave me that look in his eye and wry smile through his white mustache and beard. "Breakfast is served, mate," is all he said. Then he sort of shook his head and gave me his high-pitched giggle. *You're one enchanted sailor of legendary years gone by*, I thought.

As the ship made its way toward western Australia, a day later a shipmate discovered me and took me directly to the captain who was attending the wheel of the ship. He was smoking a long cigar. The shipmate flailed with his hands as he emotionally described the despicable situation: how a young kid managed to get on board, getting past their incompetent security guards and cameras—funny, I never even noticed any cameras--and how they must immediately notify my parents and the government and the Perth Harbor Patrol. Mr. McHenry did his best to intervene and quickly explained that I was a fine young lad traveling around the world to get back to my imprisoned parents. He crammed in some other details, but between him and the shipmate, it turned into a yell fest!

As for the captain? He just kept his hand steady at the magnificent ship's steering wheel and puffed away. He was one cool clam, this captain, if I've ever seen one. He was the *coolest* of clams of all time. I mean, that captain maintained an expression as if he were looking at a peaceful sunset.

Well, it turned out, this captain, Captain William-son, to my and Mr. McHenry's astonishment sympa-thized with my story and was amused that I was a stowaway. He said that he had been a stowaway three times in his childhood and had the best adventurous memories of it. When I told him that I helmed a two-hundred-foot cruise ship he practically choked on his cigar and started to test me on the instrument panel.

I wasn't familiar with every single gauge of this particular sea craft, but I was able to answer seven out of ten of his questions correctly. So, he casually pulled me over, stood aside, and let me take the wheel. Holy seahorses! I was now steering a football field of an ocean vessel just like that! I had only met the captain, as a stowaway, a half hour ago!

So, after many days at sea with good times and much serious instruction, I found myself steering this gigantic piece of steel into Fremantle, the Port of Perth, with Captain Williamson standing right next to me. He told me how his son died at birth but that he didn't have any kids after that. He and his wife always lived in Perth, and always thought it a fine place to live. As we got within a half mile of the dock though, he took over and *I* stood next to him. Mr. McHenry, who was welcomed by Captain Williamson to help watch over me, put his hand on my shoulder and, with a lot of pride in his voice, said, "Good job, mate. Good job."

When it was time to get off the ship, I sincerely

thanked Captain Williamson and we saluted. He said, "Please do keep in touch my son." He gave me his business card and I thanked him for that, too. When I walked away with Mr. McHenry, I started to feel a little emotional. The captain sure had been good to me and treated me like he was my father. After I walked about a hundred feet, I turned around to see if he was still there. And yes, indeed, he was still standing where we had parted, just looking at me with glossy eyes. I wiped a tear from my eye and waved; he waved back. Then, I turned around and caught up to Mr. McHenry, who had walked around a bend. At that moment, just thinking as I was walking with my head held high, that I had discovered in myself a new sense of honor.

CHAPTER 6

DESERT SOUL

M r. McHenry had told me all about "The Desert Shack" he lived in and invited me to spend some time with him there. That sounded great to me, after all, I was in no rush. I still had over five years to get back to California. So, after walking away from the docks for a few minutes, we grabbed a taxicab and headed to his place, actually a totally cool, ranch-style home in the outback, which was about a four-hour drive inland, somewhere northeast. I didn't care about knowing the specifics. I just liked the feeling that I was in the middle of nowhere... perhaps the *real* outback.

I spent about a year and a half there with Henry McHenry, except after the very first week, I just called him "Uncle Henry," and I could tell right away he liked that.

When we first got to his place, he showed me around and told me about his times with his wife, Margaret, who had died ten years ago of lung cancer. He said she smoked two packs of cigarettes a day. They had one daughter, Susan, but she had died five years ago attempting to climb a mostly unknown mountain within a hundred miles of Everest. She was one that always wanted to do the big adventures that nobody else thought of. She and her three climbing partners, all men, died in an avalanche. They were missing for three years but were found when the snow had thawed down sufficiently enough that summer, and their bodies were spotted by a passing helicopter that was on a different search-and-rescue mission. Recalling this saddened Uncle Henry, but he was not one to cry, I found.

Interestingly, because of his lack of emotion, I never cried once around him. Who knows, maybe I was becoming a person that possessed the admirable quality of being stoic. That, at the time, brought a glad thought to my mind.

Uncle Henry was extremely cheap mostly because he didn't have a lot of money. On the ship that we met on, he earned minimum wage as a "Ship's Helper." So, it wasn't long before those funds had run out. He also got a social security check which, "Was enough to buy gas, fruit, and vegetables," as he put it. We hunted and ate kangaroo, with his permit, even though it had expired several years ago. The rangers had stopped bothering the old man, seeing that he always packed up his one kill with the intent to eat it and was careful that the kangaroo wasn't carrying a joey—which is the baby in her pouch. That would be against government policy. Worse, the citizens would kill *you*, according to Uncle Henry. But I could never tell when his sarcasm was true or false. Usually, I came to determine, he spoke in half-truths. And that was okay by me. I wouldn't have changed him anymore than I could have changed Saturn.

Kangaroos, while appreciated as the national symbol, had become a pest in many of the citizens' eyes. It's a long story how this came to be, but, "Just imagine letting rats go free in your own country," as one newspaper columnist put it. He then added, "And imagine the creatures being a hundred times bigger."

Well this infuriated some citizens who wouldn't dare kill their national symbol, especially when you compared this lovable, happy mammal to a little, long-tailed, chisel-toothed rodent.

Frankly, I didn't know what to think! But, ultimately, I didn't want to argue with Uncle Henry and his ways, and I didn't want to starve either. Eating just fruits and vegetables wasn't going to do it for me.

So, I went around in his dusty jeep and watched him shoot down the hopping creatures. It was just one at a time, and that unlucky one that got shot down would last for about a month or two—after being cut up and refrigerated of course. Uncle Henry had a refrigerator and a separate, big freezer, in the garage. It was sad for me, especially when we had to load up the dead and bloody animal, but I never liked going on deer hunts with my dad, either.

I did get pretty proficient with the knife along the way, and I mean, little knives and big ones. First, with my Hawaiian fishermen friends, they had me cutting up fish to earn my keep; and secondly, Uncle Henry had me cutting up the kangaroo every which way. It took a lot of elbow grease and my arms always felt sore at bedtime.

I never believed in just sitting around. I was not going to be one just to observe. I wanted to be *in it*. Whatever the "in it" was. As long as it wouldn't be objectionable to Sister Nelly.

During the one and a half years, I learned about desert living, tolerating the heat, appreciating the nature of that part of the world, and... painting!

Indeed, Uncle Henry taught me how to paint on canvas with oil paints. He said I had a natural ability for it. *Wow*, I thought. *The more I traveled, the more I discovered my own God-given, natural abilities.* But I only thought that with much humility laced in. One side of me had always told me to be confident, to shoot to be the best that you can be, and to be thankful of all of your blessings; the other side had told me, simply put, that you're never as good as you think or hope you are.

On two occasions during my stay with Uncle Henry, we were hired hands on a tourist motorboat in Perth. This job would last for two months each time. Eventually, I got to know the crew and the captain. Lo and behold, that captain, Captain Jerry, showed me the ropes of his 120-foot tourist boat. And it wasn't long before he let me take the steering wheel, while standing next to me. I kept thinking to myself: *If I had any real natural ability, it was getting captains to have me take over their job!* I thought this half kiddingly. But only half.

My dream was so gradually coming true, of becoming an expert sailor, that the process never even occurred to me. When it eventually did occur to me many, many years later, it was at that moment, ironically, that I succumbed, willingly, to the fact that I would *never* become an expert. I always felt like I was learning something new every day.

Indeed, as time had gone on, even beyond this story, and as I got to know captains and as I got to reading about great captains and admirals--since I would read nautical books off the shelves from the ships I sailed on--the more I realized that even the best of the best, felt like they were always being challenged with something else. The overall feeling that I learned was that you must never get too confident. That the moment you think you're an expert, it just might be the moment you go down with your ship! And, after I had watched the Poseidon Adventure when I was 10, I considered myself a survivor, above anything else. Interestingly, but I didn't even realize it at the time, that it was yet another seed planted in me.

And that's why somewhere along the way, I decided I was only going to read meaningful literature. And, I was only going to watch movies that were meaningful. Yes, I had watched some rated PG-13 movies and yes, I thought they were quite foul. So, those sorts of movies were to be mostly, if not completely, avoided. I had watched only one rated R movie, and I was so shocked by the sickness and sinfulness in the first ten minutes of it, that I walked out of the theatre. Sick people! I was done with rated R movies forever.

But I have digressed, again! When Uncle Henry and I worked on the tourist boat, we called Mr. Williamson when we were in Perth. But on each occasion, there was no answer and no way to leave a message. After three rings there would be a beep, followed by a dead phone line. So, we had no idea if he was home or out at sea. His business card had a cool-looking ship's wheel on it and his name, "Captain Michael Williamson," but it only had a phone number and no address.

So, again, it was a year and five months, living with Uncle Henry, when on one late afternoon he chased off a dingo that had Uncle Henry's boot in his mouth. The dog must've been attracted to his boot because there was still dried-out blood on it from a kangaroo kill earlier that day. Those dingoes, the "coyotes of Australia" is what I called them, got into our trashcans at night and would often carry off things. This frustrated Uncle Henry to no end, especially the way it would wake him up in the middle of his sleep, but I was always amused by it.

On this occasion—with the dingo carrying off his boot—Uncle Henry grabbed his rifle and shot at the dingo as he was running off. Uncle Henry ran about a hundred or so feet into the desert scrub and then suddenly stopped and yelled out, falling to the ground. From my point of view, it looked like he vanished.

I ran up to him and found him sitting on the

ground, watching a snake slither away. "That was a death adder, Philip," he said in pain. He pulled down his knee-high sock, revealing that he had been bitten in the calf. "I always told you to be on the watch for snakes," he said as he laid back.

"What do I do?" I asked, feeling a big sense of urgency.

"There's nothing you can do," he said. "The snake's teeth sank in good and I could literally feel it injecting the venom."

Then, the following words leaped out of my mouth, "I should suck it out!"

"No!" He snapped. "You could get severely ill, if you do that, mate."

"I'll get the jeep and take you to the hospital," I quickly said.

Without further delay, I ran back to the house, grabbed the keys that he kept on a hook, and ran over to the jeep. He had never given me lessons and I had never driven a car before. So, I had to go by my observations only. It was a stick shift and I tried to figure out the sequence with the clutch and stick, but after having no luck for two minutes—it felt like the engine was violently trying to jump out of the hood--I ran into the house and got on his phone, calling the emergency number.

To cut to the chase, after much confusion with the emergency operator—which I will always remember as the "Aussie Airhead"--the ambulance arrived an hour later while during that time I had fashioned a tourniquet, hoping that it would stop the venom from moving up his leg.

When I had first gotten back to Uncle Henry, he was unconscious and barely breathing. With the help of a knife I grabbed from the kitchen counter, I made the tourniquet with cut and torn-off strips of my t-shirt and a stout twig. About twenty minutes had passed and at that point it didn't look like he was breathing at all. I carefully dragged him to the shade of a bigger bush. I checked his pulse. Nothing. I gave him chest compressions and attempted mouth-to-mouth. I had learned all this first aid as part of a safety course when I had first started my sailing lessons with the dinghy many years ago.

When the ambulance arrived, I had stopped any rescue attempts twenty minutes prior. I was sure that he had died. The two paramedics, a lady and a man, confirmed it.

"I'm sorry I couldn't save you, Uncle Henry," I whispered sincerely. "I am going to miss you." Then I kissed him on his forehead. I had never kissed him before, but it's what I did this time when my internal instinct kicked in. It was a kiss of love and thankfulness to a good uncle.

"Is there anyone else here other than you and your uncle," the lady paramedic asked.

"No, just me," I said, starting to look nervous and shifty eyed. "But I'm just visiting, and I aim to head back to my folks right away. So, I'll be okay. Don't worry about me. As for Uncle Henry, he said he wouldn't mind just being buried on his property."

The paramedics sort of looked at me strangely and then at each other, confused. "Okay, well, the police should be here shortly," the man paramedic said.

When I heard that, I knew I had to make a run for it. There was no time to waste. I immediately started to walk off and told the paramedics, "I've gotta go to the bathroom. And by the way, he keeps his will and burial instructions in the bottom drawer in his bedroom!"

"Wait," the lady paramedic said. "Come back here!" But I just ignored her and jogged to the house, went around to the other side of it, and then started to run as fast as I could toward the hills. "Hey!" I heard coming from the house. "Where are you going! Come back here!" It was the male paramedic doing all the yelling. I could barely make him out since bushes were starting to get in the way. Then, I tried to run behind some larger bushes or trees and in some cases, boulders, to stay out of any line of sight.

An hour later dusk was setting in and a helicopter arrived at the scene of Uncle Henry's "Desert Shack," which was about two or three miles away from where I now hid on a hillside that had a bunch of boulders on it. I found a shallow cave that was made by two boulders up against the other and watched the scene down in the desert valley. I could just *barely* make out police cars and other vehicles. Then, to my shock, I heard the distant bark of dogs—and they weren't dingoes. Now, I knew I must keep running. I had a huge head start on them and I was determined to not let them close in on me. I kept running in the same direction. First down the other side of the hill and then toward a desert highway. I could see occasional headlights, but it was obviously not a main thoroughfare. Then about a mile into my run I could make out an intersection, made evident by a flashing red light over it. When I got to it about a half hour later, my plan was to wait behind this small bush and then hope a pickup truck would arrive and come to a stop, and that's when I would stealthily run up to it and jump into the bed.

In the meantime, the helicopter had its searchlight on the hill that I had went up and over, which was now about three miles behind me. I couldn't make out dogs barking. I figured the helicopter might have drowned out that distant sound. About a half hour had gone by and only three cars had stopped and gone on their way. The helicopter started to make its way toward me.

Then, a big rig came to a cautious stop at the flashing signal, and to my amazement, it had a very long, low profile bed with many axles and a big sixty-foot sailing yacht on it! I noticed that the trailer had custom bracing to elevate the yacht so that the keel and rudder didn't have to be removed. I also noticed a nice-sized propeller. Without delay, I immediately ran up to it and, just as the truck was pulling away, I jumped up and grabbed onto the stern ladder, climbed up, and jumped inside the "boat". Ah-hah! This was my lucky break!

CHAPTER 7

OUT OF THE DARK, INTO
THE BRILLIANT

There I was, on this sixty-foot sailing yacht being pulled through the desert. *Now this was big riggin' in style!* It was dark but because it was a full moon, I was able to squirrel around the whole exterior--aft and forward. It had one mast, down and clamped, and a big diesel fuel tank compartment under the stern deck which was latched down without locks. While it was difficult to see clearly, I did also notice in various locations diesel fuel portable tanks, strapped down. I could also make out several crates, packs, folded and tied-up tarps, and a lot of baggage. There were also heavy duty low profile storage bins that *did* have locked latches on them. Maybe the sails and some rigging were in them.

I stepped below in its cabin, where about four or five dozen cardboard boxes of food and one-gallon water containers were stacked. There was little room to sit on the couch or make your way to the kitchen counter, small refrigerator/freezer, stovetop, and sink. Through the maze of boxes, I then found the door to the head--a convenient location. Next, I went down a short hall and opened a door to the sleeping quarters, where there was another head. I chose not to go in there, but instead went back to the cabin and found a hiding spot behind stacked boxes floor to ceiling. It was a large-sized storage cabinet. Surprisingly, it didn't seem to be utilized much. Inside it, there were a few old-looking crab or lobster traps, a decrepit life preserver, two fishing poles, a small tackle kit, and a dented lantern. These items I just sort of scooted to the back. I found two mildly dusty blankets, shook them out, and was able to lie down comfortably, but with my knees bent. I put my head on a spare couch pillow and put an even larger one in front of me just to help secure my hiding spot, in case somebody opened the cabinet door.

The big-rig ride was long, maybe three or four hours. It was long, creaky, somewhat bumpy, somewhat swaying, but very comfortable. And I was dead tired.

Next thing I knew, when I woke up in my hideout, I guessed that it was some time in the middle of the night or close to dawn. I wasn't sure. It felt like the big rig was reversing down a grooved concrete, boat ramp. After about a half hour and listening to the muffled sounds of seagulls, now several men, and cranks, it felt like the yacht got lowered into the seawater successfully. *Nice!* The voices and various sounds continued but soon after I could hear the big

rig drive up the ramp. Then forty-five minutes, perhaps, passed and I could barely make out two men
talking loudly, one with an Aussie accent, the other
also speaking English, but with a thicker accent of
some other origin.

It sounded like they were getting the mast up
and commencing with attaching necessary lines and
other rigging. This lasted for about an hour, then,
the engine fired up, and slowly but surely the yacht
picked up speed as if it were making its way out a harbor. Then, about another half hour later, I could hear
and even feel the sails getting hoisted up. It felt like
there was a wind starting to pick up that muffled out
the voices of the two sailors. Then I started to feel the
sensation of even a higher speed and the hull of the
boat slapping the waves as we moved through them.
This kept me awake for about two hours, but then I
fell back asleep.

Now, the next part might sound a little crazy, but
for the entirety of the trip, I don't know if a month
had passed or two or more; I just didn't care about
time anymore. All I know, is that I just stayed hidden
and usually at night snuck out into the cabin and got
into their supplies for food and water. Also, I would
go to the head as stealthily as possible. I could gather
what I wanted in less than three minutes, then I'd
sneak back into my storage cabinet.

It seemed to me that we were moving fast much
of the time. The engine was sparingly used to assist if the wind had calmed. I couldn't stop thinking:

Where on the Indian Ocean were we? I figured likely we were heading toward the majestic island countries of Indonesia or Malaysia... or, perhaps we were heading toward the incredibly interesting countries of Sri Lanka or India... or, maybe we were heading toward the legendary area of Persia. I remember in my geography class that India, Pakistan, Iran, Oman, and Yemen had coasts on the Arabian Sea. *Wow, the Middle East... is that where we were going?* To me, all the possibilities were dreamlike, since all I knew of these places were basic descriptions of locations and cultures that I picked up in my geography class and from world history lessons in school. *Cheers to good education and teachers*, I thought.

As each day went on, I would extend my little cabin visit for more and more minutes, to stretch out and to look through the windows out at the sea. Sometimes I could sit or stand in the cabin for as long as an hour, before I sensed that I might need to get back to my hiding spot.

On perhaps a dozen separate occasions, one of the two sailors would clunk around and come down the stairs to the cabin or open the door from the sleeping quarters and that's when I would instantly dart to my hideout. Usually, during the night, one of them slept in the sleeping quarters. But there was no exact pattern. Sometimes I wondered if one was sleeping on deck while the other steered. I couldn't exactly figure it out. My original hunch that there were two men was confirmed when I would catch the slightest glimpse of one of them as I was ducking into my hiding spot. One looked like a skinny and disheveled-looking Aussie and the other looked like an average-sized, neatly attired African. But what did I know. People could be of any origin or citizens of any country regardless of their appearance. So, I just made those observations from my gut.

One morning—and I was already awake and listening--the African-looking man opened my cabinet door and stepped back with a look of surprise. He then said, "Good morning, young man."

I replied, "Good morning."

He offered his hand to me and helped me out. Then I just stood there, face to face with him. There was a long moment of silence.

"We saw you mid journey and decided to leave you alone. You have arrived," he said.

"That's terrific. I'm so happy," I said.

"Do you know where you are?" he asked.

"No," I said.

"We have docked at Mombasa," he said with a smile.

I replied, "Fascinating. I don't even know where you're talking about. Is this a province of India or maybe a country in the Middle East?"

He got a laugh out of that one--a hearty laugh. Then, he proceeded to tell me that we had crossed the Indian Ocean and were in the port of Mombasa, Kenya, the African country that I had heard of but couldn't exactly place. He explained that it was on the eastern side of Africa. "Well," I said, "at least I got that part right."

"What part?" he asked.

"That you were African," I answered.

From that moment on we became good friends. After hearing my long-winded story, which he seemed to believe with fascination, he said his name was Monzumu Ray Adebisi. He came from a royal family from a faraway place long forgotten. He said wars and battles and whatnot pretty much destroyed the royalty aspect of his family—at least the socially recognized aspects of it. But he just held onto remnants of his family "folklore," as he put it, that was told to him orally.

He also confessed that he didn't care much for history, but that his three sisters could recite anything about it; such as, the entire family tree going back many centuries, times of great events and celebrations, each and every hostility, and even the three top secret locations of their hidden family treasures —which they never made me privy to—that mostly consisted of gold and diamonds. And his sisters were dead serious about every detail of it. They were not to be messed around with when it came to this subject matter.

So, where was the so-called Aussie that I had thought was also on board the boat? Well, turned out, he was a missionary. So, Monzumu, a fellow missionary within his own village, volunteered his sailing yacht and seamanship expertise to assist the Australian citizen with getting his supplies into Kenya. This had become a routine trip every couple of years for the last eight years. They would rent that big rig with the large yacht trailer to take it to the Australian's small desert town where all the church camp kids and their parents pitched in their portion of time for the yacht's general maintenance and repairs.

"What's the name of your yacht?" I asked. I didn't notice a name on it when I climbed up the stern ladder."

He then looked at me harshly, squinting his eyes, and whispered loudly, "That's because it's... it's the boat with *no* name." His squinting eyes turned into a glare, then he laughed and patted me on the shoulder. I just sort of giggled, thinking he was a funny man. We swapped stories as I assisted him with getting their packed goods onto the dock.

Currently, the Australian had been checking in with customs, and was unaware that I was a stowaway on the boat. I met him two hours later. His name was Mike Murphy. I said, "*Cool* name." And right after that, we were instant pals. I sooner or later found out he was 35, Monzumu 44.

It was Mike's turn to hear my life story in a nutshell and how I ended up on their boat. He thought it was very interesting but hurried me up since they needed to keep moving.

The two sailing missionaries stepped aside and quietly discussed the situation. Without much pause for analysis, they invited me to join them on their jeep ride. When I asked about where I should present my passport, Mike said he was good friends with the port authorities, and it was "no worries"--unless I wanted them to stamp it as a souvenir.

After just a little bit of thought, my reply back was, "Indeed, no worries, mate. Best we get out of here without the bureaucratic technicalities." Well, they got a chuckle out of *that.*

The jeep towed a trailer with all the supplies. Monzumu's sailing yacht was left behind at his berth. The three of us got along with good stories and good laughs like there was no tomorrow. We had to practically yell at one another because the jeep ride was so loud--no windows, loud engine, and dirt road with ruts, rocks, and dust.

And, this was one speedy, very bumpy, and very hazardous drive. Several times, I thought I was going to die by either getting into a head-on collision or swerving uncontrollably off the road or flying off a cliff, especially considering that we were pulling a trailer full of cargo; however, Monzumu turned out to be the "*Masterful Adventure Driver,*" that he proclaimed to be. Indeed, I thought he *had* gone *MAD,* but he proved himself to be the real deal when we arrived at his village safely and still intact. We were covered with dust, but all I could say out loud was, "Now this is living!"

The most memorable moment during my nearly two-year stay in Africa, and really, every day, was memorable, was when a boy who looked like he was seven-years old walked up to me and asked me if I believed in God. Not to be judgmental, but frankly, he was the best-looking and most athletic-looking young little guy in the village, and he was one of about two-hundred kids, so I didn't even know his name. When he asked me that question, it was in the middle of the day, and at that moment, there wasn't anything memorable in terms of weather or an event or anything. I had only been in the village for a week, but it seemed like it was just a typical day there. I was presently very hot, sweating up a storm, shoveling, and leveling out some ruts in the dirt road when he approached me.

So, when he asked me that question, "Do you believe in God?"

I replied sincerely and without hesitation, "I *do* believe in God."

Then he turned and walked away. I didn't know what to make of it, except that it gave me a good excuse to lean on my shovel for a spell. Well, that, for some reason was a lightning-strike memory for me. It was the sort of incident that came back to me as a random thought from time to time. "Wow," I would think to myself, "there has just *got* to be something there in that moment."

In the days to come I would occasionally catch a glimpse of that seven-year old boy at church or on the school playground. I also went to school in the village and took classes with "Master Bruno." He was an outstanding teacher and, after the two years there, convinced me that he got me all caught up with my ninth-grade level, in Kenya, or *anywhere* for that matter, including England and the United States.

Anyway, time flew by, and, indeed, a couple months shy of two years living there, it was a particularly windy day and I was saying goodbye to my two amazing friends, Monzumu Ray Adebisi and Mike Murphy, and to so many that I had come to know in the village. And yes, we cried, and we hugged, and many other family members of Monzumu were there to see me off. It was one of the most dramatic moments in my life and the clouds over the ocean, all puffy and slow moving, were a part of the spectacle.

But the icing on the cake was when that seven-year old kid, now nine--for two years had passed--walked up to me, shook my hand with a big smile, and said, "I believe in God, too." Then he told me his name was "Benny," and hoped we would meet again someday. Well we exchanged good words and I gave him a hug like he was a brother. Tears rolled down my cheeks, as I said, "And if it's okay with you, we will be pen pals." He thought that was a great idea and we shook hands again--he with his big white beautiful smile and me with tears and big gulps.

Reflecting back, I had joined Monzumu Ray Adebisi and Mike Murphy on missionary tasks, went to church every Sunday, sang in the choir with them, enjoyed outstanding town get-togethers full of games, dancing, and feasts, explored the countryside, soaked in all the wonderful nature of that part of the African continent, and just had a "brilliant" time. The word "brilliant" was a word originally said quite a bit by Mike, but by the end of the two years, we were all using that word a great deal. It became a habitual word. Not a bad habit, when you thought about it, since it had so much positive meaning behind it every time it was uttered. And, being positive and being optimistic was the lifestyle for me.

CHAPTER 8

A PILGRIMAGE

S o, now I was sailing off. Yes, sailing off! Actually, we were on a 310-foot cruise ship! No sails, but there's something nice about saying, "Sailing off," regardless of the type of boat or ship. We? *We?* Oh, my sweet goodness, I heard and felt the drums played by twelve men of the village; I felt the ebb and flow of the tide as I stood on the dock. It was a nice, mellow beat. A majestic beat. Wow. It all felt so meaningful, especially since... I was... I was sailing off with Monzumu's three sisters!

Yes, I had gotten to know these three over the nearly two years and they had gotten to know me. Now, they claimed, I was under their protective authority! Nice! They were among the best ladies I had ever known. I couldn't forget Sister Nelly. I couldn't forget my mom. I couldn't forget the mothers of my Hawaiian family and our neighbor, Mrs. Kim. I couldn't forget the girl left behind on San Nicholas, even though she was only someone I had read about in the *Island of the Blue Dolphins*. I couldn't forget my sweet girlfriend, Bella Sue, who I never stopped thinking about. I certainly couldn't forget the nice old lady, Mrs. Ruthy, from Two Harbors... wow, I guess when it came down to it, ladies were a very fine component to life. But I could only hope that one wouldn't ask me why. I never claimed to know all the answers.

Monzumu's three sisters--Tara, 22; Monzala, 26; and Qya; 35--and I were four of 266 passengers. It was a long, mellow, and easy-going trip. We went around the geographically obvious, "Horn" of Africa, and entered the Gulf of Aden. To port were the countries of Somalia and, at the far end, closer to the bottleneck, Djibouti. To starboard was the country of Yemen. On just one of those days there was a great, hard-hitting rainstorm that lasted for about two hours, then it was sunny again. That was a delightful contrast.

Days later, we entered the Red Sea, and there was something mysterious about it. When it was first announced over the loudspeaker, full of static, repeated four times over--English being one of the four languages--that we were entering that legendary and historic body of water, I just got a warm fuzzy feeling all over. It was past dusk. There were lights on the deck and coastal lights that had a mesmerizing effect to them.

I looked through a leaflet under a deck light. During this Red Sea journey, to port we would pass the countries of Eritrea, Sudan, and Egypt; to starboard we would pass more of Yemen, and a great length of Saudi Arabia. Wow, Egypt on our port side, Saudi Arabia on our starboard side. I wish I could remember all of the history lessons that now seemed like a blur to me.

As I got more tired, I headed for my room, where Monzumu's three sisters also slept. I could go on and on with the great conversations I had with these three sisters, but I will describe the one that stood out the most. It was on this very night that we had entered the Red Sea. We were all tucked in our own beds. I had one of the two upper bunks. I could look out the porthole and see the coastal lights reflecting with a flicker on the sea. I also saw a big tugboat go on by like it were some sort of big duck--except instead of quacking, it let out a big tugboat-horn sound that would cut through any fog, if there were any.

Well, right after the big-horn blast, Tara suddenly started the conversation. And we all chimed in, all in English. That was a favor to me of course. I had only picked up very little of the Kenyan language, which is called, "Swahili." Anyway, Tara expressed how she just always loved the color red and how she couldn't believe we were now on the very sea of her favorite color. That started a chain reaction of connecting the dots of everyone's favorite color, and animal, and memory, and historic event, and weather condition, and flower, and fish, and musical instrument, and book, and sport, and hobby, and figure of speech, and expression, and place visited, and friend... and, anyway, this went on and on for two hours.

We got a lot of big laughs out of this prolonged topic since we were all in good humor.

The highlight of this was when I started off with my favorite smell, that of a dirt road after a rain. Tara said her favorite smell was a flower garden. Monzala said her favorite smell was freshly baked bread. Then, Qya said, in her dead serious tone, that her favorite smell was that of a pet giraffe they once had. Well, that just threw us off. There was a moment of respectful silence, especially since Qya had sounded so earnest.

Well, I felt like I was seriously trying to control an outburst of laughter. And, I could quickly figure out that the other two sisters were also suppressing their laughter.

Qya obviously noticed the stifled giggles and asked what was wrong with what she had said. She asked it seriously, too, with a hint of hurt feelings.

Now the *big* struggle to hold back the laughter was on among me and the other two sisters. There suddenly became an awkward silence in the room with the sporadic holding back of a guffaw, a cough, a clearing of the throat, or a fake sneeze followed by a cut-off giggle. I was struggling for my dear life to hold back my laughter. I felt a few tears rolling down my cheeks.

Qya then demanded, "Just stop it!"

But that only made it worse; the horrific struggle of trying not to laugh, and then, sadly perhaps, as if it were spontaneous combustion that I learned in my biology class--but not related to laughter in that lesson--we just all busted up and couldn't stop laughing our heads off for probably five minutes. Just the three of us at first, but then, by the joy of providence, thankfully, Qya joined in. Perhaps it dawned on her eventually the silliness of a *giraffe* being a favorite smell, especially when compared to our easier-to-grasp favorites.

At the tail end of being totally out of breath with laughter, I literally fell out of my bunkbed and banged my head hard on the ground. When they suddenly sat up and were all concerned and asked if I was all right, I just rubbed my head and after a moment of silence, told them it was nothing. Well that started another two-minute session of uncontrollable laughter. It was one of those moments that you just had to be there to understand the humor of it all.

So, this conversation may have even gone on substantially longer than two hours except that that's when I fell asleep. But just as I was falling asleep, I could still remember hearing the non-stop chatter of their sweet voices and Kenyan accents.

Many days passed and going through the Suez Canal was very interesting, especially when I somehow managed, with a lot of wheeling and dealing, to convince the captain, through a befriended ship's officer, Officer Smedley, acting as translator, to allow me to pilot the ship. Well, it lasted for about 15 minutes; the captain got impatient and shoved me aside when I kept aiming directly for a prominent red buoy that

I somehow didn't notice. Well that was that! He was an Egyptian that didn't speak English and he was an impatient man, as Officer Stanley Down had told me earlier. Even though I goofed, I thanked the captain profusely and sincerely, because after all, he *did* give me a chance. He just angrily waved me off and then stomped his boot as if it were an exclamation point to his final hand motions for me to exit.

More days passed and next thing we knew, we docked at Eilat, Israel. The sisters had passports, and... I had mine. Though, this time, I simply didn't know what to expect. The sisters seemed just a little worried about my prospects in getting through. They insisted, however, that if I ran into trouble, that I just be happy and honest. *Sure*, I thought with sincere confidence. *I liked the ring of that.*

So, indeed, at customs I went through an interrogation process. After I didn't pass the test in the first two rooms, I went to a third room where there was a middle-aged lady, who spoke good English—though it didn't strike me as her first language—and who wore plain clothes and a badge. Well, I just took a big chance and told her my entire true story as quick as I could, from beginning to end. It took me at least a half hour, but maybe as much as an hour, as she took a lot of notes on a laptop.

Then an older man stepped in and they exchanged five-minutes' worth of their own language right in front of me. I found out later that they were likely speaking Hebrew. Then they walked out of the room and closed the door. I could hear pretty intense arguing between the two of them; then, ten minutes later they entered the room and closed the door.

The lady interrogator said to me very seriously, "My boss here has granted me the responsibility on this. It's my judgement call... and... I believe you."

"Thank you," I said sincerely.

"But," she said, "it's against our protocol. I hope this isn't against my better judgement, but we are making an exception here. For *you*."

"Thank you," I said again. I was at a loss for words, and... I didn't want to say anything else that would mess up her decision. It was clear to me that, ultimately, she was the gatekeeper--not just for my visit to Israel, but also, maybe for the rest of my journey around the world.

Her boss just gave me an even sterner look, then opened the door and exited. She said that she would give me temporary credentials to visit and that I absolutely must always stick with my Kenyan lady friends.

But she also granted me this luxury under one condition: that I would call her when I was reunited with my parents, as planned, which was a little more than two years away. She gave me her business card. Her name was Mary Bellman.

She then said, "My mother and father come from different backgrounds. Among my father's fine qualities, he has continued to teach me things about judgement and being tough minded. He has always told me to be a leader."

"Is your boss your father?" I asked.

"No-no," she said. "My father is tough, but he's a nice man, unlike my boss."

"I see." I said respectfully.

Then she said, "My mother is *very* nice." She just looked at me, to my surprise, with a motherly look. It melted my heart. My whole body could have melted right there on the spot.

She then added, "And she isn't so tough."

"Well I especially see her in you," I said earnestly, and then smiled.

"I suppose I'm a little bit of both... like my father, and like my mother," she said. "But I liked the part of your story that you relied on Sister Nelly's words of wisdom. I liked that a lot. You will go far, and you will do well, young Philip. I pray that God always smiles on you."

I graciously thanked her yet again and told her that I would look forward to the day when I made that call. Soon after, I was released to the hugging arms of the sisters—they all had big smiles and said how glad they were that we were now free to explore God's favorite land!

And so that's how it went down, before we knew it, we were on foot in Israel, the Holy Land! For the three sisters, this had become the realization of a long-planned pilgrimage. This was their first time there and, according to the way Monzala put it, "It could very well be our last, for God delivers and takes away. And He can kick your *butt* whenever He feels like it!"

For the next two weeks, we hit their checklist of places to see. They were so excited every moment because at last they could pay homage to nearly every place in their beloved Bible! And that would be my beloved Bible, too, going all the way back to Sister Nelly. So, all this excitement rubbed off on me, too.

Seeing these places was mostly achieved by jumping on tourist buses, local shuttles, and taxis. We saw: Eilat (the port where we docked), Masada, the Dead Sea, Jerusalem, Nazareth, Bethlehem, Capernaum, and Tabgha—the last two being coastal towns on the northwest shores of the Sea of Galilee. At each of those places there were often several points of interest. We stayed in hostels.

The two weeks flew by and the days were full of new memories. The one that stood out the most was our walk through the Garden of Gethsemane. This was a peaceful little stroll and neither I nor the three sisters said a word. It amazed me to picture Jesus in this garden, amongst the simple nature of it. Not that the other places didn't amaze me, for they did, but there was something about the simplicity of this garden that stood out in my mind. Then, midway into our walk, there was a cool misty drizzle. There was no need for an umbrella, no need to duck and hide. No, the drizzle was refreshing and later that day, Qya referred to it as "Holy Water." We all chimed in with agreement and it put a smile on all our faces.

I had really grown to love my three sisters. I started referring to them as my "sisters" when they started calling me their "brother," right after our visit to the garden. Indeed, they adopted me, and I accepted. This was not by some sort of verbal agreement or official documentation, no, it was by the heart. And it reminded me of my Hawaiian family; and it reminded me of Uncle Henry; and it reminded me of Captain Williamson, who was a father figure to me; I remembered our salutes to each other. And then, fondly, it reminded me of Mrs. Ruthy. In looking back, I wish I would have just called her Gramma Ruthy. Lastly, and again the icing on the cake, I thought of Benny... like he was my little brother. That made me get choked up.

So, the time had come to say farewell to my three sisters. They knew that this was the plan all along; that I was to make my way through the Mediterranean Sea, cross the Atlantic Ocean, and either go the long way, around Cape Horn or the short cut, through the Panama Canal, and head north to California. There was no rush, since I had a little over two years to do it, that's if I wanted to be there when my parents came out of prison. And that had certainly been a part of my master plan all along.

CHAPTER 9

WORK

The sisters had just enough money to get back home to Kenya, but I was dead broke. With the help of my sisters and Officer Smedley, though, I managed to find a job on a mid-sized Mediterranean cruise ship, as a janitor. This was part of the same company fleet as the one that had gotten us to Israel. While it was sad to part courses with my sisters, and I did hug each one of them, it was a less emotional good-bye since they were running behind schedule getting back to their cruise ship. They didn't have a minute to spare. Furthermore, my new job was to commence in about three hours, when I was to find myself heading toward Turkey on the Mediterranean Sea.

Being a janitor for the next month was one big un-ending burden. The janitors, unlike the maids, were all given special duties, that were mostly determined by the "Chief Sanitation Engineer," Señor Durazo—my boss. My specific duties, and I was one janitor out of a dozen janitors, were to clean toilets, mop bathroom floors, clean mirrors, and scrub the decks. The three dozen maids mostly did all matters concerning the bedrooms and other rooms, but not bathrooms.

Señor Durazo on day one sat me down for a brief meeting in the late afternoon. He spoke Spanglish to me, but he also had a ship's assistant, Maria Smith, with him to help correctly translate his rules. He was mean and warned me sternly that if I were to step one foot off the ship, before reaching our final destination in Malaga, Spain, I would lose my job and would never be welcome on board again. He also warned me that if I were to get "lost" on the ship, that I would be treated as a stowaway and be thrown overboard without a blessing. Maria reiterated this more clearly. Frankly, I couldn't tell if it was a joke that she was in on or if it was for real. Well, I never did figure out if it was a bluff, but if it was, it worked, because I never dared test him on it.

He also continued to say that I was only to get paid in full at the end of the month-long trip. And that sum was going to be four-hundred-dollars' worth of Euros. He knew how to speak this sort of currency lingo because much of his profession was dealing with tourists from the United States. Once in Malaga, if at that point I decided to go back to Israel, which was another tourist cruise that stopped at different places, I would get another four hundred dollars. He also said that if I were a diligent worker, that it wasn't uncommon that the maids would give janitors nice tips.

After I left the big sit-down session and headed to

my very small, shared room down below that didn't even have a porthole, I blurted out in frustration, "Rats! And to think that I thought I had this ship-travelin' business down to an art!" Then I kicked an empty metal beer keg and it made a lot of noise. A maid waved her finger at me with that worried look on her face. What a dreadful situation I had found myself in!

The next morning, I asked several other maids and janitors if there was really to be pay at the end of the trip for the amount promised. Each of them—speaking either in Spanglish or broken English--convinced me that while the boss was mean, he actually did pay them the agreed upon amount without fail, but that it was always at the end of the trip, either docked at Malaga, Spain, or docked at Eilat, Israel. Since the ship stayed at Malaga for about two weeks and at Eilat for about two weeks, it allowed for roughly four of these roundtrip cruises per year.

So, just imagine, as we made stops along the way, I was essentially trapped on this big boat and practically treated like a slave; though, in all fairness, it was just a tough and dirty job.

When we docked at the island of Cypress—nope, I couldn't get off the ship. I had to recall the strict rule that I had silently agreed to. When we docked at Antalya and Izmir, Turkey—nope, I was reminded that I couldn't get off. When we visited a variety of ports and islands of Greece—nope, there was no way I could get off, especially since Señor Don Juan Durazo had only gotten meaner. When we made brief stops at the countries of Albania, Montenegro, and Croatia, all I could do is scrub the decks and yearn to set foot on those foreign lands. Foreign to me, that is; to them, I would be the foreigner. I once saw photos and videos of Croatia on the internet and thought it looked absolutely wonderful.

As the cruise ship went on its course and when we stopped at Venice, Naples, Rome, and Genoa in Italy —nope, I couldn't even consider getting off the big boat, for Maria Smith continued to sense my wanderlust needs and warned me that "the boss" was a no-nonsense man and that he could also be cruel and ruthless.

But then when we stopped at Nice and Marseille and Montpellier in France--nope, by my own self-torture to actually follow the stupid rules, I still couldn't get off. However, when we visited the island of Palma and landed at Barcelona, Spain--nope, still, I couldn't get off, because I kept thinking I just needed to keep holding my breath, like when I got the fifth-grade record for doing the most underwater laps in the school pool--the width of the pool, that is. And that was 10 laps. Only one other fifth grader had done 8 laps, and that was 10 years prior to the new record I set.

All this time, I had never worked so hard and so fast in all of my life, figuring that I just had to suffer for one month and then be rewarded with the decent sum of money, and hopefully, a lot of tips, for I had gotten to know many of the maids well and they all complimented me on my hard work daily. Plus, I shared a good sense of humor with most of them. It was pretty much the best weapon one had against drudgery—the ability to laugh--at yourself, at someone else, at a joke, at the world, whatever it took. Now I was never into making fun of someone, like a bully. But, for example, if a fellow employee accidentally broke an ornament or plate or whatever, it was perfectly okay to say something like, "Good job." And that would surely get a chuckle out of the other employees standing nearby.

Humor, subtle or otherwise, and situational comedy was almost a non-stop daily part of life on this cruise ship. Stories, observations, spontaneous jokes, puns, pranks, it was all fair game. The maids always seemed to enjoy it when I was working in the bathroom of their room, because I, for one, always tried to keep things lighthearted. We also whistled and sang songs, many of them I made up, and many of those I made up were of a humorous nature that were typically just out-and-out silly or ridiculous.

When at last we reached Malaga, Spain, Don Juan Durazo and Maria Smith sat at a big desk in a big conference room and there was a long line of maids and janitors and other ship helpers. Since the maids got paid substantially more than the janitors and ship helpers, they were first in line to collect their pay. The door closed behind the last maid and we janitors and other ship helpers had to wait outside.

After about an hour had passed, the door opened,

and my fellow janitors and I funneled in. From the back of the room, I could see that there were about twenty large jars that were painted white and had metal screw-down caps. They sat atop tables lined up on both sides of the big desk. There was a large slot in each cap. Each jar had a label with a name neatly written on it with a black marker. One of those labels, and it was the jar closest to Señor Durazo, had *my* name on it, "Philip Wilburton." *Wow,* I continued to think, *these were the tip jars that fellow janitors had described to me.* And sure enough, each of the janitors would open his jar, empty it out, count the money, and walk away. Most of them looked satisfied. A couple looked less than satisfied and a couple looked very satisfied.

For whatever reason, I had decided to be at the end of the line. As I got closer and closer to the big desk, my heart pounded a little faster and faster. I don't know if it was because I was scared or excited or a combination of the two, but at last I stood face-to-face with Señor Durazo. He looked at me very grimly and then handed over an envelope. Maria said it was four hundred dollars' worth of Euros, as promised.

Then Señor Durazo stood up and offered his hand to be shaken, "Good job, my little amigo," he said. His facial expression suddenly turned to one of the sincerest ones I had ever seen, upturned eyebrows and all. So, I shook his hand and smiled. Then he handed me the jar with my name on it. A couple bills were sticking out the slot, unlike the others. "I never see such stuffing jar in all my vida," he said. "And muchas, muchas times buenas words from maids about you my little amigo."

Then I unscrewed the cap and was utterly amazed to see such a totally stuffed jar full of bills and coins, mostly of Euros and foreign currencies.

Then, practically in a state of shock, Maria Smith said, "That's the most I've ever seen in one of these tip jars, and I've been on this cruise ship for three years. Only once I saw one that was barely half full." She was so taken aback by it, that she grabbed a tissue as she fought back tears.

"I hoping you stay with us, Felipe," Señor Durazo said with his eyes welling up just a little. "I give you better pay, and better job, and you get off ship when you wanting."

"Thank you," I said. "I am suddenly overwhelmed by everyone's kindness--yours and the maids."

"Everyone loves you, my little amigo," he said.

For the first time, and it never even occurred to me, I felt like I was part of this family of shipmates. Maybe that sounded like a stretch and maybe it was, but suddenly I was overcome with a heartfelt sense of joy.

And even more suddenly, the maids and janitors and helpers came barging into the conference room with a birthday cake and seventeen lit candles on it. Someone turned off the lights and they sang, "Happy Birthday," since indeed, it was. I had only told one fellow janitor earlier that morning, but, well, word traveled fast among us all, because in many ways we were like a family.

After I made a wish and blew out the candles, I said, "My dear friends. You will always be my family of the Mediterranean. Some people see the nations that border her waters, but I, I got to know all of you instead." I saw hands go up to mouths and other hands wipe away a tear. Other hands were put around a nearby shoulder.

I continued, "I'm not going to lie to you. While this was the hardest job I ever had, a job I really struggled with, I have come to realize that a job well done, regardless of the work, is a worthy effort in life. I have also come to realize that when you are among wonderful people, that even difficult work can often be fun. Anyway, thank you, for making my job enjoyable and for being so good to me. Thank you for treating me like I was your little brother. I really appreciated it." Now, even Señor Durazo had tears rolling down his cheeks.

They moved in on me with hugs and praises and kisses and it was such a splendid moment in time that it all passed by in a blur and the next thing I knew, Señor Durazo and Maria Smith were walking me down the very long gangplank. I had been given a backpack that now had my belongings, mostly clothes, in it.

Taking a step back, Maria Smith had made special arrangements for me. A customs officer met me at the cruise ship's exit and stamped my passport without any hassle whatsoever. She said that she had made a call to "Spain" and that I was to be considered an exception. She further explained to me, saying, "Everyone knows at the port authority that you're just trying to get back to your parents and that you're making this amazing journey around the world."

So, I finally felt free at last walking down the very long gangplank, finally about to set foot in Europe. *Wow*, I thought, *Malaga, Spain*. At the midway point, Señor Durazo grabbed a call on his cell phone, then quickly said to me, "Goodbye and good luck." He put his hand on my shoulder, turned, and headed back toward the ship with the phone pressed up against his ear with one hand, while the other one gesticulated.

DINGHY TO SUPERTANKER

CHAPTER 10

FROM WITHIN THE HEART

M aria Smith and I kept walking down the long stretch of the gangplank as we talked. At the end of it, we walked right past some guards, right past two security stations, and we just kept walking right toward the first intersection we came across in the city. It had never ceased to amaze me how you can so quickly move from one environment to another. And using this occasion as an example: one moment I was in the environment of the cruise ship that I had eventually gotten to know very well, the next moment I was on the grounds of a foreign city that I knew *nothing* about! That sort of contrast that the brain had to sort out was the sort of thing that always fascinated me. Change.

Maria Smith had proceeded to tell me from the gangplank to the intersection—a bit of a distance away--that the owners of a superb bed and breakfast home were expecting me and that there would be no concern for the expense. She explained that her friends were the owners and were supportive of me and my story. She wrote down the address, located in Malaga, on one of those small yellow square sheets and told me to give it to a taxi driver. She also gave me some money. I protested immediately but she stuffed it in my hand and gave me a kiss on the forehead. She said, "Please don't forget me." When she said that, I fought back my emotions as I was trying to regain any sort of ability to be stoic.

We said goodbye, I sincerely thanked her again, and I promised her that I would send word to her once I made it back to California. Then, she kissed my hand, turned around, and started to walk back to the cruise ship.

Now I was all alone for the first time in a long time. I was alone in Spain with no plan as to how I was going to make do with the next part of my journey, except to go to the bed and breakfast. So, that was very comforting. It was also comforting that I felt as rich as the time "Gramma" Ruthy gave me all my earnings.

I noticed that the pedestrian light turned green, so I stepped out into the intersection, not even knowing why I chose to start walking that way. But then, an incredible event happened right before my eyes. Two cars collided in the intersection at a pretty high velocity. At that moment I had no idea who was at fault, but one of the cars spun off, hitting an old lady, and flipped on its side plowing into the back end of a regular-sized tow truck, and the other car spun out of control right toward *me*. I jumped and rolled over its hood as it slammed into the heavy, intersection light post. The heavy metallic light post crashed down, up and over the two-door sedan-style car, denting in the hood, shattering the windshield, and crushing down its top shell about eight inches. Flames and smoke erupted from the bottom of the car and from the open gaps of the hood.

There was instant pandemonium from pedestrians and people getting out of their vehicles. Many of them rushed to the car flipped on its side and to the old woman that was laying just outside the crosswalk.

I stood up and felt a big bump on my forehead, ironically the exact spot where Maria Smith had seconds ago kissed me. The fact that I even mentally processed *that* was a curiosity to me.

Next and in a flash, I saw what looked like a baby boy strapped in a child seat in the back seat of the burning car that I had rolled over. I was only fifteen feet away, but I immediately went into action. I got right to the passenger door and tried to open it up. It was jammed as the signal light post had crushed down the body of the car, again, what looked like eight inches, and partially crumpled out and shattered its side windows. I saw a few people trying to open the driver's door, but to no avail.

The baby boy started to scream and the driver, a man in his thirties, was unconscious and slumped down with the ceiling of the car pressed down on him. More fire erupted from beneath the car and from the gaps of the crumpled hood. Smoke started to fill the interior. I quickly took off my shirt and broke away the shattered pieces of window glass of the door, though there were still jagged and slightly protruding pieces. I then quickly crawled into the passenger front seat with my legs hanging out the window from the knees. I got a little scratched up in the process, but I wasn't even thinking about it.

I then pushed the red release button for the driver's seatbelt and shook the driver, yelling at him to wake up. Others from his window had backed off since the flames were higher on that side of the car. The driver was totally out. There was no time. I had to go for the baby. I completely climbed into the tight space of the passenger seat and reached back, struggling to find the seatbelt release of the child seat. The baby boy was now coughing uncontrollably as I was also coughing quite a bit. By the second, it was getting harder and harder to breath. The flames were inching up higher with each passing second.

Maria Smith showed up at the window that I had crawled through and yelled, "Hand me the baby, Philip! Quickly! And then get yourself out quickly!"

With quite a struggle, especially since the ceiling was crushed in, I managed to free the baby from the seat and carefully draw him toward me--which was quite a squeeze. I then brought him around my lap while he was coughing and crying and super red in the face, and handed him over to her.

Then, the black smoke got even thicker and I was coughing and gasping just trying to find whatever remnants of oxygen! I grabbed the side seat lever to my right and got myself leaning back, then I reached over, and grabbed the driver by his collar and gave him several yanks toward me. He was now over my lap and I was slunk down in the passenger seat as low as I could get. Blood dripped from the top of his head onto my lap. At that moment, the flames and more black smoke were entering the car and I could barely breath. I felt like my face and my legs were getting extremely hot. The driver's clothes were catching on fire and I felt like I was starting to catch on fire, too. My heart was racing as I tried to move but couldn't.

A man and a woman showed up at the window, yelling words in Spanish, and quickly pulled the driver over me and out the window. No longer trapped, just as I was trying to crawl out the window, the couple frantically pulled me out, too. There was a big eruption of flames that practically spat me out as they pulled me out. They fell backward and I dropped, hitting my head hard on a glass shard on the asphalt....

....The next thing I knew, I was looking up at a white ceiling. It took me about thirty seconds, at least that's what I remember, to figure out that I was in a hospital bed. Flashbacks of the car accident and my rescue attempts sprinkled into my thoughts. I felt bandages on my arms, legs, and head. I felt some pain in those areas. I felt and saw tubes, not having any idea what they were for, except I remember seeing that sort of thing on TV shows and movies. In other words, I soon realized I was hospitalized. Interesting, I thought. Very interesting. Then I started to process what had happened. On the one hand, I was glad that it all seemed so vivid to me, that whatever happened to me, it didn't seem like I sustained critical damage. On the other hand, I was concerned for the boy and the driver. I wondered if I had done enough. I wondered if I had been too late.

Just then a nurse came in and looked at me with great concern. "You're awake," she said with a surprised look.

"Yes," I replied. "Is the baby okay?"

She put her hand to her mouth, taken aback. She put her other hand on my forehead and her eyes were welling up. "He's fine. He's perfectly fine. You saved him. You're a hero. People took video of the rescue from their phones. The whole thing has gone viral all over the world. You're a hero, young man, and the whole world is praying for your recovery."

I was stunned to hear that and didn't know what to make of it. "And the driver?" I asked.

She looked at me with just the slightest look of anguish, "You saved him too my dear."

To make a long story short, much of my hair, eyebrows, eyelashes, and arm hairs had been burnt or singed off. I did have two small areas that were second-degree burns, the right side of my neck, my left wrist, and my left ankle, but the rest of my face, arms, and parts of my body, the doctors described as being somewhere between first-degree and second-degree burns. In other words, with creams and treatments, the doctors told me that the redness would likely and eventually go away, some in a few months, some in a few years. Though, they added that some of the burn spots might show as scars for life. They weren't sure since everyone healed a little differently. I also had to get eight stitches on my head above my right ear. Additionally, I had some bruises, abrasions, and soreness throughout my body.

So, what had happened on that fateful day? Well, a 30-year-old man, on drugs, had snatched a purse and was in hot foot pursuit by two park security guards on mountain bikes. As a lady was getting into her car, the purse snatcher grabbed her keys, threw her aside, jumped in, and drove off. Two blocks away later, he ran through a red light, collided with another car, sending that one spinning into a tow truck, while his stolen car slid right toward *me!* My instinctive reflexes kicked in when I jumped and rolled over the hood of it. The car then slammed into the intersection signal light post, knocking it over right on top of the vehicle!

There were several injuries resulting from the other car involved. That car had spun, flipped on its side, and crashed into the back half of the tow truck. These injuries mostly consisted of a few broken bones, abrasions, and a couple punctures wounds. One of the victims, a four-year old girl, lost her right eye. To make matters worse, a six-month-old German shepherd puppy, flew out of the girl's hands and was ejected from the car. It died at the veterinary hospital several hours later.

Also, a pedestrian, a 65-year-old lady, was barely grazed at the hip by that spinning car, but it was enough to throw her hard on the ground, and she hit her head on the white line of the crosswalk leaving a blood splat. She was hospitalized for many days and just wasn't the same ever since. Her only son, 45, immediately put her in a round-the-clock care facility, which was a major financial stretch for him, according to a reporter.

The one-year old baby boy that Maria Smith had taken from my hands was reunited with his mother shortly after. He only temporarily suffered from smoke inhalation.

The driver, Javier Santiago Rey, that I had tried to pull across my lap was pulled out by Juan and Cecilia Perez, a husband and wife in their 40s, married exactly fifteen years with five children, but their children were back home with a babysitter, since their parents were on their own little anniversary dinner date.

This married couple had rushed to the burning car only when their own car had inched up to the intersection a minute or so after the accident had happened, and they noticed what they deemed might be an emergency situation. Some of the bystanders had raced to the other vehicle, especially since it didn't catch fire and help was needed there. Other bystanders--some documenting the event with their cell phones as video cameras--just stood far away from the burning vehicle, afraid that it could blow up any second, according to reporter interviews later. Besides, the driver's door was jammed and had higher flames. They didn't want to completely break out the crumpled window for fear that it would only allow the flames to more easily get inside the vehicle.

Just as Juan and Cecilia Perez were yanking me out, a bigger eruption of flames appeared to cough out the window. They successfully yanked me out completely, but they fell backwards in the process, inadvertently letting me go, which is when I banged my head on the ground and piece of glass--and passed out. A teenager ran up to the car and sprayed it with a fire extinguisher, which was too little too late for the car, as a few other people pulled me away. A minute later a fire truck arrived, when the car was totally engulfed, and put out the flames. Other fire vehicles and ambulances and police cars arrived, very shortly after, but I was oblivious to all that, since it was the next morning that I woke up in the hospital bed.

The driver, who had been pulled out by Juan and Cecilia Perez and dragged several feet away, also suffered from burns, like me, and had a severe concussion from the ceiling crunch-down.

Juan and Cecilia Perez suffered some first-degree burns, mostly on their faces, necks, and arms. Juan cut his wrist on the jagged glass and needed eight stitches.

The news and amateur footage of all this went worldwide in a matter of minutes after the actual event. I watched some of the footage from my hospital bed. It was strange seeing it at different angles, and it was really strange thinking about how those were my own legs sticking out of the burning car when I first crawled in. I thought I must have been crazy.

But really, on second thought, no, I had always been taught to step up to the rescue. To never hesitate. To always put others first. I attributed this way of thinking partly from my first-aid instructor, Mark Henson, who was the epitome of a lifeguard stud. I got part of this line of thinking from Sister Nelly's teachings and sayings. I picked up much of this way of thought from Jesus and the Bible and going to church. I also always liked war-and-disaster movies where rescues were the just the thing to do. What more can I say; when it came down to it, springing into action was programmed into me.

Thankfully, in this case, there seemed to mostly be a good outcome, but I would have understood if the outcome would have been different, because there were no guarantees. Anyway, I was happy to be alive and I was especially happy that the little boy and the driver made it out alive.

I was free to leave the hospital the next morning. I was still in my bandages and looked somewhat like a clothed mummy. Even my face and head were half covered in bandages. I immediately realized, whether I liked it or not, that I had become the latest overnight sensation, and everyone wanted to hear my story. And everywhere I went, cell phones were held up in such a way that I knew people were taking photos of me or shooting video. I was asked to give my autograph constantly. Often, I found myself talking into a news microphone or bunch of microphones.

The first two days, I was overwhelmed with it all. I had grown so used to just being my own self without this huge spotlight, that it was all pretty scary to me. So, much of the time, I just stayed in my room at Abila's Bed and Breakfast, ignoring inquiries on the room intercom or ignoring knocks at the door. But, after the second day of it all, therefore, on the third day, when I woke up, I decided I would have a new attitude. It was time to accept it, and just embrace the mostly caring nature of it all.

So, for the next several weeks, I was treated like royalty in Spain and I had letters coming to the Bed and Breakfast address from all over the world. The owners, Mr. and Mrs. Abila, were absolutely the best. They were super generous and kind and everything you'd want from an older couple in terms of friendliness and hospitality.

They also told me that since all the big news surrounding me, that their six bedrooms were completely booked for the next two years!

Maria Smith visited me, and we had a lively conversation. She said she recently decided, much to Don

Juan Dorazo's chagrin, to not go off on the cruise ship this time. Then, she volunteered to help handle all my new affairs. She said that she would help out with the letters, with the press, and with anything else. Reluctantly, I agreed. I didn't want her to feel burdened, but Sister Nelly always told me that when someone wants to give, that's if it's good and from the heart, that it's usually best to accept. The giver wants or even needs to give! And those who give store up their rewards in heaven, provided they eventually got there—and that she would mention with somewhat of a stern look in her eye and a poke on my shoulder.

When I was invited onto a Spanish television talk show, and the hostess asked what I thought about the treacherous driver, Javier Santiago Rey, I replied, "I sure hope he's recovering from everything just fine."

Her mouth dropped and there were boo's in the audience.

She then added, "After all that he caused? Just look at yourself!"

Indeed, I still had all my bandages on, again, which made me look partly like a mummy. "Well, I forgive him. I heard that after he's released from the hospital, that they have set up a court hearing and intend to send him straight to jail. I don't know what his punishment should be. I have no idea. All I'm saying, that from my end, I forgive him."

That statement of mine stirred up a lot of controversy around the world for days. Some people thought it was ridiculous for me to say that, others understood why I said it but had their reservations, others agreed with my sentiment, and still others gradually came to agree. I wasn't trying to stir up anything, I was just speaking out honestly, the way Sister Nelly always told me I ought to be.

Then, the day before the scheduled court hearing, while Javier Santiago Rey was still in the hospital, his parents arranged to have a priest visit him. After the priest had left, the nurses said that Javier spent the afternoon writing and rewriting a note, crying much of the time, and said that he wanted the message to be read on the news. That evening, he passed away.

His death stunned the world especially when the hospital spokeswoman, at a news conference, read the note that Javier had written to *me*. They had called me to see if it was okay that they read it publicly and I said it was fine.

The spokeswoman reading the note, now translated in English, said: "Dear Felipe, my dear friend. I am so sorry for all the trouble I caused. I am so ashamed of what has become of me. Despite my mother's wishes and despite my father's wishes, I got involved with the wrong groups of people. I did drugs. I resorted to stealing. I beat up some people. I got into stealing. I stole from stores. I stole from homes. My friends, mostly, didn't even like me. Then all in one afternoon, I stole a purse, I stole a car, and I kidnapped a child, except at the time, I had no idea the boy was in the car. Then I got into the big accident. Then, you saved my body. You saved my body but as for my spirit, there was nothing to save since I thought that was already dead. Then the nurse told me that you forgave me and hoped that I would get better. Well, my little Felipe, that broke my heart, and I have been crying ever since. I don't know what to do with myself. I want to be punished. I want to serve my time in prison. I understand why everyone hates me. I understand. But as of right now, as I write these words, I feel forgiven. And I repent from all my evil ways and deeds. And I feel alive again. By the love of sweet Jesus and all that you've done for me, Felipe. Thank you and may God bless you and all your family." Sincerely, Javier Santiago Rey.

Watching that on TV in the living room at Abila's Bed and Breakfast really—in a big way-- touched my heart, and all the other guests in the room were teary eyed and mostly just plain silent.

The next day, the news on TV, on the internet, and in print was all about the hospital news conference, which became a message of love and forgiveness. For days, that was all the talk.

Then, it was a Saturday, Javier Santiago Rey's mother, father, family, relatives, and friends, were laying him to rest. Except it wasn't just them. There were hundreds of people that showed up for his funeral at a big Catholic church in Malaga. It turned out that these people were from all over Europe, not just Spain. There were even people that flew in from different parts of the world to pay their respects.

I had been invited to be one to walk with the casket and so there I found myself, in suit and tie, still all bandaged up, in this magnificent church, holding onto a handle of the coffin, with five others, who happened to be his four brothers and father. As we were very slowly walking with the casket, the people, with the most earnest expressions, and many of them with tears rolling down their cheeks, reached out to touch me or the father or a brother or the casket.

A pretty little girl with a pink patch over her eye walked over and put a single stem pink rose on the casket, then walked back to her mother. A 45-year-old man stood behind a 65-year-old lady in a wheelchair. As the casket went by her she held up a white piece of paper that, written in black marker, read, "I forgive you, Javier. May you rest in peace." Juan and Cecilia Perez and their five children were present! Cecilia walked over and put a white single stem rose on the casket. Maria Smith was also present and made the sign of the cross, as did many, as the casket passed. Last but not least, when we came to a stop right before the alter, there stood a lady with her two-year old boy in her arms. I remembered that face so vividly in the car seat, except that at the time it was red and scared. Now, instead of coughing crying and coughing, he looked like he was at peace—as was his mother.

I could go on and on about this beautiful event. Somehow, while it was indeed sad, the overall feeling expressed by all was that it was a worldwide event of *beauty* and *healing*. Those two words somehow became *the* two words.

In terms of money, I never asked for a dime; however, Maria Smith had me set up a bank account because I had an endless stream of donations coming in from around the world. These donations were sent to the hospital and sent to the Abila's Bed and Breakfast address, but the checks were all specifically in my name. It amounted to $264,545.00!

I told Maria to make sure that 10% of it was tithed to that magnificent church in Malaga and she was delighted to hear that. I also wanted to make sure all of the emergency and medical bills were paid in full. I also told her to keep 50% of the rest of it, for herself. She absolutely insisted that she would have none of that. I gradually suggested a smaller and smaller percentage to her, and she continued to insist that she didn't want a cent of it. The irony to this was that I figured that with her good job on the cruise ship, she was able to get by fine. However, judging by her old, somewhat dusty car and her modest clothes, I could tell she wasn't particularly well off. In my eyes, Maria Smith was right up there with Sister Nelly—just plain saintly.

Maria Smith had found out early on that letters and donations had also been sent to the other victims such as the little girl who lost her eye, the 60-year-old lady and her son, those others that were injured, and last but certainly not least, the husband and wife that literally saved *my* life and Santiago's. I had visited all these folks, each separately, and there was always at least one newsperson present with microphone and camera. It had nothing to do with the way I wanted it, but according to Maria Smith, and I trusted her of course, the world couldn't get enough of it. The story had gotten so big, that everyone wanted to know how everyone was doing. There was real-life drama there.

Along with these donations, there were notes and letters of amazing words, and prayers. I took the time to write back to each and every person or couple or group that sent me a letter or donation or both. It's partly why I stuck around for six months. It was all very time consuming, but it was all spiritually rewarding, too.

One day, Maria Smith got a call, walked into the bathroom, closed the door, and spoke softly enough so that I couldn't hear what she was saying. After several minutes, she exited and walked up to me putting her hands on my shoulders, looking at me in the eyes. But I also noticed she was looking at my mouth, which was one of the areas that didn't suffer from any burn whatsoever, probably because it was mostly blocked by Javier's head when the flames caught us on fire.

She then said to me, "Philip, that was a doctor from the hospital. He informed me that he knows a plastic surgeon, who's a true specialist for those with your condition. He wants to donate the whole procedure to you. It's all on him!"

"What procedure?" I asked ever so curiously.

"He thinks he can mostly fix your cleft lip, so that it will be barely visible."

I put my fingers to my cleft lip, and I couldn't believe what I had just heard. "When?" I asked.

"Tomorrow morning," she said. "I already made the appointment."

Next thing I knew, it was 24-hours later, I was walking out the doors of that hospital after having undergone a somewhat lengthy surgery. My new head bandages included being wrapped under my nose. Now I was really looking like a mummy! Dr. Fritzmeyer had a dry sense of humor, which I found particularly funny. It helped to ease my fears before, during, and after the surgery.

Since the accident, I had continuously been invited to more television talk shows, radio shows, and other events—but because of my surgery, I had to put off those engagements for two months.

When my stitches had been taken out and another month had passed, I was really impressed with the surgery. I looked practically 100% better. There was going to be a slightly noticeable scar but the harelip had somehow miraculously disappeared. There was still going to be redness for some time, but I was already accustomed to that aspect since I was going to have to wait for my burn redness to go away. And that might not ever go away.

When the engagements resumed, my favorite event was one that was all about classic cars—and it was held in Paris. Amazing cars, amazing BBQ eats, and amazingly cute girls my age. Though, I couldn't help but to think about Bella Sue.

The organizers of these events, like this one, paid for my travel, my hotel, my food, everything. And Maria Smith was my assistant, they paid for all her expenses, too. On top of all that, they paid us an additional five hundred to a thousand dollars. Now that money I insisted that Maria Smith take for herself, and she was okay with that and even very thankful.

All I had to do at these events was to give a twenty-minute speech, but it always ended up being at least an hour to two-hour long affair. As always, I would become very engaged and sincere in what I was saying, and people would sometimes laugh and sometimes cry in the audience. While I'd try to be as stoic as possible, sometimes I would cave and get teary-eyed myself. The last thirty minutes or so were always reserved for "Questions and Answers." Then I would end with a prayer.

So, what would I talk about? Well, every speech was different. No two were alike, mostly since I always enjoyed spontaneity. However, many of the topics I would touch upon were: 1. My ongoing journey around the world. 2. How my plan, ultimately, was to make my parents proud of me for not sitting around while they were in prison. 3. The big car accident and all the aspects that became a part of it. 4. Forgiveness and healing. 5. My observations at sea and in the various countries. 6. My successful cleft lip surgery and how I wanted to donate half of the donations that had come to me, to provide funds for both children and adults with the same defect. 7. Etc., etc., etc... For me, it became very easy to just talk. I never considered myself of having the gift of gab, but I guess when there was so much going on all the time, it was just flat-out easy to talk about all of it, without even trying.

Anyway, somehow, I had become somewhat of a celebrity. It wasn't a dream of mine; it just happened. Did I like it? Honestly, I mostly did. I guess I liked being liked and I liked being popular. On the downside, it sometimes grew a bit tiresome and sometimes I missed just being alone. Yeah, that was it... alone. I missed being by myself. I missed the quiet, the solitude, the adventure, and the challenge of not knowing what to expect next.

So, as the weeks and the months went on, I became more and more eager to get back to the order of my journey. My bandages, depending on the burn severity, were gradually removed, but by the third month, they were completely off, but my burn areas were evident. When six months had passed, most of the burns had faded except for the three second-degree burn locations—the right side of my neck, my left wrist, and my left ankle. As for the area above my mouth and the shape of my mouth and smile, it looked terrific. I couldn't be happier. All thanks to Dr. Fritzmeyer! He was my hero right up there with Mr. and Mrs. Perez... and, of course, Steve and Mac.

Interestingly, after the sixth months, all the hoopla had pretty-much *faded*, as well. The word "fade" turned out to be one of my favorite words of all time—especially when things *faded* away. But silly me, with thoughts like this I could tell I was starting to go beyond stir crazy. I still had to get around a third of the world and there were no plans in place.

Furthermore, even for Maria Smith, she felt it was time for her to get back to the cruise ship, especially when Don Juan Durazo was desperate for her help, had called her, and offered her a raise. Two days later I walked with her to the cruise ship gangplank. I told her to say "Hello," to the boss, Señor Durazo, and all my cruise-ship family. We exchanged a few more nice and thoughtful words, promised to keep in touch, hugged, and said goodbye. Then she walked up the very long and low-angled gangplank with her one large piece of luggage on wheels in tow. She had been so good to me.

Indeed, the time had come! I must sail away into my next leg of the journey. And, despite many offers in the last six months to go on a free cruise or ocean liner or sailing outfit or you name it... I just wanted to head out on my own with no modern technologies, such as GPS or radar. I wanted old school, like the days of the 1970s and earlier.

So, I went around in a taxi to three different places that sold boats in Malaga and found a basic 27-foot sloop, with a smallish cabin, outboard motor, and nothing else too fancy. I also got to keep it where it was docked for one month for free. As far as I was concerned, that was all the time I needed. I named her,

"Feliz Sails," and they put the decaled lettering on her as part of the deal. Nice!

I knew that if the word got out of my plans, that there would be all this news, a big send-off, and boaters and news people tracking me all along the way. Well, I didn't want that. I just wanted to slip away into the ocean. I wanted it to be between me, my boat, and what God might toss my way. And as I thought that, I felt a wave of fear sweep through me. It even made the hair on my arms stand up. And it was nice to see that those hairs, as with all of my hair, had nicely grown back. Anyway, I knew that sailing solo across the Atlantic Ocean was definitely *not* going to be a small undertaking.

Except, this time, when my month was almost up, I felt like I was prepared! When I thought back of my original escape in the 8-foot dinghy, when I had brought so few supplies, well, this time I was going to be supplied to the hilt. In the course of the month, I bought and stowed away on the boat all sorts of food, two hundred gallons of water, five 5-gallon tanks of diesel, spare sails, tools for my specific boat, lots of clothes, especially for stormy weather, etc. I had studied up on the internet, and this time, I was going to be prepared for anything. Also, thanks to what I had learned from my Hawaiian friends, I brought along a sextant, a compass, and some navigational maps. I decided my plan was to head for the Northeast coast of South America. It seemed like a target I couldn't miss!

So, I said goodbye to Mr. and Mrs. Abila, who respectfully agreed not tell anyone of my departure. Then I slid out of my Bed and Breakfast room, wearing sunglasses and a beach-style straw hat. I walked four blocks and flagged down a taxi, taking it to the harbor. It was dusk when I stepped onto the deck of my new boat, *Feliz Sails*. I felt both fear and freedom at that same moment. But then I just bit down, tightening my jaws, and said to myself, "Fear *not*."

CHAPTER 11

ALONE AGAIN

I untied the sloop and sailed off.

As the night set in, it was rather peaceful. There were boats and ships hither and thither. And as I got farther away from the shore and farther out to sea, it felt lonelier and lonelier. But somehow, perhaps by the grace of God, I embraced the feeling of it. I liked it! I was free at last! The next day, I was sailing through the Strait of Gibraltar and the entire Atlantic Ocean was before me. What a moment of awe it was.

And for the next ten days it was smooth sailing. There was nothing but saltwater all around me. It's such an unusual existence compared to the comforts and variety of activities and companionship of people and friends afforded on land or even on a cruise ship for that matter. But again, this is what I had always wanted. To go out on a big solo adventure. Just me, my boat, and God. It was important to keep myself psyched up about it. Because every now and then, I would get a hint of doubt or fear that would start to creep in, but then I would just start singing a song to change my thought pattern.

I also liked to see how many pushups I could do. Not only would this refocus my attention, but it kept me fit. My latest record was 112 pushups. I had no idea if others could do a lot more than that, but for me, it took every ounce of my strength. Next, I would do the same thing, but with sit-ups. My record was 146.

Eleven days into the trip, I found myself in the worst storm I had ever been in. As I could see the storm approaching, I had taken down the two sails, the main sail and foresail, also referred to as the jib, and I went down below and just curled up in my bed. I wasn't sure if this seemed cowardly or wimpy or what. But, despite all the research I had done before the trip, I just didn't know what to do. Or, maybe I had some ideas as to what I was supposed to do, but I was so weary and scared, that I didn't know where to begin. I just somehow couldn't remember or get a grip on the step-by-steps.

In the course of two hours, the wind gradually blew harder and harder and the rain came down stronger and stronger. Within another hour, I could hear thunder and I could see lightning in the distance. Then the lightning got closer and the thunder roared louder. The swell got bigger and bigger, too. And there were moments I thought the boat was going to capsize. I suddenly got extremely nervous and seriously wondered if I should be at the helm--that way I could help to steer the boat in such a manner that would help prevent it from rolling over. "Of course, you idiot!" I yelled. I was so angry with myself.

This realization came at the height of the thunderstorm, though, and I was concerned that I would get hit by lightning. "That's right!" I also said aloud. So, maybe I had inadvertently done the right thing.

The boat continued to toss and turn and every now and then felt like it was going to capsize, but then it would right itself. When the lightning passed, I flipped on two switches for the exterior lights. I got on deck now donning my foul-weather clothes. I turned on the engine, kept it humming low just to provide a little forward speed to make the boat steerable, and grabbed the wheel with both hands. The rain continued to come in hard at a slant with the howling wind. Wow, what a ride! It was pitch black beyond the lights cast out by the boat, but I could make out that I was going up and over the big waves that never quite crashed, teasing like they would, and must have been at least the height of the sloop's mast. I mostly got this estimated measurement when the boat was in the low spot. While it was scary, I just clamped down hard on my jaw and put on that fierce look in my eye. This wasn't pretend like at my fifth birthday pirate-themed party. No! I was in the middle of the *real* deal!

I laughed out loud in a wicked manner. Suddenly, I took on that pirate-like demeanor. "Arrr! Let the devil bring it on!" I yelled.

Then the high adventure of it all really kicked in, as the wind picked up even more, the waves got bigger, and the rain just pelted harder and relentlessly against my raincoat. Maybe it was a bad idea to prod the devil I thought. But then I just yelled rebelliously, "No!" to that, and proceeded to just have the time of my life. Yes, I was soaking wet, and yes it was very cold, and yes it took up all the energy I had just to hold onto the wheel, stay standing, and negotiate the waves, but in my mind it was all totally doable and, with a surge of confidence, I yelled out, "I like this more than anything! Never had so much fun!"

So, that storm lasted for fifteen-hours straight, gradually dying down from the climax that I just described. At the end of it all, when it was dawn and the sun came out and the wind died down to about three knots, I slouched behind the steering wheel, with one hand resting on the bottom part of it, turned off the engine, and fell asleep.

When I woke up, it was midafternoon, and I put up the sails again. I had survived my first storm at sea, sailing solo. The accomplishment was exhilarating to me! I went down below and made myself tuna fish crackers.

Now, I could go on and on about the wondrous aspects of sailing across the Atlantic. The first thing that would spring to mind, though, is one word: Grand.

It was many, many days of an enriching experience. It filled my spirit and my soul.

The one very sketchy moment, however, was when a huge cargo carrier that looked like it was the length of two football fields, nearly ran me over. All along I was waving at the approaching vessel with a big smile on my face. As it got closer and closer, I slowly realized that they couldn't see my boat, let alone my ridiculously invisible smile and hand waving, and I was only able to steer the boat out of the way in the last thirty seconds. It missed me by only thirty feet and I only saw one sailor at the rail casually waving at me as it went by, like nothing happened! The wake of the beast felt like it was going to capsize my boat, but I quickly steered into it, preventing that possibility. I hate to admit it, but I furiously cursed that man waving at me. Later in the day, though, I felt bad about that and forgave him--not that he had any idea of my sentiments at the time.

A few weeks later, I was sailing into, according to my maps and calculations, the island of Barbados —relatively speaking, pretty close to South America. When I first saw it on the distant horizon, I jumped up and down with joy.

As I got closer, I sort of followed other boats. There weren't many. Just three actually in the distance. One was a cruise ship. Anyway, I resorted to my maps and realized it might be best to swing around the island of Barbados, which is exactly what I ended up doing. It was a very cloudy day, but it was warm. The clouds were of the white, puffy variety. They were my favorite type to see.

I sailed into what I believed was a harbor of Bridge-town and found an empty slip where many docks and many boats were located. I decided that I would just pretend that I knew what I was doing and that I was expected. In my mind, anyway, it was the truth. According to Sister Nelly, God expected us to just show up according to his master plan, whatever that plan might be. Well, who was I to know what that plan was?

With ropes forward and aft, I fastened *Feliz Sails* to the dock and stepped out. Wow, it was nice to be on land again—to feel the boardwalk under me. However, I was wobbly and for a moment I thought, and I said it aloud as I thought it, "Maybe this isn't so great." I suddenly got dizzy and had to sit down right on the wood planks of the dock. I managed to get a splinter on my thumb, but then pulled it out cleanly with my teeth. While I was sitting, I was half asleep. I wanted to snap out of it and enjoy land (!) but I was so tired and completely worn out—both physically and mentally.

CHAPTER 12

BEAUTIFUL BALANCE

I barely woke up lying on my back on the edge of the dock, still coming out of a mysterious dream, when a very old man in shorts, not wearing shoes or a shirt, walked up to me and said something in a language I didn't understand, but it sounded like Spanish. I told him that I only spoke and understood English. He smiled, turned back around, kicked up his heels, literally, and skipped off whistling. *Funny old man*, I thought.

I stretched like a cat and fell back asleep. The next thing I knew, I woke up looking into the eyes of a man in his 50s with a sailor's cap—the sort with an anchor embroidered on the front of it.

"Ahoy there," he said with a smile. Then I noticed the old man without a shirt, standing right behind him. I was still on the dock and still waking up, but felt like I had had a great rest.

I rubbed my eyes and asked, "Is this Bridgetown, Barbados?"

"Yes," he said with a smile.

"Oh, wonderful. Maybe I've got this navigation thing down then," I said with an inner-feeling of delight.

Before I knew it, this good-vibes man, Alexandro Loreto, who explained that he spoke French, English, and Spanish, invited me to his very large house up on a hill. We drove in his 1990 Ford F250, Crew cab. The old man, Jose Loreto, who was his father, sat in the back seat.

As we conversed, I referred to Alexandro as Señor Loreto and his father as "your dad." Anyway, Señor Loreto told me not to worry about my boat. It was a guest slip. Any guest of the thousand or so yacht club members could dock there. He said that he had already put in a call to security as they were leaving the harbor. He also said that crime was almost unheard of especially since the gate locked as you came or left.

I had the best seafood dinner in my life. His hospitable and pretty wife, Linda Loreto, prepared hammerhead shark and pasta with a marinara sauce and spices. I just called her Señora Loreto. The shark had been caught by Señor Loreto the day before. He was a sports fisherman and sold much of what he caught to the local fish markets. But he was also a retired attorney. Apparently, I gathered, he was a very successful one from Mexico City.

Then, out of the blue, Señora Loreto, who spoke Spanish and English, asked me if I was all better since the car accident. "The car accident?" I asked. "So, *you* know about it? Way out here on this obscure island?"

"Of course," she said. "Who no have satellite television estes dias?"

Well then it broke into a whole new conversation, but the upshot was, I was on the fence trying to decide if I should head to the Panama Canal or head south and go around Cape Horn.

Señor Loreto advised me that if I was looking for the shortcut, that I should take the canal; but, if I had a whole lot of time, that sailing around the Cape Horn would be a little more epic.

"Epic?" I said with a laugh. "While I like the sound of that, my main goal is to just get back to Ventura, California, on time. I have less than a year and a half left."

"Oh, well that's plenty of time to go around the Cape," he said.

"Well, probably not," I protested. "The more I think about it, the more I realize that my journey has continuously been interrupted by stopping for whatever length of time at different places. And I've really enjoyed that aspect, because it gives me time to soak in those experiences. You know, to not rush things."

"Of course," Señora Loreto said. "You can stay with

us for a while then."

"Oh, but I didn't mean to impose, I—"

"No-no," she said. "Is all fine, we love to have you stay as long as you wish. That is right, Alexandro?"

"Of course, Linda. In fact, I am wanting to fly him down to Port of Spain, Trinidad, for visiting my little brother, Raul."

"Fly?" I said excitedly.

"Yes, I am a pilot," he said. "I own a twin-engine propeller plane. We can go down there, doing island hopping and staying in hotels. Then we stay two days with my brother, and fly back, We can do everything in two weeks' time. You know, with a few stops for fuel and go-to-sleep in hotel each way. Island hopping is the fun life. Take it easy. And you know what's nice for you on these islands, actually even here in Barbados, the main language is English. I speak maybe not very good English, because my first language is Spanish."

I replied, "Your English is very good. As for me, I know very, very little Spanish. Just some easy words like 'taco' and 'bueno.' Anyway, I'm excited. When would we leave?" I asked.

"Sooner than you think, mi amigo," he said with a wry smile.

"What about my boat?" I asked.

"Oh, mi padre, my father that is, will keep his eye on it. He works down there as the dock manager," he said.

"That's great," I said.

He then threw a dart at a dartboard, hitting the bullseye on his first throw. Then he put down the other two darts.

"Wow, you're good!" I practically yelled. "Keep throwing."

Then he just waved his finger at me and said, "Is already perfecto." Then he smiled and ruffled up my hair.

I slept well that night, and before dawn, we were driving to the airport. Next thing I knew, we were taking off in his twin-engine airplane. As we flew off, I could start to make out the island. After several minutes, he made a few turns and then pointed at the harbor. He then specifically pointed down at my approaching boat and as we whizzed off to the side of it, he said, "See, your boat, Feliz Sails, is just fine. Oh, how I liking that name. It's good Spanglish." That sure put a smile on my face.

Well this had to be the most amazing experience I had ever had. It was my first time in an airplane, and I think I found a new love—flying! It was so thrilling, it was so fast, it was like being a bird! I was flabbergasted. "Whoo-hooo!"

It took us four days to get to Port of Spain, Trinidad, since we stopped at three airports along the way near the cities of—Kingstown, St. Vincent... St. George's, Grenada, and... Scarborough, Tobago. Each day, we flew for several hours, land, and then take a taxi to the nearest hotel—each one had a lot of character and I really enjoyed staying in them. As we walked around, not too often, but occasionally someone would recognize me and ask for my autograph. Sometimes, they would ask me to be in a photo with them. It was all good. Again, I liked that I was liked. People would say how great I looked—no more bandages, burn scars faded, my smile. It all made me feel so grateful to all the nurses and doctors, especially Dr. Fritzmeyer, who fixed me up.

After getting off the plane at our final destination in Port of Spain, Trinidad, meeting his brother, Raul, at the airport was terrific. He gave me what looked like a chocolate candy bar but was actually chocolate-flavored chewing gum and he gave his older brother a cigar that squirted water. He was a real jokester and always had the best, upbeat attitude.

We all got along great for the two days. We did some sightseeing, saw some shows, hung out at the beach, had fantastic food, it was all just super. I found that the citizens of Trinidad were a particularly fun sort of people.

When we went to church on Sunday, it was a wonderfully reverent church setting and the music was some of the best I had ever heard. It was as if the choir had come down from a cloud in heaven.

The trip back to Barbados went as fast as the trip down to Trinidad. We dropped by the same airports but checked into different hotels, because Mr. Loreto liked variety. I guess when it came down to it, as I loved every moment of it all, the time flew by. And yes, it *literally* flew by. I was so grateful to Señor Loreto for paying for everything. I offered to pay several times, but he always refused.

When we got back to his house on the hill, one day led to another, and one week led to another, and one month led to another, and in the end, I stayed with the Loretos for about a year! During this time, I enrolled in a home-schooling co-op where I attended classes at different people's homes. At *his* own home, Señor Loreto volunteered as a guitar teacher. That was *his* thing. So, I learned the basics of guitar which was a real pleasure to me. All in all, there were about thirty students of various ages.

During this time, I also really learned how to relax —that was something the Loretos insisted that I do. Initially, they said I worried too much and was a little too hyperactive. So, during my time there, I painted with oils and played darts. I hiked around the island of Barbados whenever I felt like it. I made a few friends my age on the other side of the island, went on fishing excursions with Señor Loreto, played a lot of chess with now "Grampa Loreto," and went to church every Sunday. I celebrated my eighteenth birthday, enjoyed other birthdays and holiday festivities, and on four separate days sailed for a few hours in *Feliz Sails* with Señor Loreto. I read Moby Dick, books on oceanography and yachting, and books on drawing and painting. I ate great food, learned cooking techniques, and played the congas. Señor Loreto played the guitar, of course, and Señora Loreto played the flute. We all sang songs, too. Occasionally, I would play guitar in our trio and the Loretos said I was getting better and better at it. So, all in all, this particular style of island life was the closest thing I had experienced to a well-balanced sense of joy and tranquility.

But it really did feel like I needed to be on my way! I had no idea what to expect in my sailing journey and I still had a long way to go. When you looked at a globe, everything seemed so close—that it would be no big deal to just jump in a boat and get there like snapping your fingers. In reality, it was all very slow going and it took a tremendous amount of patience, especially once you had a destination in mind. But the patience came with passion. I had a love for boats and sailing and the ocean and the seas. Whenever I started to feel weary or discouraged or scared or sad, I had to remind myself, "Hey, you're doing what you love to do!"

Next thing I knew, it was dawn and the Loretos were waving at me from the dock. They had resupplied *Feliz Sails* with food and fuel and a few other things. I really appreciated all of it and thanked them profusely. Now, as I was starting to sail off, waving goodbye to them, I was glad that I didn't shed a tear this time. Maybe I was growing up at last. The thought of that made me get a feeling inside that warmed me up with a sense of pride.

Then, Señor Loreto yelled out to me when I was a hundred feet away, "I love you, Felipe!" And he stood there for about twenty seconds, stoic, like a real man.

Then, suddenly, I could tell he broke down in tears, holding onto his wife and father, who both were trying to hold it together, too. Well, that's when I jumped on my feet and yelled back, "I love you, too!" Then, *I* started to cry. "You're the best! Thank you for everything! I'll let you know when I make it!" Then I sat down at the steering wheel and cried some more... so much for that newfound sense of pride!

CHAPTER 13

ONE NEVER KNOWS WHAT HAPPENS NEXT

I had about eight months to get back. If I sailed through the Panama Canal and straight up to California, it could all be done in two, three, or four months, but I just knew that I would run into delays. I started to think of them as, "Happy delays." You know, to break up the monotony of boating and to discover new experiences. Besides, it all came down to timing. I didn't want to arrive in California, only to have to wait around for my parents to get out of prison. No, the whole idea was that I wanted to arrive just as they were getting out. Why that was so important to me, remained a mystery. But it's what I was going with!

On to the Canal! That was my next step! I sailed right through the Caribbean Sea, avoiding the temptation to drop by the variety of her historic islands.

I also avoided the temptation to find a port on the north coast of South America. I could imagine new experiences to be found there. No, I was dead set to head toward the Panama Canal. I wanted this part of my journey behind me and under my belt. My pirate belt, if you will. Harr-har-harr.

Well, I knew I was on course when I just started following these huge cargo carriers and oil tankers. They would gradually pass me as I had learned how to get out of their way and not tempt fate. But, with the additional aid of my topographical maps and navigational instruments, the sextant and compass, I just pressed on.

There was an occasional squall, bringing both higher wind gusts and lots of rain. Sometimes they brought along some thunder and lightning, too, which, when I thought about it, I always liked. I suppose one stopped liking lightning when he actually got hit by it. Until then, lightning was way cool. These squalls were very tame compared to what I had already been through. In my mind they were like kitten weather when compared to the tiger storm I'd been through in the middle of the Atlantic. Thinking back at *that* storm, indeed, that lightning had me scared. But then again, it was night, during high seas, and it sounded like it was going to hit the boat, which all things considered, could've sunk me.

With all this confidence, another squall came along when I knew I was probably a day away from the canal. This one hit me and my boat hard though. I was unprepared. The boat almost capsized and a wave came onto the boat that even soaked the cabin since I had left the door open. I barely turned the boat to headwind on time which uprighted her. I lowered and tied the mainsail and jib, and fired up the diesel engine. I decided to travel at the speed of about four knots. I got up and quickly glanced in the cabin to inspect. Everything was a wet mess. My clothes, supplies, food, even some of my bed, had all gotten a good soaking. Kitchen supplies were floating around, and a few boxes of goods were soaked.

I closed the cabin door as the rain kept pouring down at an angle. The wind almost blew me off the boat, but I leaped and grabbed the steering wheel in the nick of time. The boat almost started to capsize again but I corrected her direction. I shouldn't have downplayed squalls, I thought! This one was kicking my butt!

Then I saw a waterspout in the distance approaching my way. Wow, I had never seen one before. I had only seen photos of them. This one was very long and very slender--a real beauty. It didn't look so menacing. But as it got closer, it looked bigger. "Sorry," I said with a newfound sense of fear, "you're scary! You're very scary!" It was headed right for my boat. I accelerated the engine for the first time to her maximum twenty-five knots per hour to get out of the way. As it grazed by my boat, but forty feet away, I could feel the pull of her vortex as if it were trying to grab us. But I got out of there so fast, it made my head spin! Now that was a near miss if I ever had one. Holy monster! The thing was dark and majestic and huge and just went on its merry way!

Apparently, I survived the climax and the rest of the day the weather very gradually eased off. I fought out the "squall" and by the end of the day when it had completely passed, I was totally worn out. Then I saw a magnificent rainbow. Sister Nelly had always told me that that means God's smiling at you. Well, did I ever need that smile. I turned off the engine and turned on the exterior lights. Then, I managed to find a dry spot on my bed, curled up, and went to sleep.

I woke up in the morning and had a hard time figuring out which way was which. It was overcast so I couldn't exactly figure out where the sun was. I decided to just keep the engine off, the sails down, and drift. The wind was only at two knots. Four hours later, the clouds cleared, and the sun was overhead. I still couldn't figure out which way I was going. Another hour passed and a pretty big sports fishing boat came within fifty yards of me. I took a chance and waved them over. It was a husband and wife and their two teenaged daughters cruising the Caribbean on vacation. I asked them, yelling, which way to the Panama Canal and the man yelled back over the noise of his big, idling engine, "Follow us! Do you have enough fuel!" I gave him the thumbs up and followed them at about twenty knots per hour.

"Now this is the way to move," I said aloud.

To my surprise, we got to the Panama Canal by late afternoon. I thanked them, yelling and waving, when they were twenty yards away. For some reason, they didn't go into the canal; instead, they headed north. We continued to wave goodbye to each other as they got farther and farther away. Nice family, I thought. Nice family. Godspeed to them.

When I sailed up to the first canal station, the authorities—four uniformed men in their 30s perhaps-- soon figured out who I was. They had me dock *Feliz Sails* and before I knew it, I was sitting down in an office with a big window overlooking one of the new and greatly expanded locks of the canal. I spent an hour of what I would consider to be a soft interrogation. It was actually more a thing of storytelling, interpreted by a very pretty Brazilian lady in her 20s— I found that out because I told her all about my plane trip. She said I should've kept flying down to Brazil! She told me her name was Mary Townson and we shook hands.

Well amidst the men's cigar smoke and laughs and interpreting, they eventually got around to telling me I needed to follow right behind *that* tanker. They pointed out the window at an oil tanker that was the biggest man-made thing I had ever seen. It was docked, assisted by tugboats, as night was setting in, but it was scheduled to depart at the crack of dawn.

They further explained that "to follow right behind" meant at least a half-mile behind and that I was always to give tugboats, patrol boats, or other vessels the right of way.

Then they were called out of the room by a Spanish-speaking voice on an intercom. They left me alone for about two minutes and came back in. They then notified me that I wouldn't need to check in anywhere along the way since the other station personnel were going to be notified of my crossing. I was getting a "free pass" from the big chief, they said with laughs and big smiles. They also asked that I give them each an autograph which I was more than happy to provide. Then they wanted a group photo which Mary took with each of their cell phones. Then, I was dismissed and just as I was leaving, they gave me hugs and pats on the head and back. What a great group of guys I thought! Then, the interpreter hugged me and gave me a kiss on the cheek. Wow. She was so pretty in quite the exotic way, and her long, dark brown hair smelled so good, too. It was going to be one lucky man whoever found her to marry.

At the crack of dawn, I woke up in my docked boat and followed the gigantic oil tanker as it shoved off. Sailing in the Panama Canal was fascinating. I looked at it all as an engineering wonder--how many decades ago, people figured out a way, with early technologies to dig and blast through the thread of land, like tissue, that connected the two continents of North and South America.

Thinking back about recently meeting Mary Townson, who said she was from New York, she had told me during the lively "interrogation" that *that* ship was just a bit shorter in length than the Empire State Building was in height! It was called a "supertanker." She even showed an online site that visually compared the heights of the tallest buildings with the lengths of the biggest supertankers.

Anyway, she also told me that this supertanker was en route to Alaska making several stops along the way, including Long Beach, California. Hearing that practically made my heart stop. It sounded like I was getting closer to home! Home? Funny, how I never really thought of home. I always thought of getting back to my parents, but "home" wasn't the word that popped up in my mind. But... of course! Home! *My* home. It's where I grew up. It's where I made many friends at school and outside of school. It was where all my sailing buddies were....

Then, it struck me. Ever since I had made my escape, I really hadn't thought much about my friends back home, especially my sailing buddies, and indeed I had many of them. I did have a best friend, Mike Donner, who liked to sail his dinghy but didn't compete. Sadly, though, we had a falling out, which occurred about two weeks before my escape. I thought he cheated when we were playing the board game, Risk.

What had happened was, after I had gone to the bathroom, I came back and noticed that he had fortified his armies on each of his territories. It was subtle, the increases of his troops, that is, but it was definitely noticeable. We got into a huge argument and I then stormed out of his house, yelling back, "No friend of mine is a cheater!"

Now, all these years later, I felt a pang of guilt.

Maybe I was too hard.

My new thought was: *If you find somebody being dishonest, deal with it. Don't kill the relationship. No person is perfect, and everyone has his or her own faults. Maybe by dealing with it, that person can change for the better.*

I wasn't sure if I got all that from Sister Nelly, or from church, or if I sort of figured it out from all that I had learned.

But it was about forgiveness. Indeed, "forgiveness." That had become a key word in my life. As I thought about it even more, it was also about self-control. That is, having the ability to refrain from whatever the wrongdoing was. My best friend, Mike, should not have cheated in the first place. And I, should not have been a hot head and stormed out.

Anyway, as I was sailing through the canal, and during one of the stops at the locks, it was the third one, a uniformed man, not unlike the ones I had met, except he was Caucasian, waved me over. So, I lowered my sails, fired up my little diesel engine, and eased my way over to him. He said, in perfect English, that the captain, Captain Steve Howitzer, of the super-tanker I was following, wanted to crane my boat on board and invite me to ride along. He explained to me that the captain knew that I had already steered big ships, since he gathered this knowledge from news stories that revealed my impromptu world journey and my desire to learn how to be an accomplished sailor of all vessels, big and small. Well I was blown away by his invitation.

I couldn't tell if I was dreaming or what, but next thing I knew, my tiny little, adorable sloop, *Feliz Sails*, was being craned on board what looked like the mothership of modern watercraft. Her name was *Magnificent Lizzie*.

Before I knew it, the very talkative security guard escorted me to the tower elevator and took me up to what he referred to as, "the pilot's nest." On the way, he explained that the captain of *this* mighty ship was pretty much the pilot most of the time. "But," he added, "that the captain really preferred to be called a "helmsman," because that's what his father, a professional fisherman, always told him he was destined to be. And that *that* was the highest achievement according to his father.

So, when I exited the elevator, that's when I first saw Captain Howitzer. He was a stern man that didn't seem to smile or laugh. He had white hair and a white beard but looked as fit and healthy as a young marine. His perfectly ironed uniform with stripes and badges, complete with captain's cap with the official patch of the ship, suggested that he was one that heralded great attention and respect. It was no wonder that a man of his stature was the sort to be put in command of such a monstrous-sized vessel.

When I first walked up to him, standing at the ship's wheel, he didn't look my way. With a few gestures, he had another officer take over the wheel —perhaps a genuine pilot, other than himself, of course. There were other officers as well, monitoring or managing or operating computer systems, navigational equipment, maps, camera and security systems, levers, meters, and gauges. All in all, it was a large room high in the tower that was enclosed by large windows allowing to visually look out, I learned later, 260 degrees.

The captain turned to me and said, "Young Philip Wilburton, *Mr.* Wilburton, welcome aboard." The look in his eyes was so piercing, I could have fallen back. Instead, I stood my ground and said, "Thank you, Captain Howitzer, it's very good to meet you, and I thank you immensely for this opportunity." I could have kicked myself for not deepening my voice, instead, it sounded a little high pitched with a hint of nervousness.

CHAPTER 14

PEACEFUL IS THE PACIFIC...
NOT ALWAYS

I n the days to come, while we passed through the canal, entered the Pacific Ocean, and then started to head along the coast of Central America, northbound, I was taken on a tour through the ship by yet another pretty lady named, Lola Day. She said that she spoke five languages: English, Spanish, Italian, French, and German, but that she was hoping to learn a whole dozen before she hit 40. Currently, she was 33 years old, a graduate from Johns Hopkins University, where she got a master's degree in International Studies. That sincerely impressed me, and I felt like I was in the presence of a very important person; so, I always did my best to be as respectful as possible.

I learned a great deal about the ship in the course of the first week. Much of the time Ms. Day sat me down in a conference room and we watched all sorts of videos which included: the making of *Magnificent Lizzie* and her specifications, the oil industry, trade and commerce of today, currents and weather, disastrous weather, emergency protocol on an oil tanker, training, the ship's engines, the roles of the officers and ship personnel, the navigational equipment, steering the ship and understanding her gauges, instruments and systems--pretty much everything. I never grew bored. I was just ever more fascinated with obtaining the knowledge and then putting it all into perspective. It was still a mystery to me regarding the business or operations behind the shipping company or its corporation, because none of that was in the videos and we never really talked about it. But big business was always a mystery to me anyway, so it didn't matter.

Then, one dawn, Captain Howitzer, to my surprise, summoned me up and, after a brief exchange of words, let me take over the ship's wheel. He was standing over my shoulder, of course, and gave me tips or instructions to whatever degree needed. Well, I was astonished. After standing there for the first five minutes, I literally pinched my arm as hard as I could to feel the pain of it. I wanted to *make sure* it was painful to confirm that I wasn't dreaming. Stupidly, I cried out, "Youch!" The captain gave me a perplexed look, the kind with only one eyebrow up. I assured him that I was okay but felt embarrassed.

"That will be enough for now, young Philip," he said.

The rest of the morning I moped around the deck of the ship feeling like I really blew an opportunity. It was so lame that I revealed my cards; that, in truth, I was just a wannabe helmsman of such a grand ship that obviously lacked the skill and maturity to even seriously consider it.

After I had lunch with Ms. Day, I explained to her what had happened—how I pinched my arm in front of the captain. We took a walk on the deck and she then explained to me that *Magnificent Lizzie*, the newest ship of its class, was mostly owned by President and CEO, Darko Meyerhof, an eccentric seventy-year old billionaire who, for forty years built and ran the shipping company, DMWW OIL Corporation. It had a fleet of a dozen oil tankers and cargo carriers and a network of businesses that amounted to a total of some twenty-thousand employees. Anyway, when word had leaked from the canal authorities about my whereabouts, Mr. Meyerhof, who had followed my story in Spain, was the one that heard I was sailing in the canal right behind his supertanker. This amused him to no end. So, upon hearing this news, *he* was the one that put the order in to Captain Howitzer to get me behind the wheel of the ship and to train me.

"Wow, I said to Ms. Day, "maybe I *am* dreaming." She assured me I wasn't and even gave me a pretty hard pinch in the arm. "Youch!" I exclaimed and we both laughed.

Ms. Day then said, "This ship is unlike other supertankers in some ways. For example, Mr. Meyerhof put a walking or jogging track around its perimeter, since he has always believed that his crew should routinely, during breaks, put in the laps to stay in shape. He also put in two deck shuffleboards, partly because he's a champion in the sport, and partly because he thinks it's a great way for the crew to relax during any days off."

"He sounds like a great guy," I said. "Man, I mean. An accomplished, great man."

"I'll let him know you said that," she said with a friendly wink.

As it was getting close to dusk, I was by myself and stood at the bow, the enormous bow of the super-tanker, and felt the majesty of the Pacific Ocean right before me. We were moving at about 15 knots and I loved the feel of the breeze at my face and body.

Then in the distance, maybe a mile ahead of us, I spotted what looked like a very small sailboat potentially crossing in front of us. I turned around and waved for attention, yelling, "Hey, let's watch out for that boat!" I half turned and pointed toward it. I didn't notice anyone but hoped that they saw me through the observation windows or on camera. Then I turned around again, looking at the enormous body of the vessel; I noticed an officer and I did what looked like jumping jacks. "Hey, slow down! There's a boat up ahead!" It was now about a half mile away and the supertanker hadn't slowed down a bit. Furthermore, by the looks of it, the little sailboat was crossing in our direct path! It looked like a sailing dinghy, not too unlike the one that my whole journey started with years ago!

I ran up to the officer and told him we must stop the ship! I alerted him that there was a sailboat up ahead. He shook his head and said, "It'll get out of the way."

"We must at least slow down," I pleaded!

He walked to the bow and the distance had closed to about a quarter mile. The officer stood there calculating in his mind what he was looking at. He then calmly spoke into his radio relaying the observation in a manner that was both calm and intense at the same time. How can that be? Well, I figure there's some sort of art to this non-panic style, emergency situation.

Moments later, the ship started to slow down and turn. A kid, maybe a young teenager, was in the sailing dinghy waving both his arms at us as our ship closed in. We just couldn't slow down or turn fast enough. By the time the ship had slowed down to about five knots, we grazed the dinghy on our starboard side. At first the little sailboat, luckily, sort of spat outward like it had caught a wave, but then it suddenly capsized, audibly slapping the salty water, and soon after got somewhat mangled up as the ship kept moving forward, even though it was slowing down.

Worse, we couldn't see the kid. At this point, several officers and shipmates were at the rail. We were mostly walking aft keeping an eye on what was left of the sailing dinghy, hoping that the kid was in its proximity. Then, a shipmate, a janitor actually, spotted him. Compared to the enormous walls of the ship, it looked like a tiny head bobbing in the sea water. He had come up from under the sail and was holding onto the tip of the boat's little tiller as the ship was passing. The tiny, now splintering dinghy continued to get scraped up by our passing ship.

The officers and ship's hands yelled at one another, while the emergency alarm was sounding off. It wasn't long when all of them scrambled to engage the system to lower an emergency lifeboat.

I suddenly ran as fast as I could, two hundred feet aft and grabbed two life preserver rings on hooks. They also had thin white ropes attached. The ship was still trying to slow down, but it was still moving at about four knots. I threw one of the rings down to the kid, but it missed him by thirty feet. He didn't swim for it and it looked like he was struggling and barely hanging on for dear life to the tiller. Next, I took off my shoes and socks, keeping my white pants and shirt on, got up on the rail, and looked down at the very distant 80 feet! I was scared beyond belief, but I couldn't just let the kid drown! I quickly tied the rope to my belt loop, hating myself for doing what I was about to do, flung the life preserver as hard as I could and jumped! This was probably not the best way, but I jumped going cannon ball style because I was afraid that I'd break an arm or a leg or my neck! Well, I hit that water so hard that it felt like it slapped me senseless. And it hurt! I barely missed the mast of the dinghy and plunged probably twenty feet. At least that's what it felt like when I slowly rose to the surface. Wow, this was scary stuff! The wind had been knocked out of me and I barely managed to grab onto a piece of the sail that was completely in the water and in disarray. I had no idea where either life preserver was, but at least we had pieces of the crippled boat to hold onto.

I was struggling to get air and finally, after about ten seconds which seemed like a minute at the time, I managed to start breathing. Next, I made my way over to the kid, who looked very worried and in a state of shock. Blood was pouring out of his forehead—not massive volumes but steadily. I took off my shirt, wadded it up, and applied pressure to his wound. The tiller broke off and he started to drift away flailing with his arms. "Swim to me!" I yelled now holding onto the rudder of the upside-down boat with one hand and reaching out with the other toward him. He swam frantically with all his remaining strength and I just barely reached over far enough to grab him at the wrist. I pulled him in, but it now required all of *my* strength. We were both panting and exhausted. The bloody wadded shirt had gotten caught up in the rigging and I managed to rip it free. I wadded it up again and applied pressure to his head wound again.

I abruptly found myself hoping that this blood of his *wasn't going to attract you know what!* Well, I thought that too soon! Because that's when I saw two dorsal fins slowly making their way toward us—and they weren't of the dolphin variety! Indeed, they were on the blood trail!

"Help!" I yelled desperately as loud as I possibly

could. "Sharks! Sharks! Help!

The emergency boat, a pretty big one, was just being lowered to the water. However, it was plain to see that it was going to be too late! Now one of the sharks revealed himself by biting into the mast lying in the water just five feet from us! The one eye that I could see was a sinister deep shiny black and his sharp, white teeth were plentiful! He must've thought that mast was one of our limbs! But now he had seen me eye to eye! I was next! If not by that shark, surely the other!

Then, like it was lightning from heaven, several gun shots rang out! The sharks were being shot at from an officer with rifle and scope from the very rail that I had leaped from! He must've been a marksman because those sharks were getting peppered, evident by little splashes and their dorsal fins getting shot up. Then pools of blood came up from the sharks, not us! As the ship kept moving forward, our splintered boat kept moving aft until the ship passed us and we were left out in the open water. The severely injured or dead sharks were about fifty feet away from us and were now being eaten up by their own!

Soon after, we were rescued. The kid, a 13-year old Guatemalan, named Jose Mares Gomez, and I, were successfully extracted out of the water by the ship's crew via standard emergency procedures. We were taken to the ship's urgent care facility. There were two doctors and four nurses on board this vessel, so Jose and I got top care instantly. It turned out he was mostly okay, just severely dehydrated, hungry, and needed eight stitches on his forehead. I was treated for sore muscles, a mildly strained neck, and a few scratches. The doctors said it was a miracle that Jose survived such an ordeal and credited me, according to a few witness reports, for saving his life.

And what was the ordeal? Well, this is what Lola Day told me after she had spoken with Jose: He was the son of a fisherman and had observed routes of large, passing ships all his life. He was always the curious sort and often wondered where these big "boats" were coming from and going to. His father also had a brother who had access to commercial shipping schedules, since he worked in the oil industry. Jose confided with his uncle to find out when *Magnificent Lizzie* would be passing by their coastal town, claiming he wanted to look at it with binoculars. The long and the short of it is that he knew *I* was on board this ship.

News—world news that is--had leaked out from those fun and goofy canal officers that I had been taken on board the *Magnificent Lizzie* and heading to California (with several port stops along the way). The supertanker was en route to Mexico, passing along the coast of Guatemala by some ten nautical miles out. Jose wanted to see if he could somehow hitch a ride to try to join me on the last leg of my journey!

His intention wasn't to wreck his sailing dinghy, but he had hoped that the supertanker would stop to pick him up. The news had mentioned that my sloop had been hauled aboard with a crane onto the super-tanker. So, he thought to himself: *Maybe the same can be done with my boat!* In the end, while it didn't work out as he had planned, he did succeed in getting on the supertanker and meeting me in person. I think I was just as amazed to see him as he was me! I had no idea that anyone would go to such lengths to join me as a traveling companion. So, indeed we became friends, but I had the hardest time communicating with him, since I really didn't know but a handful of words in Spanish and he didn't know an ounce of English. Lola Day helped out when she could, but she had other matters to tend to regularly—one of them was figuring out what to do, according to the ship's proto-col, with our new unexpected visitor. She confided that with me, but also told me to just keep Jose busy and happy.

Well that was my pleasure, especially since it broke up what was typical routine stuff. Jose and I sort of hung out with each other for the next two days. We played shuffleboard quite a bit, threw darts, and jogged around the deck. Apparently, he was a star soccer player in his youth league and was a very fast runner. Even I, a few years older, had a very hard time keeping up with him. So, all in all, we had great com-petitive fun, good laughs, and enjoyed teaching each other words.

To my disappointment, I soon found out that he was to be dropped off at Mexico's Port of Lazaro Cardenez, one of the supertanker's stops. There was a strict policy, that under no circumstances whatsoever, stowaways or rescued people were to be kept onboard. It was all business and clear cut.

Also, Ms. Day had been able to notify Guatemalan authorities, and made arrangements to have Jose bussed back south to his small coastal town, where his greatly relieved mother, father, family members, and community would await his arrival with great anticipation. He had gone missing for three days without a word. Since he was last spotted going out in his sailing dinghy, family members and volunteers went out on fishing boats for the three days searching for him but came back with ever-increasing fear and sadness that he had likely perished. So, the news that he safe and that plans were in place to get him back home safely, was joyous news to them—all a wonderful answer to their endless prayers.

I could definitely imagine the celebration that was going to be and was tempted to invite myself to go back home with him; but then again, I seemed to be right on time for my own long-anticipated homecoming.

Actually, I was ahead of schedule but figured there was always the unexpected something or other that would slow things up. My new vision, though, was to pilot the supertanker, just as my parents—fresh out of prison--were meeting me at the dock in Port Hueneme, right there in Ventura, California. This was a planned stop for this monumental and technological beast, the one and only, *Magnificent Lizzie*. This, I figured, could all be arranged by Ms. Day, though I hadn't discussed it with her yet. There was something inside me that said, *Don't ask her. Or, at least, don't ask her yet.*

Anyway, we arrived at the first of three stops in Mexico--Port of Lazaro Cardenez. Once docked, Jose and I shook hands and said "goodbye" to each other. As I watched him walk down the gangplank, escorted by Ms. Day, I felt sad, but... I was so glad that I didn't break down in tears! I was so done with that. It was time to man up. In fact, I almost felt like giving him a swift kick in the butt--to send him off! I would have then said, "Nice knowing ya, kid, now get lost." But... when it came right down to it, that would have been too extreme. Instead, I "allowed" myself to feel sad, but I emotionally held it together no problem.

Next, the craziest thing happened. As Jose disappeared, what looked like a dirty, long-legged, hairy chihuahua, ran up the gangplank. It let out only a couple barks and ran right by me. The three, armed security guards, who were exchanging an argumentative conversation off to the side, didn't even notice. The dog just took off and I saw him duck into a crevice between two large metallic containers.

I went hunting for that "mangy mutt"—those were my feelings at the time--for the next hour or so, but it was nowhere to be found.

The next dawn, I was woken up and summoned by Captain Howitzer. I jumped into a new outfit they had given me. It was all white. It also came with a shiny black belt and shiny black shoes and a shiny officer-style cap; though, it was plain. The whole effect is that it made me feel like an officer, even though there were no stripes, badges, nautical patches, or ship's logos—like the real officers had to one degree or another. Maybe what they gave me was the beginner of beginners ranking uniform, like having a white belt in martial arts. So, yeah, I was stoked! Now I was officially invited into the fold, even if unofficially!

Next thing I knew, Captain Howitzer was having me steer away from the dock and out of the port. I was able to further observe and then participate in the reversing and the throttling—a new first for me! I paid close attention to the instrument panels in front of me and even to the right and left of me. At the same time, I keenly listened to the words exchanged by the captain and his fellow officers. *Wow,* I was doing it. I have to admit and mention that the captain had his hand on the wheel much of the time but allowed me to take over because I listened to his crisp and detailed instructions. It was an unbelievable experience... but there was no way in *hell* that I was going to let him see me pinch my arm again. From here on out, I was going to stand erect, keep my chin up, bite down on my jaw, and sharpen my eyes like an eagle—a sea eagle.

I found out later while talking about it with Ms. Day, that "sea eagle" is the common name for a genus in the bird kingdom. She wrote down the name of the genus for me, "Haliaeetus." One of the species of these birds, for example, is the bald eagle, or, "Haliaeetus leucocephalus," which she also wrote down. Well guess what? From that point forward I decided I would just stick to common names! "Bald eagle" would be the bird for me... not that garbled-up gobbledygook. However, I will acknowledge that there's a place for that sort of language in the community of scientists. And while I have always appreciated scientific matters, I knew that I didn't have the IQ or passion to pursue it as a real interest. My interest was sailing and swimming and... well, come to think of it, I had discovered art and music along the way... and people... and traveling... and cultures... okay, for the first time I started to realize that I was a person, as young as I was, that was multi-faceted. Maybe a lot of individuals were of the same nature, but just had a different combination of interests or hobbies or sports or passions. Wow, the more I thought about it, the more it fascinated me--how *you* define who you are. Then I added the thought: *as long as it wasn't an offense to Sister Nelly.* Because she always seemed to know what pleased God... and what didn't.

As we got farther out in the ocean, Captain Howitzer relieved me of my duty, thanking me, and telling me that I did a "fine job." I sincerely thanked him in return but refrained from getting syrupy about it. Only kids do that. Indeed, I was starting to figure out this man business more and more. And it suited me fine. Very fine. That's right. When he said I did a "fine" job, I figured that "fine" was perhaps the finest word to use. From now on, I would be careful not to use words like "awesome" or "great" or "fantastic"—those words tended to make one sound like an exaggerator. And who wants that sort of image or reputation? Not me. I wanted to sound accurate and credible—like Captain Howitzer.

A day later as we were heading north along the coast of Mexico, I was having a fine lunch with Ms. Day. We were having a sophisticated conversation and I was feeling like I was on top of the world. I even told her how few men, such as myself, had the fine privilege to enjoy the fine intricacies of world cultures firsthand. That's when suddenly, she slammed down her fork that still had scrambled egg on it and accidentally knocked over her glass of water. She didn't flinch; instead, she just angrily looked me in the eyes and said, "What has gotten into you, Philip!"

"What do you mean?" I asked surprisingly.

"You have been putting on these airs like you're some sort of head honcho. Like you're the big man on campus, like you're... anyway, please get back to the way you were!" Then she got up and stormed out of the dining room. Some of the other shipmates at other tables sort of laughed or shrugged their shoulders and went on minding their own conversations.

Well, that was a big slap in my face. I realized that all this newfound manliness had taken over my usual personality. I was no longer the fun, light-hearted, nice guy anymore. Sure, even in my previous personality, I could be serious and... anyway, she was right of course, and I felt embarrassed. Somehow, I just needed to be me again. Indeed, it was okay to learn manly ways and, in some ways, start behaving as such, but maybe it needed to be a lot more gradual and natural. The transition to manhood, I quickly figured out, definitely shouldn't come across as contrived. And it certainly shouldn't turn a nice teenaged kid into a haughty jerk. The thought of that made me sick. Seasick. And I rarely had gotten seasick. God had somehow graced me with sea legs and a sound sense of balance in both body and brain. I went to my room and rested. While it made me feel less sick, I still couldn't get over the incident with Ms. Day.

When we happened to come across each other later in the hallway that evening, we practically both started to apologize at the same time. But I stopped her in her tracks and said, "No, I get it. You were right, Ms. Day. And I'm thankful that you put me in my place. I promise that I'll go back to my good-ol' self if you will forgive me." She smiled and gave me a hug. Wow, I loved the smell of her perfume. It wasn't strong, but just right. Anyway, we exchanged a few nice words and parted to our separate sleeping quarters. Another day had passed, partly restful and partly restless, but now it was time for a good night's rest. I must've stared out the porthole for two hours. I partly couldn't fall asleep because I had already rested for a couple hours in the afternoon. And it was partly because there was so much to think about. Looking at the surface of the ocean; however, always had a calming effect on me. Finally, I said a prayer and fell asleep.

A fog had set in during the middle of the night and the supertanker collided into a huge cargo carrier! There were explosions, and pandemonium, and people running all over the place. Captain Howitzer yelled out orders. One of the large metal containers slid and shoved three nurses overboard. I got into the emergency lifeboat and swung it around on a large cable, connected to huge chain-links, knocking out the smokestack of the other ship. Storm clouds showered down sheets of hail and lightning hit a very tall stack of pancakes in the kitchen. The pancakes flew out the window like they were flying saucers. One of the ship's officers was trying to make light of it all by telling everyone to stay calm and not panic. He even started doing jumping jacks on the bowsprit. Then, he started laughing his head off and punted a football which flew about fifty yards, right into the hands of Ms. Ruthy! She really didn't appreciate that, and thought it was insanely disrespectful. So, I just slid down the smokestack that had ocean water pouring into it. Somehow, I just couldn't slide fast enough even though I was pushing with my hands, trying to save the day. I hit an oil spot and dropped instantly into the flooded chamber. I submerged and struggled underwater, tumbling. I couldn't get out! I couldn't breathe! It was dark! I couldn't scream for help! Then I woke up.

I blinked a few times, wiped my eyes, rubbed my head, and looked out the porthole. It looked like the dawning of a new day. Wow, now that was a nightmare! Horrifying, but... strangely, I sort of wanted to drift back to sleep to try to figure out the missing pieces of the puzzle and to try to somehow rewrite its ending. But then I thought how silly that was. What's the point of figuring out or rewriting a dream when it's all just a non-sensical series of events, that don't really add up to anything. So, instead, I got up and decided to go for a jog on the deck, like I had done with Jose.

On my second lap, the dirty, long-legged, hairy chihuahua started running along with me. He looked like he was skinnier than before. He didn't bark and he didn't even look up at me. It was as if he was my new jogging buddy. *What a curious dog*, I thought. I didn't stop to pet it, because I wanted him to feel like there was nothing unusual about what he was doing. Instead, I very gradually slowed down and came to a stop. Then I sat down on a small wooden crate. He came right up to my ankle, sat down, and looked up at me with sad eyes. I petted him behind the ears and that made his tail wag a little.

Fast forward to a day later, we were heading into the Port of Manzanillo, Mexico, and I had made a new friend. I had fed him, gave him lots of water, bathed him with shampoo, combed him—this dog of mine looked great! And now we were on the forward deck looking out at the approaching commercial harbor.

When the captain and crew had found out about my new pet, and that I had named him, "Poncho," they were all okay by it. Lola Day thought he was just adorable. Pets were not allowed, but everyone was happy I had a friend to keep me company. Besides, even *I* was an exception to the ship's rules.

Ms. Day had me leash Poncho to a rail when Captain

Howitzer called me up again and had me steer the ship into the port... steer the ship into *the port*? What!

With the closest of scrutiny and directives, he even had me dock her! He had to take over as we got very close, but wow, this was my biggest "sailing" feat to date. I was all kid and all man wrapped up in one at that moment! Later in the evening, indeed, I got to thinking and finally figured out that aspect of myself. Being myself at this stage in my life was *all about* my transitional years. In my mind it was the best of both worlds. Boyhood? Manhood? No and no. I was somewhere right in between. Nice! It was great to come full circle and finally understand it like it was some sort of epiphany.

Fast forwarding, we spent days cruising north along Mexico; eventually Baja California was to our starboard. Our next destination was Ensenada. It felt like we were getting ever so close to home. My home. But I had to remind myself that these days wouldn't last forever, and that I had to enjoy the experience and learn as much as I could before it was all ended.

As we continued to move along the long coast of Baja California, a wooden ship came into view also at our starboard side. As we were slowly passing it, about a nautical mile away from us. Ms. Day looked at it through binoculars and then handed them to me.

She said, "It looks like a replica or near replica of Richard Henry Dana's brig that he had spent much of his *two years before the mast* and wrote about in a book by that name."

"I read it," I said.

"I love that book," she said. "It really captures that capsule in time."

Seeing that old-style, wooden ship, with its majestic sails was so heart-warming. Ms. Day explained that those ships were pretty common in the Pacific back in his day, which I had sort of gathered when I read the book; but, hearing it from her helped to reconfirm what I had learned. It was refreshing to see a visual representation of the past, especially when you consider that Baja California looked so much like old southern California in terms of land features and sparse vegetation.

A few hours later, we were hit by an unusual storm. It rained very hard, but we were all inside warm and cozy. Many of the shipmates were in raincoats on deck performing whatever storm duties they had, but this supertanker just pushed forward like it was nothing. Lightning could be seen on the mainland, which was spectacular to see, but it never made its way out to us. It was the best lightning show I had ever seen. Even an occasional spider web of lightning spread out for miles over the mainland. The thunder was loud, but in-the-distance loud, not like when I was in the middle of it all in the Atlantic—when thunder and lightning passed directly over my sloop!

When I explained that part of my journey to Ms. Day, she said that I was extremely lucky that a bolt didn't hit my mast and potentially even sink the boat from its damage. She told me that on an average annual basis that roughly one per thousand insured boat owners make a lightning claim. Finally, she said that *that* was the second reason why she would never consider sailing in the ocean in a small boat. When I asked her what her first reason was, she said, "Pirates."

"I never ran into that sort of trouble," I said.

"Well, you're lucky. Because they're out there," she said. "We're even trained on this ship how to deal with the different types of pirate encounters. Basically, just look at it as high-seas robbery. That's all it is. Criminals that prefer sea over land."

Without further ado, she said she had three videos on the subject matter. So, we watched those, and it really opened my eyes and gave me ideas as to what to do in the various circumstances. Every scenario, regardless, is sketchy and much of what you do relies on reading the situation or potential situation and assessing what the best matter of action is. Sometimes the best thing to do is nothing. For example, if a suspicious boat comes around, sometimes it's best to not act friendly and to not act unfriendly. Stay confidently neutral. Sometimes that's enough to psyche out the intruder, since he doesn't or they don't know what you're "made of," and it makes him or them go away.

Another day went by and we saw a pod of whales to port. Seeing the plumes was fascinating to me because in all the days I spent around Ventura and on this circumnavigational voyage, I had never recalled seeing a whale plume. Now, not only did I see them spouting away, I saw part of their upper bodies and tails. Looking through the binoculars, Ms. Day told me they were grey whales. Then, just as I was looking through her binoculars, one of them popped his head high in the air and splashed down. I waved at it excitedly, "Ahoy there! Hey! Hey you! Happy travels!" Ms. Day got a laugh out of that and also waved. Wow, amazing creatures. Just amazing. And what a day! What an awesome day! My favorite white puffy popcorn-like clouds were out, too!

And there was Poncho sitting inside a discarded cardboard box that was sitting up on its side. He looked happy and comfortable. "Come here, boy," I said. He ran up to me, jumped in my arms, and gave me a lick on the cheek. Poncho turned in my arms and then sat up and gave Ms. Day a surprise lick on the chin. She smiled and fluffed up his hairy head. I wish someone could have taken a picture of the three of us then. It was such an easy-going, supremely pleasant part of the trip.

CHAPTER 15

RITE OF PASSAGE?

Time continued to pass. It seemed like ever since we had left the Panama Canal, time flew--like a frigatebird! Minutes hurled themselves into hours and hours hurled themselves into days. Lots of things happened, some aforementioned—all in a flash—and next thing I knew, we were pulling into Ensenada, Baja California, Mexico.

Captain Howitzer invited me to do more maneuvering. He said I was getting better at it, but regardless, he absolutely couldn't let his guard down and needed to be right there with me, sometimes taking over a little bit—or a lot... or completely! There were also the other officers that were always assisting with controls and instruments. If I ever had any aspect of controlling the ship, it could be taken away from me in an instant, and often it was. That was the level of scrutiny and preciseness that Captain Howitzer demanded. There was no room for error with a vessel of this magnitude. If for example, one was to get into a fender bender with a car, it might run into the hundreds of dollars to fix it. A "fender bender" with this ship; however, Ms. Day had explained to me, would cost tens of millions of dollars.

Anyway, once docked, after lunch, Ms. Day announced to me that I had a visitor. A visitor? For me? We walked to the gangplank with Poncho on a leash. That's when we saw Jose Gomez come running up the long ramp with the biggest smile on his face. "Jose!" I called out to him. He ran up to me and we hugged like pals and jumped up and down, excited to see each other. Pancho was barking all the while. "What are you doing here!" I said excitedly.

Well, it turned out that news had leaked out to the world about my run-in with Jose and his boat. People just ate up the story and their excitement of my journey was reaching a fever pitch.

A wealthy businessman, Stuart Blacksmith, in San Diego made arrangements to have Jose, my new buddy, reunited with me to go on the Ensenada to San Diego leg of my journey. Indeed, the Port of San Diego was to be our next stop and Mr. Blacksmith wanted Jose and me to do a promotional photo shoot with his new soda product, "BestFree." It was going to be a new carbonated beverage that promised to be as refreshing as soda but also made with a variety of real fruit juices. The following were the three different flavors that consisted of real juice combinations all mixed with lemon-lime soda: Orange-Banana; Pineapple-Coconut; and Guava-Mango. I couldn't wait to try them!

Lola Day explained to me that I didn't have to do it, but that the shipping company and Captain Howitzer thought it was just fine, since San Diego was going to be a lengthy four-day stop. She said that even the shipping company and her sister companies thought it was very good publicity. So, I said, "Sure! Sounds fun!"

Then she added, "Oh, by the way, you and Jose are going to get paid fifty thousand dollars each, as long as you give the okay to allow them to have you in their advertising photos or videos. These could go nationwide and worldwide. In other words, welcome to the world of advertising."

"It's okay by me. Sounds real good," I said.

Jose was already on board with it, and I never saw a kid look so full of positive energy.

The rest of that day and the next, while at sea, we got back into our competitive regime with shuffleboard, darts, and running. It was good times. When Ms. Day challenged us at shuffleboard, she beat us handily. Apparently, she had that as a hidden talent up her sleeve and made us look like we were real novices at it. We were embarrassed and humiliated. But when we got over it, and it didn't take long, we realized it was all a part of the fun. Anyway, we didn't hesitate to give Ms. Day a handshake and acknowledge her easy victory.

That made me think a little later: *Wouldn't it be nice*

to marry a woman someday that had everything going for her like Lola Day.

Then I thought about Bella Sue. I thought about what a great girl she was. I thought about how she was the first girl I kissed and how nice she was to me. I thought... well, honestly, I thought, I had gotten over her. For whatever reason, I didn't think she was the one for me. I didn't think I had to run back to her arms and marry her. I felt a little bad, because at the time, I had a big crush on her and couldn't stop thinking about her. But enough time had passed, that I just didn't think about her anymore. I still had fond memories and could replay the brief and beautiful moments with her. However--and I didn't think I wanted to mention this--but here goes: I had noticed for weeks that she was somewhat of a flirt before she walked up to me at the big island party. I was amazed and love-stricken when we hit it off the way we did, and I wouldn't want to change any of that. It was super sweet. Anyway, after I had left Hawaii, I figured she wouldn't have any trouble finding someone else— maybe she already had. Regardless, and after factoring in everything, I now felt like the sort of girl that would be more up my alley would be someone like Lola Day. She was it! Too bad she was almost twice my age!

At dusk, with the peaceful Pacific Ocean all around us, I was going for a jog with Poncho on the enormous deck of *Magnificent Lizzie*; somehow, I could never quite get over the size of her. Amidst the tranquility, I found myself reflecting on this whole aspect of girls or ladies... and even life for that matter; well, this is what I came up with: *Life is meaningful and confusing at the same time, so just make the best of it!*

In the dining hall that night, I had a lively conversation with Jose, Ms. Day, and Hector Green, who was a totally cool service crew member on this ship that I had gotten to know. After a half hour went by, Ms. Day sort of cleared her throat, looking unusually nervous, and changed the course of the conversation. At that moment, as if urgently, even though she was keeping an even keel, she informed me that there was going to be a huge celebration for me upon our arrival in California. She explained how the news of the recent dramatic event, when Jose had sought me out so many miles out at sea and that I was the instrumental person in saving his life, that *that* really stirred the pot all over again. She threw in that my nineteenth birthday was going to be in ten days, a bit beyond the time of arrival but that this big event was going to celebrate my birthday anyway, along with everything else.

"This is craziness," I said. Actually, I was both astounded and confused at the same time.

Ms. Day continued to explain that when one prominent female news anchor had coined me, "The young man of adventure, heroism, and forgiveness," that *that* somehow hit the right chord with the world at large. Those three words set off an avalanche of commentary in all media and conversation in many households. Everyone following the story wanted to know of my whereabouts, my health, *all* the details of my journey since Spain, and if I was still on track with the planned rendezvous with my parents; this part of the story they were already well-acquainted with.

Now, I must mention that as Ms. Day was speaking, all the following literally flashed through my mind: First of all, all I could think was, *Wow.* Did everyone have the wrong person? What did I do exactly? I just felt like I was an ordinary guy just doing my thing. Heck, unashamedly and purposely, I was a bum not too long ago in Tasmania! I had lived in a tire igloo, that *I* had built, as a stowaway! I was a desert rat and wasn't very helpful at skinning the kill of the day, but I'd go ahead and eat it for supper! I had hidden in a dark cabinet, like a coward, crossing the Indian Ocean! And even in the grand and historic Mediterranean Sea, and I mean history that went back to ancient times of monumental occurrences, I was a janitor that cleaned out toilets! Well... I had explained all of this in previous interviews in Spain! I felt like I had always been transparent—*just tell it like it is*, was my motto. So, the news of this celebration of my arrival to California, which had something to do with my circumnavigating of the globe—which took between six and seven long years--was beyond my comprehension. This was no great feat. Anyone could buy a plane ticket or two and go around the world within a couple days! So, when it came right down to it, there wasn't a whole lot there. I wasn't anyone special.

With that said, somehow my mind still managed to filter that the news of this planned event really excited me. I felt important. I especially liked the part of *forgiveness*. If I had a message at all, I rejoiced that it was *forgiveness*! I pictured in my mind that Sister Nelly would be glad.

Anyway, while my brain was processing all this a nautical mile a minute, Ms. Day continued explaining that thousands of people, even from around the world, were expected to be at the Port of San Diego. This was shaping up to be a well-organized event with news people and celebrities and government officials and rock bands. I couldn't believe it.

She also added that I would have time to meet with many of my friends who awaited me at the hotel. These friends included Sister Nelly, Ms. Ruthy, some of my Hawaiian friends—family really--a handsome little kid from Kenya, a captain from Perth, a surgeon from Spain—and she said that with a wink--and someone that claimed he was my best friend, even though he had lost at Risk. She didn't know what to make of that, but I waved my hand and my mouth sort of dropped halfway open... I gulped... my heart pounded and thumped with joy. As much as I hate to say it, I fought back tears. This was all overwhelming to me.

I was dumbstruck and overjoyed all in one fell swoop.

The excitement was building, and I could even feel it in the lively wind that afternoon—not that this monstrous ship without sails needed it, but... *my sloop sure would have enjoyed it*, I thought.

And that's when my heart leapt a little. Suddenly, I realized I hadn't given much thought about my little boat. Her mast had been lowered and a heavy-duty blue tarp had been wrapped around her. She had then been wedged in between two large metallic containers. These containers were designated to be delivered somewhere in Canada, so I was to get her back when I was dropped off in Ventura.

Next thing I knew, I walked up to her with Poncho on a leash. I raised up one corner of the tarp and put my hand on the hull, just to feel it. I said, "Thank you, Feliz Sails, for all that you did. We shall sail again."

I started to consider the possibility of sailing from San Diego to Ventura. I had gotten a great deal of experience on this large ship, already. But now I had a longing once again to be back in my little boat and to feel the wind fill her sails.

In bed that night, I thought about the big day that was planned for tomorrow. I thought about the crowds, the planned celebrations, my friends, and everything else. And then I thought about my new plan, how nice it was going to be to get back on *Feliz Sails*, and to have the company of Poncho. I would set sail from San Diego on my sloop, head up to Ventura, and arrive just on time as my parents would have at that point been released from prison. I wouldn't be weeks ahead of schedule, as it was looking like it would be the case if I stayed on *Magnificent Lizzie*. Wow, there was so much to look forward to.

Dawn arrived. I looked around and made sure

everything seemed normal and that I wasn't dreaming. I had come to realize that normal everyday things don't happen a whole lot in dreams. I even jumped out of bed and looked out the porthole. Indeed, it was a pretty plain ocean. Nothing spectacular was happening like World War II bombers nosediving into its waters into the mouths of whales. Haha, I guess I've had a lot of really wild and bizarre dreams. Anyway, currently, I knew for certain I was not in a dream! It was a new day and one full of new possibilities!

In a jiffy, I met Jose and Ms. Day for a quick breakfast in the dining hall. The ship was starting its turn toward the Port of San Diego, but it was still many nautical miles off in the distance. Curiously, it seemed like it had slowed down somewhat. Maybe we were ahead of schedule. I had learned that everything runs on tight schedules in ports with oil tankers—arrivals and departures. Ms. Day was unusually quiet. The few words exchanged were mostly Ms. Day translating between Jose and me. Anyway, we were eating and all the while, secretly, I was hoping to get the call. That's why I was already in my plain but sharp-looking uniform.

And... I did! Captain Howitzer radioed Ms. Day and sure enough, I was being called up to the ship's bridge. Ms. Day, who was looking like an international model but in a conservative, maritime style, escorted me to the tower elevator and up to the ship's bridge.

This time, however, she directed me to sit down off

to the far side of the room. I sat with her at a small table with two chairs on each side of it. We could see Captain Howitzer, who glanced over at me with a serious look, and his fellow officers all doing their thing as they steered the ship toward its new destination—not the final one, but a destination.

Ms. Day said to me, "Philip, I have good news for you, and I have sad news, too. Very sad."

That worried me. What could the sad news be? "What is it?" I asked.

She took my hands with both of hers, which she had never done before, and looked at me so peacefully, being very hesitant about saying whatever it was that she wanted to say. It was like looking at an older sister. That thought had never occurred to me. There was something in her look that even reminded me of... of my real mother. A surprise flashback occurred in that instant that took me all the way back to when I was only three years old. I was sitting by the Christmas tree, and my parents lovingly helped me open a package: it was a firetruck! Ms. Day didn't look anything like my real mother, but the expression she gave me, did! In the flashback, I saw that my parents were quite young and happy. My father was handsome, and my mother looked beautiful and saintly. I hugged them and my dad lifted me up in his arms. *After all these years, why did I recall this now?*

"The good news is," Ms. Day then said breaking the silence, "is that your parents continued to hear of all that you've been doing and were absolutely overjoyed. They wanted to send you their love and words of joy, but they had bigger plans for you. They wanted to be in San Diego as you arrived. They were released from prison a month ago for good behavior and wanted to throw a surprise party for you on a huge scale. And that's when they really got the ball rolling."

"Really?" I said with a heavy breath.

Then there was a long pause. Ms. Day's eyes were starting to look glassy, but she held it together.

"Philip, I'm sorry to report that your mother had a stroke a week ago and was put into intensive care."

"Oh no," I gasped.

"Everyone was hoping that it was a mild stroke and that she would get better, but it took a turn for the worse and, after having her on life support for a day... she died last night."

"Oh no," I was stunned and didn't know what to make of it.

Then Ms. Day said, "Your father who expressed how proud he was of you..." then she started to get choked up. "I'm sorry, Philip." She moved in and put her arms around me.

"What?" is all that came out of my mouth.

She continued while holding onto me, "He was in very poor health while in prison and actually got worse when he got out. He complained of severe muscle soreness and headaches. When he was present at the hospital when your mother died, he then walked out to the parking lot... and... had a heart at-tack." Her arms around my shoulders tightened, as she continued, "A doctor, who saw him as he was passing by, quickly came to his aid. He said that your father's last dying words were, 'Tell Philip we love him. Don't let this stop his party.' Ms. Day broke down in tears and held onto me. I was shocked be-yond belief. I didn't know what to think. I couldn't believe that I wasn't crying myself. *Why did this hap-pen?*

Then, Captain Howitzer had an officer take over the wheel and he walked over to me. He stood there for a while looking down at me with his big earnest eyes. He said, "Philip, my condolences. I am truly, truly, truly sorry to hear of this news." He got teary eyed.

He stood there and I sat there with Lola Day—her arms still around me, comforting me in my sorrow. There was a reverent quietness for about a minute.

"Now, my son," Captain Howitzer said. "I sum-moned you up here to take a hold of that wheel and steer this ship into the harbor. You deserve the honor. You deserve the honor on behalf of your parents, from this shipping company, and... from *me* personally." Tears were now rolling down the captain's cheeks. He held his hand out to me and, slowly, I took it.

I slowly got up out of my seat, feeling extremely dizzy. He steadied me and we stood there for another minute, his arm around my shoulder. Then, he slowly began to walk me toward the helm of the supertanker. As I walked side by side with him, ever so slowly toward the steering wheel, the room was slowly spinning around me. Emotions were spinning in my head, the world was spinning in my head, all that had happened in the last six or so years was spinning in my head...

I could see the Japanese kite maker and how he, poetically, lifted his creations into the sky... then I saw the cop who lifted me up off the Australian beach.... I could see the three sisters of Africa... then I saw the lady interrogator in the Holy Land.... I could see the two guys who lifted me out of my sailing dinghy.... I kept being lifted. People kept lifting me up... that man who took me up in the plane... the couple that pulled me out of the burning car, but instead of falling to the asphalt, interestingly, they lifted me up! The room kept slowly spinning. I saw that old man-- the old salt of the desert. I saw his wry smile and twinkle in his eye. I saw the Mediterranean cruise ship lady, moving up the cruise ship gangplank, waving goodbye to me. I saw my African schoolmaster. I saw all sorts of kids and all sorts of people in all sorts of lands and buildings.... Then I was in that holy garden--it was drizzling—and, out of the mist, Jesus approached me. As he reached out with one arm and lifted the palm of his hand upward, my feet lifted from the ground. But where was I really? I could see ship's officers. I could see Captain Howitzer, though he was the only one in the eye of my slow-motion emotional hurricane. It was me... and it was him... and one foot... was leading the other.

But when the officer at the helm stepped aside, I

started to come out of my deep emotional spell. The captain reached over, took my left hand, and put it on the wheel, then he did the same with my right hand. It was all respectful like. In some ways it felt like I was in the middle of a ceremony. I couldn't quite figure things out.

After a long moment of silence, I felt that the more I gripped onto the ship's wheel, the more I came back to my normal senses. Then I looked over at the captain, standing off to my right side. All I could remember is that I must have had a look of sincerity. He put his left hand on my right shoulder and just looked at me like the father figure he was.

"Bring her in," he said quietly. Then, after another moment of silence, he said it again a little more loudly and firmly, "Bring her in, helmsman."

Then, I knew...

Then, I *knew*.

That's when everything came into focus.

Things weren't spinning anymore.

Amazingly, my body and my brain and my spirit started to snap into order.

It was as if the storm clouds cleared, and it was open blue skies. I could see things more clearly than ever.

I wiped some tears away with the back of my hand.

I looked around at the mighty ocean and the approaching port, now just two miles away. I looked at the real sky, not the figurative one, and it was gray and overcast, but glory be to God, that was okay by me! Sister Nelly used to say things like that, and it was always comforting and encouraging.

Then I saw seven pelicans fly by, in perfect formation, skimming the ocean surface.

At that moment, I stood just a little taller; and that's when I stood realizing the earnest responsibility that was gracefully granted to me.

I then said with:

pride...

thanksgiving...

and confidence...

"Aye aye, captain."

LAILAMINDI THE MERMAID

I went down to the beach at dawn and headed south toward the point, which was essentially land some one hundred fifty feet above sea level, meeting the edge of the Pacific Ocean. In other words, it's where one found narrow stretches at sea level, usually rocky, but some parts sandy, to walk along the base of these massive cliffs or bluffs.

It was going to be a warm day in May 1979. The only thing I could think of was to hike around the rocky bluff and enter that secret cove. So secret, that I did not ever discuss its location--not the name of the beach or its town or even the state. Though, anyone who knew me could have likely at least guessed one of two counties of the secret cove's whereabouts. Except that I never even mentioned the cove to anybody... that's, not until now.

It didn't seem like the cove could be so secret because it only took less than fifteen minutes to hike from the beach to the big rock blocking the way. However, the beach was not very frequented except by a handful of local surfers and the occasional walkers, joggers, or good old-fashioned beachcombers.

Getting to the cove on foot required hiking about a hundred yards on the very rough rocks. Since the rocks were difficult to walk on with bare feet and there was that one big rock that had to be climbed over, I never once saw a person anywhere in or near the cove. I enjoyed being barefooted and didn't care much for sandals. So, my feet had toughened up and I actually enjoyed walking and climbing on the rocks.

As summer would eventually roll in, the beach did get a little busy on the weekends. But this was a Tuesday in May. There was one surfer just getting into the water and a couple strolling off in the distance down the beach. It felt like, once again, I was going to have the cove, that was completely out of site from the beach, all to myself.

Being eighteen, I was somewhat of a minimalist. I only wore a white tank top and bathing suit. I brought fins, mask, and snorkel, that I kept slung on a thin nylon rope over my shoulder. The articles hung over and lightly banged about my back. I liked the overall feel of it.

I brought no food or water. I had a pretty big breakfast in the morning and drank a lot of orange juice-- that routine always seemed enough to last me several hours or even all day. My energy derived from soaking in the sun, splashing around in the ocean, and diving amidst the kelp. Ah yes, the kelp was a heaven-on-earth to me. Under the water and swimming in and out of that dull-green wilderness was the means for me to forget all worries and really *feel* life. Just seeing the varieties of fish dart around, small or big, opaque or flashy looking, didn't matter to me. I just meditated on the tranquility of floating and diving and swimming. I mostly liked the motions of swimming underwater. The sheer freedom of it was refreshing and exhilarating.

Climbing up and over the big rock seemed pretty easy to me, even barefooted, but I could imagine that it could be quite difficult for the everyday person or kid. Besides, I was a mean, lean, fighting machine. And when I said that, I meant it literally. I got into four or five fights in any given school year. I always tried to avoid them to the best of my ability; however, I would still get into them—fist fights.

On one occasion a few years back, for example, a junior was picking on a sophomore at my high school. Clearly, the former had the advantage in physique. Also clear was that he was just being a flat-out bully. I stepped in, a fellow sophomore but not knowing either one, just to break it up. I even had a pretty soft-hearted voice. Since I was at six-foot even, the junior had three inches on me. He attempted to shove me aside three times, but it was on that third time, I wrestled him to the ground and punched him in the cheek very hard. He immediately gave up, yelling out, "Okay, stop! I was just playing around!"

I thought, *wow, that was easy*. I punched him in the cheek because I wasn't of the nature to want to break a nose or damage an eye or take out a tooth—though even a punch to the cheek could potentially break a jaw, so I even hated that as a target. I just always wanted to effectively end a bad situation. Was I the best fighter around? No. I had lost one out of every three of them. When I lost, it was not that I gave up, it just somehow got broken up. As for me, I didn't quit. But it was a good thing when the losing fights did get broken up; otherwise, in some situations, I'd get beaten to a pulp. Some guys were ruthless.

The last two times, in fact, my girlfriend--a beautiful gymnast--was the one who jumped in and broke up the brawl. When she sprained her wrist on the second occasion, that was it. The next day, she told me her parents were furious, and... she went ahead and broke up with me. Sad, but that's what happened. I was miserable all the last month about it but was just beginning to get over it.

Anyway, as I had started climbing up that 20-foot rock that blocked the way to the cove, the handholds got extremely thin, so much so, that I felt like I was practically hanging on my fingernails for the last five feet. I must confess that it had always felt devilishly scary up there. When it came down to it, I could see why I never saw anybody in that cove for the dozen times I had visited it in the course of four years. I mean, I never once saw *anyone* in this dream world, which always amazed me since it was so close to civilization.

Well, this was the first time on this big rock that I slipped and fell back some twenty feet, slamming against the jagged rocks, maybe busting some ribs, slashing my right side, and landing into the crashing sea in a backflipping motion. I gulped up sea water, flailed around since the waves were big that day, but managed to grab onto the nearest rock. I jumped onto my feet with the push of some whitewash. In those moments that lasted under a minute, I wasn't in any sort of a panic whatsoever as I had body surfed my whole life, well, since I was six. The abrasions on my side were somewhat red, somewhat bleeding, but it was only superficial.

This was my playground: The sand, the rocks, and the ocean. I really loved all the elements of body-surfing especially the crashing of waves, the stroking of arms, the kicking of feet, the negotiating of bodily position, bobbing up and down, tumbling underwater, holding my breath--I lived for that stuff.

I climbed back up and over that twenty-foot rock with a vengeance despite that my hands were wet and slippery. I think it had to do with grabbing the right little protrusions and finding the slightest footholds in the right order. Besides, it was muscle memory since I had done it successfully on so many previous occasions. I guess it just went to show that one can eventually get a little careless with too much confidence.

When I went over that rock and downclimbed it, I felt the incredible delight of having that cove all to myself, once again.

I looked up at the clear sky with distant, feathery clouds, and absorbed the scent and beauty of the sea.

Several seagulls flew off and two cormorants stood on a nearby ledge on the other end of the cove, which was only three-hundred feet long, arching inward.

There was only a twenty-foot band of sand from one end to the other and the backdrop was steep bluff, unclimbable. Many smaller boulders, rocks, and pebbles were strewn in clusters and individually. In fact, oftentimes, I found myself picking up a little rock or seashell just observing all its mini intricacies. Nature never ceased to amaze me, and I always felt myself lost in it.

Just as I was putting on my mask, fins, and snorkel, I glanced up and saw the back end of a pretty big fish tail slip back into the water. It was a split fin joined up at a bottleneck. I had never seen a fish that big in that cove. Also, it was strange, but it didn't seem like an ordinary fish. It looked like the tail of a mermaid, but I knew how ridiculous that sounded. Still it was bewildering and enchanting and I savored the moment. It wasn't a sunset. It wasn't a dream. It was just an ordinary day. Still morning. But what I thought I had just seen sent shivers up and down my body.

Three hours went by. I was snorkeling and really enjoying life.

When I came up for air after going through an underwater sea cave--one only fifteen-feet long that I had been in many times--I enjoyed the up and down ride of what I called "the sea elevator." I was in the middle of a big flat sea rock, shaped somewhat like a donut. Indeed, there was a hole in the middle of it. As the tide ebbed, I took the elevator down for the fifth time, held my breath, and went back through the underwater cave. When I came up for air, blowing the water out of my snorkel, I looked around and saw a lone sailboat close to the horizon. How peaceful I thought. Even though it was close to midday, the boat looked like a silhouette. It must have been the angle of the sun and distant clouds dimming the light where the boat was located that made it a very peaceful effect.

Then I looked over my left shoulder for I sensed movement. And that's when I saw a mermaid sitting on the far end of the cove, near the cormorants that were now flying off.

A mermaid? In a way I didn't think too much of it because I thought it must've been a young lady in some sort of mermaid get-up. I was surprised to see anyone in the cove. I had never seen anyone in this cove before other than about three times in the past I had seen scuba divers just doing their thing, but they entered the waters from a boat about a hundred yards out.

So, I didn't stare at the costumed girl; she must have swum in a northerly direction from the other end of the point.

I snorkeled off in the other direction as if I didn't notice. I was a little embarrassed. Indeed, I felt embarrassed. I wanted to just swim around, outside the cove, and head back to the beach, snorkeling.

Then I heard a squeal that sounded like a seal, or a whale, or, I wasn't sure. I hadn't heard that exact sound before--it was higher pitched. I turned around with mask and snorkel barely sticking out of the water. That's when I saw the mermaid jump back into the ocean. She disappeared. I was impressed that this person in costume could hold her breath for so long. A whole minute went by, then two minutes, and there wasn't a trace of her. I couldn't see how she could have possibly vanished. It would take her at least a few minutes swimming underwater if she were trying to exit the cove heading back from where I thought she came from. If she were heading toward me, same thing, it would take several minutes of holding her breath. I kept my eyes peeled to see if she came up for air, but there was no sign of her whatsoever.

I started to worry. Maybe she was drowning, caught in the kelp or snagged on an underwater rock. *Now*, I thought, *I must not hesitate a second longer and go rescue her.*

I had taken several classes in junior lifeguard training; and, well... this was my first opportunity to put those lessons to work.

I found myself swimming frantically toward the far end of the cove. I was worried that I was going to be too worn out by the time I got to her. I was afraid that if I did find her, she might inadvertently pull me under. I just kept swimming and when I got to the other end, I dove underwater. Normally, I could hold my breath for thirty seconds to a minute. However, I was so worn out from the swim that I was amazed how I couldn't hold my breath for more than ten seconds.

Furthermore, this girl or lady in mermaid costume was nowhere to be seen. I dove under a dozen times in different spots, looking all around, and all I could see was the usual kelp, rocks, fish, and sandy bottom that

I was already well-acquainted with.

I rested on a rock, gasping for air. I was exhausted and became even more worried. I had failed in my first life-saving mission. Maybe I should have become a junior lifeguard after all so that I could know what to do in this situation. I was angry and scared and sad all at the same time. Where was this mermaid girl!

Where was this beautiful... yes, beautiful... *mermaid*?

I thought I had better hightail it to civilization and call for emergency help. But as I started to run along the beach, I couldn't help but to feel how futile it was. It would take me thirty minutes at best to reach someone. Then, it would take another thirty minutes to an hour before help arrived at the scene. I kept running toward the big rock that I would have to climb over, but thought the whole situation seemed hopeless.

Then, she popped up through the donut-hole sea rock and sat at the edge of the hole.

I yelled, "Where did you go! Are you okay!"

She waved her left arm at me and smiled. Her long, wet, flowing, dark-blond hair fell over her shoulders and back all the way down to her waist. The lower part of her body, all fish-like simply sat on the rock—like a woman sitting on a chair with a long dress. It all looked so real. What an amazing costume! And what an amazing swimmer to go with it! She looked my age!

I waved back and smiled. She jumped back in the hole. When the tide flowed, the sea rose up to the level of the rock and she waved again. Then as the tide ebbed, she went back down.

I swam out to the rock with my mask, fins, and snorkel. It took me two minutes to get out there, then I held my breath, dove underwater, swam through the fifteen-foot long cave, and popped up for air in the hole. As the water rose, I quickly sat up on the rock, sitting opposite of the mermaid, only about six feet away!

And that's when I was blown away. If this was a costume, it was unbelievably real looking. Her face and upper part of her body looked human, sort of, but from the waist down it was a seamless transition of what looked genuinely scaly and shiny, like that of a real fish.

Still, there was something about her face and body that didn't look exactly human. It looked primitive, but it looked beautiful. She was beautiful. She looked at me with her mysterious green eyes and didn't say a word. She made the slightest squeal sound and it felt like she was starting to hypnotize me with her gaze.

"Hello," I said.

She held her hand out to me. I reached out and our fingertips barely touched. Strangely, I felt like we were instantly attracted to each other, like love at first sight. My heart was pounding, and I could almost sense that hers was too. I felt like I was being carried away into another realm. The sea, the lapping and crashing of the small waves, the light breeze, the sound of a couple seals on a buoy a half mile away, but most of all, looking into her tranquil eyes and the sweetness of her face.

"What's your name?" I asked.

Instead of going down the hole in the middle of the flat sea rock, she rolled sideways over it toward the horizon and fell into the sea.

There was a brief moment of what seemed liked nothingness—a minute passed--then with amazing speed, she popped up and swam two laps around the rock, even jumped twice in and out of the water like a dolphin. I couldn't believe what I was seeing. I couldn't believe it. This was no person. This was a mermaid. A real mermaid. I was astonished.

I looked around to see if anyone was watching. There wasn't a person in sight. I felt like I had stumbled upon a treasure that I didn't want anyone else to see or discover. If word were to get out that there was a mermaid in these waters, that would be it. Her life would be in peril and this cove would never be a secret again. My whole new wonderous world would be destroyed.

But now what? She popped up the hole again and sat on the rock, now a quarter distance closer to me. Indeed, she now didn't sit across from me; instead, she had come in a quarter of the circumference of the hole and now sat only three feet away. She reached her left hand out toward me and we held hands. She looked both timid and confident at the same time, if that's even possible.

"Can you speak at all? Do you understand me?" I asked politely.

"Lailamindi," she said softly.

"Is that your name? Lailamindi?"

She made a very soft squeal sound. Then she looked a little embarrassed. I looked sincerely in her eyes and gently touched her cheek. She scooted closer still looking into my eyes in the most mesmerizing way. We got very close and as if by instinct, she looked even deeper into my eyes. Again, it was hypnotizing. I was absorbing every second of it. I wanted it to last forever.

She looked a bit sad but also a bit happy. The emotion in me was a deep purple. I wasn't sure what that meant, but I liked it immensely. And, I felt like I was a mirror of whatever her emotion was. It was profound and earnest, and it went outside the boundaries of time. I was lost in time. The only thing for me was the right here and now, with her, at that moment.

Then she slid into the hole and disappeared. She popped out near the exit of the underwater cave and waved. It looked like a wave of goodbye. I waved back halfheartedly. Then she dove back underwater and swam off toward the horizon, jumping in and out of the water like a dolphin one last time as she headed out.

That was it. That was the last time I saw her.

I have been to the secret cove a dozen times in the last five years and she never came back.

Meantime, I had eventually found a regular mainland-style human female that I became very fond of. She got me into horses and going to church functions. We got married last year and we already have a kid on the way. We're soon going to move to Texas. I never told her about Lailamindi. She would have never believed me and besides, she was the jealous type. It only would have made her angry and she only would have taken me as some sort of weirdo. I didn't need that. That's for sure.

When three years had gone by since the day that I met Lailamindi, that's about the time I met my wife-to-be, and... it was also when I soon after got over my emotional attachment to that mystical sea creature, lovely as she was.

Anyway, it was a precious memory, but... I got over it, and now I can honestly say that I *do* believe in mermaids. I don't have any idea what they're all about, but when it comes right down to it, maybe the same thing can be said about females in general, human or otherwise.

PIRATE SKULL

A hoy there! Now this be a treacherous tale. Arrr, this be an ugly one at that. You've seen the cust'mary skull and crossbones flag, have ye? Well, every time I see that skull, it has a whole different meaning. Jolly? No, I don't think so.

This here story be not for the weak at heart. You there, if yer a lad or lassie, go into another room or go outside and play!

You have been warned. Savvy? Not running a rig here, so I'm going to wait now for several seconds, because sometimes that's all there be to make up yer mind... especially for an ol' seadog like me. An' if you want to know the truth, since I'm just a grumpy old man, I prefer thinking of myself as a big ol' rusty lobster.

Ready to set sail?

Onwards then!

Fifty-two years ago, the year 1722, 'twas a balmy January day in the Caribbean. A mutiny had unfolded. Our pirate cap'n, Cap'n Fiddlestealth, just got his head--well, how should I put this politely--anyway, it was *off* with his head. I hated any sort of punishment to any sort of person for any sort of reason, so I turned my head and closed my eyes when it happened. I did hear the chop. Then one of the crew, Henry Crimson, said out loud, "Would you look at that. All that red wine he drank today now looks like a fount'n." It got a few chuckles and after a moment of silence, everyone applauded and cheered. Not me though.

To reflect on what had *just* happened: Cap'n Fiddlestealth had been tied to the main mast and was tried by his rebellious crew. And I, an English lad of nineteen years of age, was a part o' it. I had been on the ship for just a tad over a year. 'Twas a trial of spontaneous words. But they were words of truth for certain. This cap'n was cruel, dog-headed, and just plain too harsh. For weeks, "Death to him," had become the quiet call... the quiet call by all. An' that's when the biggest man o' the crew, Henry Crimson, volunteered to be the ex'cutioner. And soon after, that's when the captain's lights went out for good.

And, just for a li'l further reflection on the event, keel hauling Cap'n Fiddlestealth wouldn't have been the right punishment lest we be hypocrites. He had keel hauled many o' the crew, twelve in all, in the last year, for insubordination and other crimes unbecoming to the cap'n. To be keel hauled was a torture not one of ye would ever want to endure. As any one of you might be aware, keel hauling be tying up the mate, pushing him over the starboard side of the ship, and dragging him under her belly, barnacles and all, and back up to her port side. This would be done repeatedly until the young mate or old seadog be scraped up beyond repair and drowned. Twice he had mates walk the plank, plunging into the middle of the sea, and three times he used decapitation measures. He found new recruits from the very ships and towns we raided, as crazy as that sounds.

Anyway, once the guilt of Cap'n Fiddlestealth was easily and gleefully confirmed, without further ado, he got *his* punishment. So, at the time, it was "cheers," an' a big swallow of rum. Then, an' I only saw it in the corner of my eye since I was tending to the bowline that his body was thrown overboard in the same manner that he had done to those he had punished. I just shook my head and felt a little sorry for him, even though he had been such a wicked captain.

Alas, now I admit, that I had put myself in the company of evil-spirited men. I was a young fool for certain! Our sea rover, the best pirate ship ever, *Serpente Linda* was her name, raided other ships, and we also raided small island communities—some native, some civilized. We raided whatever we might, all to get for ourselves the booty. Booty be gold, jewelry, wine, rum, muskets and ammunition, canon balls for sure, swords and daggers, food and rations, lemons to prevent the scurvy, water, clothes, an' all sorts o' other trinkets.

We'd be kind to women and children, though, and always rounded them up an' kept an eye on them until we sailed off. For the men who surrendered, which were often the case, ahh, we didn't bring harm to them neither. We only killed when men fought back. That was the crew's moral code if you'll permit me saying so, though now I see the wrongness in all of it.

Cap'n Fiddlestealth didn't care for moral codes but he went along with the crew on this aspect, just to keep what little order there was. Also, we made sure that for the many people we spared, we left them plenty of their own food and goods to survive in comfort.

After our heinous victories of pillaging a sea town or winning a prize, we would then, at the end of the exhausting day, drink wine and rum, laugh out loud, sing sea songs, frolic around the island or prize we captured, and just have one hellish time. The prize? Yea, that would be another ship, pirate or otherwise. We had lots of tricks up our sleeves and masts, but we had no friends in the Caribbean. Ours was the life of the long past days of the buccaneer. And one grand ol' time it were, if ye can call it that. Indeed, we were *one bad bunch of buccaneers.*

Alas, as for me I no longer feel that way 'bout it all. Indeed, I now feel great shame and I might repent a thousand times and a thousand times moreover. For the pirate's life isn't for me. 'Twas a long, long time ago. I became old. As each year marched on beyond my wild-eyed youth, I came to realize the harsh evil of it all, ye see. But, once again, I have fallen into the trap of melancholy. So never mind that for now!

After our mission of plunder, whichever one of many in our miserable history, we'd weigh anchor and head for the distant mysteries of the next horizon. 'Twas one new adventure after the other. Call it good, call it bad, but adventure it were to be, an' we just threw our fighting fists with the wind, or into it.

At dusk or even into the night, our call out to

the stars—which gradually turned into a chant—was, "Head banging, canon balls, Devil go to bed! Drink mates, tonight! For tomorrow, you'll be dead!"

The cook came up with those words on one drunken night an' for some reason, don't ask me why, it stuck with the crew. Then we'd break into singing. On a few occasions, one, two, or three of the drunks dared to dance along with a song but he was always laughed at, mocked, and kicked off the deck. As silly as it were for us grown men, 'twas some of the heartiest laughs back then. Ye can't understand it unless ye were there.

But I shall no longer divert course from this tale that I aim to tell.

We thought 'twas high tide to bury the overage of our treasure on a very small uncharted island. We had treasure coming out our portholes—our spoils of war if ye will. So, we just dug eight feet down and threw the treasure in as a big pile. We called this island, *W Island*... "W" for Wonderful. This would serve as our reserve of funds in case our ship were ever taken. Henry Crimson then threw in a small canvas bag with something in it--on top of the pile, before we buried it. I had wondered what it was, but it could've been anything and I thought it be best that I mind my own business, 'specially with the ex'cutioner.

We, the crew that is, had decided not to put this booty in chests because we needed our eleven chests for the treasure kept aboard *Serpente Linda*. The treasure we buried was merely the leftovers, but still a small fortune no doubt. Prob'ly would have filled four, maybe five chests!

On a side note, during all the digging down to make a hole big enough for the treasure, I snuck off a hundred feet away and relieved myself of water and rum. It went down a curious hole in the ground, about two-feet wide. It was like a monstrous rabbit hole. And strangely, I felt cool air coming up from it, like it were some sort of vent. Then I noticed several more of them down the way, some even bigger, but a mate spotted me and told me to get my arse over there an' help out! Never sweated so much in my life, digging that hole in the rocky dirt, after all that cutting and blazing of a trail getting' there.

Now as far as accounting goes, and as it were explained by our good-ol' cap'n, our buried treasure consisted of over two thousand pieces of eight, two hundred pounds of gold bars, bundles of silver coins of all sorts, other foreign coins by a couple bushels, mostly Spanish and French, and probably a hundred pounds of jewelry an' trinkets. Thrown all together, it looked like rubbish! A tangled dung heap of rubbish! *Keep it buried* was my thought at the time. *We had our eleven chests an' that were plenty!* Maybe we best aim our sails back to England and just blend back in with our motherland--with our riches, of course. An' call it quits whilst we be ahead. But it just didn't happen that way. Life sometimes don't happen in the course of events in any way you expect it to.

Hear me this lesson if ye don't hear anything else: Don't get y'rself on a-ship o' thieves or with anyone that even slightly resembles 'em. It only leads to an endless whirlpool of sin an' broken dreams. An' you'll likely die begging or screaming for mercy for one reason or another. Only it'll be too late.

An' one more bit o' advice I came up with myself: Never trust a coxswain with rum on his breath, lest ye want to be on the next shipwreck! Har-har, and here's just one more for ye! I learnt this the hard way more than once. Here it is, my own words of wisdom: Respect girls and ladies with all yer heart, and listen to their thoughtful comments and rebukes. For without 'em, boys and men are nothing but dirt dogs and mischief-makers.

But I have diverted, so back to my true tale, and I swear it on my future grave, the treasure spot 'twas at the base of a rocky cliff, where we were standing 'proximately fifty to a hundred feet above sea level. Indeed, this part of the island leading up to the base of the cliffs was quite flat, however, on the way we did go up and over a few large mounds—where we discovered hot springs! Oh goody! This island must've had plenty o' water in its bowels. But we'd go up them mounds and right back down them, so until we got to the base of the cliffs which veered off all the way back to the sea, it didn't really seem like there were much of any high ground, unless you wanted to climb up those steep and jagged rocks. And there was no reason for that.

Arrgh, and to even describe it further where we decided to bury all that treasure, we had to cut through a big swath of heavy veg'tation and palm trees, maybe not quite a mile long. I never sweated so much in me entire life. Insect bites o' every kind. One matey got bitten by a snake and died an hour later, another sprained his ankle in a hole an' we made him a cane in about a minute, another two o' our crew got a mean red rash on their arms and faces. All nasty going. We all did indeed cut through it, though, with blade and song. But just try singing a song when you're getting bitten to death. No jolly holiday, if ye know what I'm saying.

Aside from that, this tiny little uncharted island had nice little beaches. An' it had cliffs that quietly laughed and cried at the sea. The whole feeling was ebb and flow in a good ol' way. It was a pleasant island. Ye can't imagine such a peaceful and lovely lil' paradise. Light blue sea. Sweet waves of tranquility. Swaying palms of the long-neck variety. The best sunset I ever seen as we hoisted up anchor and sailed off. Well, I live for that moment. That moment was the seed that brought me back to my sanity and what little goodness were left in me.

A map was drawn by the boatswain who happened to have that artistic touch. Our newly-elected cap'n, Cap'n Brownstone, made him to draw up four maps all exactly the same—one for himself, one for the cox-swain, one for his right-hand man, who was the most liked among the crew--a Caribbean native with the name of "Gogogo"--and the fourth map was for the cook. The cook ye might ask? Aye, Cap'n Brownstone thought that cook made the best seafood in the world and that he be the most humorous man in the world to boot. Cap'n Brownstone swore that the cook was the best man he ever knew. Giving him the map was an expression of his loy'lty. As for the boatswain, he didn't draw one up for himself since he said he'd have it all mem'rized.

Cap'n Brownstone ordered all these identical twin maps—quadruplets if you will--be made so that at least one of these selected men, hopefully, with fellow mates, would someday make it back to W Island and reclaim the loot. He captivated our attention and explained to us that maybe those who made it back, could start a civilized island township. But, he added, one that would know how to protect itself against the likes of us! When Cap'n Brownstone explained that last part, we all got one belly full of good humor out of it.

Sadly though, it also put us in our place--scum of the seven seas. Ahh, I wince at the thought of it. We were robbing and killing men, in the mix o' bad men of course, that seemed to be minding their own island existence. 'Twas one thing to attack a fellow pirate ship, you know, in the same dirty-dog business as us, but attacking settlers or other regular folk, now that was just plain bad. Alas... an' that were us. We didn't engage in battle when it was clear that there be no booty or rations to get our grubby hands on. An' we did spare those who didn't fight back or just plain surrendered. Indeedy, we just let the minnows go and there be many o' them. Just like in the belly of the ocean—no dif'rent really.

Avast, keep the next part of this tale secret and I mean batten down yer own hatches, partic'ly yer latch. That means yer mouth! An' mind ye, this tale be not one of the tall varieties. Therefore, listen to me careful now. Arrr, please do pay close 'tension to its details.

So much time had passed. So much plundering and high-sea events had passed. But us pirates under the command of Cap'n Brownstone found that our luck had finally run out when two Spanish galleons come sailing along, prob'ly having hunted us down. Well it was a bloody sea battle like none I ever known. 'Twas deadlier than sin itself. An' punishment was finally dished out to our shipmates, according to the Bible as far as I was concerned. I'm not one to pull out a quote, but let's face it, the good book sayeth that the wicked shall payeth for their evil deeds. I even remember me mum telling me *that*, when I was a fine five-year old lad. How I ever got into bad company and bad habits as a teenager continues to be a mist'ry to me this day.

Anyway, *Serpente Linda*, Cap'n Brownstone with her, an' all but four of the entire crew was sent to the bottom of the sea. Arrgh, the Caribbean Sea. I wonder if Davy Jones Locker is real. If it is, sounds scary enough, but if it be a myth, oh go stuff it in a giant clam! I hate sup'stitions and myths 'specially when I'm giving a real account of a tale--as in a real story, and *not* the tail of a whale.

Anyhow, why God spared *me*--one of the four mates that escaped--I don't know. 'Twas me, Gogogo, and two others of the crew, "One-eye" and George Tanner.

During the battle, there was so much mast and crossbeam and sail blasted to pieces this way an' that way, that through all the gun fire, canon blasts, cut-lass clanking, groaning, screaming, sabre clinking, yelling, gore, fire, and commotion we somehow were able to lower a boat and row off in the same direction of the drifting smoke. We just paddled as fast as we might, taking our turns with two sets of oars.

Besides that, we figured that both remaining gal-leons were afloat but so severely crippled with not many sailors left alive on them, that even if any o' them got a glimpse of us, they couldn't catch us. No way, no how.

Anyway, 'twas a good piece of providence that Go-gogo grabbed his treasure map, 'cause we had no idea where that W Island lay in this wide open sea. The whole idea o' the map was not so much to pinpoint the treasure spot on the island; no, we knew where to go once we got to the island. Instead, the map pointed out the right longitude and latitude an' navigational points of interest. It also showed the location of the treasure with the standard X, which we got a chuckle out of. How can ye forget the carving out of all them plants and trees? How can ye forget the cliffs and how they arched a bit right where we dug our hole? So, ye hear what I'm saying? We just needed to get our hands on a sextant, compass, some shovels, and lar-ger boat--large enough to haul away the treasure once we got back to it.

Instead of having all those items, though, the four of us were lost at sea in the rowboat! Gogogo and George Tanner navigated the boat in a westerly direc-tion, if I remember correctly, primarily by looking at the stars at night and not fighting the current. But we had no idea if it would get us to an island. We really had no exact point of ref'rence if ye get what I'm trying to say. In other words, blast it if we weren't lost! And hungry! And thirsty! And sunburnt! And feeling sicker and sicker as the days progressed. After four days, mostly drifting, since we gave up on rowing after the first two hours, George Tanner died. Then One-eye died on the seventh day. Then Gogogo and I just about died on the eighth day, but then through the uplifting of a very small squall, we saw a rainbow, and by great providence, shortly after, got picked up by one of our own class, a pirate ship. 'Twas even waving at us with the blackjack—that sinister black flag with the white skull and crossbones. Funny thing was, looking back at our recent hist'ry, we never hoisted a blackjack up the mast of *Serpente Linda*, since we were always about being as sneaky as pos'ble.

Can you "beerlieve" it that some stupid-drunk pirates even started lifting the flag that be called the *Jolly Roger*! A smiling skull and crossbones? Oh, how cute and how funny. Really? Who was the inspired dimwit who came up with that! Ye might as well put up a mocking-like sign that proclaims, "Here's a target for your canon fire! Now come sink our ship!" No-no, those of us of the *Serpente Linda*--an' may she rest on the sea floor in peace--were slick and inconspicuous as eels.

When Gogogo and I woke up in a cabin with bunk beds, the crew gave us water, fed us, and of course, wanted to know all about the map. This went on for two days as they nursed us back to life. Then on the third morning the cap'n stepped in. He was Cap'n Ruckmaster. He was an' ol' barnacle, but he talked a tough game. He demanded that we tell him all about the map and I mean everything about it, or that we'd each be placed over a canon and made into shark bait.

So, Gogogo and I just took one look at each other and knew that we better wholly co-op'rate and parley without trick'ry. And I made one condition though, in front of the cap'n and a dozen of his crew, that the deal be struck only that we, Gogogo and me, be a part of the sharing of the booty, equally amongst all the men.

Well, Cap'n Ruckmaster agreed except he said he himself would get six times the portion of everyone else, since he be the cap'n. All agreed and passed around a jug of rum to one another. When ye look at the situation, they *had* to agree! 'Twas that or mutiny. An' mutinies sometimes be just too plain complicated to organize. Instead, all were in good spirits. Pirates, aye, they're a bad lot, indeed, but they can be orderly when need be.

Now finding W Island? There wasn't much to it. Just eight days getting there. An' Cap'n Ruckmaster made Gogogo and me scrub the deck, batten down the hatches--not figur'tively--and shine all the rigging 'round the clock like we were his personal slaves. Funny thing be and maybe it weren't so funny, we were in hot pursuit by two British warship frigates as we arrived into the island cove, a large cove, almost a bay.

An' so 'twas dusk when they commenced firing

away at us. Their first three canon shots to show us some disrespect put a couple holes in our mizzen sail, but even worse, one of 'em took out our bowsprit! 'Twas the sort of nose punch that enraged cap'n and crew and thus the brutal battle of these sea beasts begat.

And now, this is one of my proudest parts o' the story; that being, Gogogo and myself repeated our previous escape! I suppose ye can say that we got pretty good at it! We were real escape artists an' I still pat myself on the shoulder for that with a big smile on my face. Once again, we lowered the lil' boat during the heat o' the engagement and rowed off. However, we were clever enough this time to grab several jugs of water, a bottle of rum, a bag full of grub, a sword, an' two shovels. The cap'n had the map that he took from us hidden away for certain, but we no longer needed it anyway! When I mentioned this to Gogogo, we got a chuckle out of it. How we hoped that map would go down with cap'n Ruckmaster's ship! We didn't even know her name nor cared to know.

We rowed away with the drifting smoke just like the first time, except now the angry sea kept kicking up big waves. Our lil' rowboat took in much o' that salty water and we were struggling to keep her afloat, even bailing her out with our oars. An' all o' a sudden, we caught a big wave. We then fell backwards on our arses and the wave crashed with a tremendous roar! We nearly bounced out, but by some sort o' miracle held on for our dear lives. The tumbling white wash of the wave pushed us several hundred feet an' guided us, not by our steering, mind ye--'cause we had no control of her whatsoever--right into a sea cave.

"Jolly jumping jellyfish, a sea cave!" I cried out and listened to the almighty echo. It even had its own little beach about two hundred feet inside it, which is where the water calmed, an' we landed. "Yo, ho, ho!" I yelled with excitement and, again, listened to the deep and distant echo with delight. Gogogo sort of looked at me with that hushed look. I got the hint an' decided we should keep our hideout on the down low.

Gogogo and me were quite glad that we made it alive. We could see that this cave with some sort of sea stream went farther and farther back but it had gotten too dark to explore. We could still hear the muffled sound of the crashing surf outside the cave an' the 'casional canon blast, but then there was a long lull as we just sat an' listened for prob'ly less than an hour. So, just as it were getting pitch black, we just pulled the boat as high up the pebbly and rocky beach, up against the rock wall, and, dead tired, fell asleep on each side of the rowboat.

An' on a side note, I had the best dream in my life that night. I simply spread my arms out and was able to fly. I skimmed the white caps of the ocean; I skimmed the rocky shoreline; I skimmed along both bluff and field; I flew high above island forts; I scooped down across their towered fort'fications made of block; I flew under canon and over musket —all blasting and firing away; I flew atop the ship's crow's nest, then dove down and hovered over her deck; then I flapped my arms and went high into the clouds and got lost in them; an' all o'sudden lightning an' hail; then I barely escaped a bolt and flew around the moon an' back. Imagine that! The moon! Then I coughed 'cause I was choking on some grains o' sand, and I woke up. I woke up! A dream! How disappointed was I. But, oh, what a beautiful dream. Oh, how I wish it were all real to this day.

Anyhow, back to the story. It was dawn and I woke up to the cave's sea water lapping at my heels. Gogogo was already awake an' chewing on some grub. The tide had gotten much higher! We had probably arrived at low tide when there was just a big pool of water, however, even then it had appeared that this pool was just the head of what appeared to be a sea stream, if you can call it that, which kept moving deeper into the cave. That fascinated me, 'cause I gathered from my observation, then and now, that it didn't matter if the tide were high or low--that this island's cave always seemed to be thirsty and just continued to gulp in the sea water no matter what the tide was up to! Currently, now that we had woke up, it looked like a much bigger pool and we only had about ten feet of rocky embankment left. It was a good thing that Gogogo and me found high ground when we had gone to sleep.

Soon after, we jumped in our rowboat and begat to paddling farther back into the cave, really, a bon'fide sea cavern! We paddled for a hundred yards or so an' it started to get dark, then we plummeted down a ten-foot waterfall at an angle. What a thrill it were! We were now coasting along and light shined through holes in the ceiling of this magnificent cave. Holes that were every hundred feet or so. Apparently, the ceiling of the cave, some twenty to sixty feet high depending on where ye were, was close to the surface of the island. So, sunlight spilled in hither and thither an' offered highlights to the cavities of the sea cave or cavern, whatever ye might call it, that otherwise could never have been seen without a torch—which we had not.

Coming around a bend we went down another waterfall that was much longer than the previous one, but also at an' an angle. It even had a bend in it. The wind whooshing by my ears and my belly dropping made for a sensation like no other. But you'd have to experience it for yerselves to know what I'm talking about.

So, after going deeper and deeper into this sea cave, we came across some treasure just sprawled out on its embankments. Ah, no big deal, just some good ol' fashioned... What! Treasure!

Wow, W Island was the place that just kept giving!

Gogogo and me looked at each other an' didn't know whether to giggle with glee or shed tears of delight. I suppose, we were just dumbfounded.

The cave still kept on going deeper, but we landed our rowboat and decided to step out and take a closer look. Try to imagine being in treasure heaven. Ye probably can't. But what were we to do! We had no way of hauling out all this treasure. An' where would we go with it! Imagine being rich beyond yer wildest dreams but having no way, at least no immediate way, to make good with it.

An' aside from all this, we still had the treasure to dig up at the base of the cliffs--another cache of booty!

What a big problem this was indeed!

Anyway, we decided to keep exploring. After all, we were bored with our riches, apparently, an' wanted to know what was around the next bend in this deep dark sea cave—though, again, we could see highlights of it as light spilled in from a variety of holes in the ceiling. So, we drifted with the slow an' calm current. Occasionally we heard whispers. Was it the wind whistling through the ceiling holes or was it the ghosts o' this dreary place. Well, I say that in jest, ye see. Gogogo an' me didn't believe in ghosts an' we didn't find the place dreary at all. We were over-whelmed with the coolness of the cave and its fascin-ating features.

There were even places in the cave or call it a cavern that had these long, pointed rocks coming down from the ceiling and nearly meeting up with its match down below. Looked like teeth of a shark, both the upper and lower teeth.

Anyway, after going for what seemed to be a mile or so, we came to a very large area of the cave—perhaps a hundred-foot high ceiling, an' there was a small hole of sunlight beaming from the top of it. Well, that light pointed right down into our little sea stream where there was deposited yet another large pile of treasure! An' oh how it shined where the sunlight hit it!

Lo an' behold! And 'twas just twenty feet in front

of us. It was the treasure we had buried! Evidently, it had eventually fallen through the thin ceiling. I suppose the ceiling was thicker in areas and thinner in dif'rent spots. 'Cause hell's bells, we had only buried our little treasure trove, har-har-har, only eight feet down--all righty, maybe 'twas ten! It's not like we carried around a measuring rod. All I got in my head is memory and estimation, for all I know, a foot in my mind may have grown to one an' a half. Or perhaps, a foot had shrunk down to eight inches. I'm just trying to relay what truly and really happened without exaggerating none. This is not some sort of big fish story mind ye!

The cavern wall next to the creek must have extended all the way up and out into the world where it became the cliffs. Or you can figure the cliffs went into the earth and became the walls of the cavern.

Anyway, Gogogo an' me recognized our buried loot an' some of the trinkets right away. We started to drift right over it. Some of it was spilled over on each side of the embankment. Then to our astonishment, we saw a human skull on the sandy bottom just beyond the rich rubbish. There was still a hint of hair on top, an' fragments of beard at the chin an' cheek bones. Hmm... I thought. Looked familiar. Then I saw the small canvas bag, that Henry Crimson had thrown on the treasure pile, up on the embankment. This was none other than the skull of Cap'n Fiddlestealth! Just as I thought that, a small crab crawled out of one of his eye sockets. Several other crabs were about underwater and on the treasure. Suddenly, two seagulls fluttered off downstream.

But what a way to go! To find yerself, in the end, just a skull. Amongst your own booty. In the dark crevices of a sea cavern. Underwater. Forgotten in time. I don't know, maybe, knowing his character, he would've wanted it that way.

Curiously, the part of the stream flowing downward forked off into a cave that only had a one-foot ceiling. The water went into that pocket and simply disappeared. The only thing I could figure, when I later contemplated it, was that it was supplying the island with spring water after all the salt be filtered out of it. Anyway, the other part of the fork went upstream. So, there we were: turning back would be upstream, an' if we kept going, that would be upstream, too, with a very mild current. Apparently, the Cap'n's skull found itself on the lowest part of the sea cave.

Well, deciding to just let the skull be, Gogogo and me loaded up what we could in the rowboat, which wasn't a lot, an' then just kept going. It took a lot of paddling an' a many, many hours a-going. It was all a mild upstream current, but we eventually found the route out, after being misled by two dead ends. What a joy it was to be back on a beach again, an' on another part of the island.

Then, we were stranded on W Island for five years, but that's another story an' a good one at that! I'll save that one for a rainy day. Anyway, when we were discovered by an Irish ship an' crew, all friendly, they took us back to where would you think? That's right. Ireland!

To make a long story short, we shared our treasure discoveries with all those on that ship; though, we left some of the trove behind for other explorers, since the Irish crew thought it be bad luck to greedily take it all. We all became the best of good mateys. And in Ireland, Gogogo and me bought a big fabulous cottage together. We each got married to fine ladies a year later and then went our separate ways.

I gave most of my wealth to the poor. My wife and me for many years helped clean up the grounds of the church, became expert gardeners, an' helped out at all o' the festivals and events.

I once pleaded with the government to send me to prison or hang me or do anything of the sort for my offences to innocent folks in my pirate days. Instead, they just forgive me an' told me to be all that is good.

That was very kindhearted. That's showing mercy. That's the sort of material that now appeals to me most. Not treasure here on Earth, but all the treasure stored up in heaven by kindness, char'table giving, and good works.

My dearly beloved wife died five years ago. She's buried in the boneyard behind the church. I have a reserved plot right next to her. I know I'm going to die soon. But, in the meantime, I must share joy to all that cross my path. A smile, a handshake, a telling o' my story. Whatever it takes. I wrote this short verse when I was pondering one evening. It goes like this:

"Live short or live long, sayeth me. But do it for the Creator o' our land and sea."

So, finally... to cap off this tale... as for Cap'n Fiddlestealth—and I cannot help but to think o' his skull at the bottom of the cavern stream since even the Irish left it there, saying that the cavern was just as good a tomb as any—well, I dearly forgive him, and I pray for his soul.

With a moment of silence then, indeed, a moment of respectful silence...

I hoist up this bottle with my good right arm:

Cheers to ye all, an' a sip o' rum.

QUOTES RELATING TO THE SEA
FROM FAVORITE AUTHORS

There are no foreign lands. It is the traveler only who is foreign.
   --Robert Louis Stevenson

Twenty years from now you will be more disappointed by the things that you didn't do than by the ones you did do. So throw off the bowlines. Sail away for the safe harbor. Catch the trade winds in your sails. Explore! Dream! Discover!
   --Mark Twain

Four hoarse blasts of a ship's whistle still raise the hair on my neck and set my feet to tapping.
   --John Steinbeck

All loose things seem to drift down to the sea, and so did I.
   --Louis L'Amour

From the first time I ventured from the shore in a boat, I felt that my spirit was touched.
   --Steven Callahan

Life's a voyage that's homeward bound.
--Herman Melville

He always thought of the sea as "la mar" which is what people call her in Spanish when they love her.
--Ernest Hemingway

There is no prettier sight in the world than a full-rigged, clipper-built brig, sailing sharp on the wind.
--Richard Henry Dana, Jr.

We don't understand who we are until we see what we can do.
--Martha Grimes... the renowned detective fiction author and my favorite teacher at Johns Hopkins University (JHU).

Speaking of that, a special thanks to President (at the time) Steven Muller, JHU, who was instrumental in spearheading my scholarship. He passed away 2013. Prayers and blessings.

Psalm 95:5 *The sea is His for it was He who made it, And His hand formed the dry land.*
--David

James 1:6 *But he must ask in faith without any doubting, for the one who doubts is like the surf of the sea, driven and tossed by the wind.*
--James

Shipwrecked sailor. Poor wretch. Folks living along the coast take pity on a shipwrecked sailor and take him in and feed him.
--B. Traven

I saw the Cloud, though I did not foresee the Storm.

--Daniel Defoe

Don't press your luck in unsuitable weather. Do the necessary things around the house, when it rains and storms.

On calm days, and perhaps when the full moon accompanies the quiet sea, the time is ripe for visiting friends. Get your boat, set sails, and visit other places. The chores around your house and property will wait for another day.

--Carl M. Heinz Wiebach (commenting on island living in his book, *Escape from Rat-Race*)

Favorite Maritime Music

This motley list is not necessarily in order of favorites since different music fits better with different occasions:

Jaws soundtrack by John Williams

The main theme of *Castaway by* Alan Anthony Silvestri

Bands: The Beach Boys, The Ventures, and The Lively Ones

La Mer by Claude Debussy

Instrumental island or oceanic music

Traditional sea songs and shanties

Music artists: Yanni and David Arkenstone

The soundtrack of *The Spy Who Loved Me*, for a unique adventurous and nautical mix

The soundtracks of surf movies are generally good to excellent. Three favorites: *Endless Summer, Big Wednesday, Step Into Liquid*

Chill or new age music of an aquatic nature

The following sea songs:

Day-o and *Jamaica Farewell* by Harry Belefonte

Redemption Song by Bob Marley

Red Sails in the Sunset, by Hugh Williams and Jimmy Kennedy

The Ocean and *Down by the Seaside* by Led Zeppelin

Under the Boardwalk recorded by The Drifters

Pirates and *Take A Pebble* by Emerson, Lake & Palmer

Pipeline by The Chantays

Underwater by Midnight Oil

Uncle Albert/Admiral Halsey by Paul and Linda McCartney

Yellow Submarine and *Octopus's Garden* by The Beatles

One Tree Hill by U2

And You and I <u>and</u> *Don't Kill the Whale* by Yes

Rock Lobster by The B-52s

Calypso by John Denver

Sailing by Christopher Cross

On the Border by Al Stewart

Beyond the Sea by Bobby Darin

Dock of the Bay by Otis Redding

ABOUT THE AUTHOR

From 1982 to 1985, Gregory L. Kinney (Kinney) went to San Diego State University (SDSU). His primary focus of study was art, writing, and film. His regular favorite surf spots near the campus were Sunset Cliffs, Ocean Beach, especially near the pier, where he enjoyed riding waves through the piles, and... of course, Baja California, Mexico (too many misc. spots to name).

While at SDSU, he wrote a three-volume series and roleplaying game, *World Action and Adventure*. At the time, those types of games were very popular and he sold the product and books nationwide. Kinney points out that this only happened through the enthusiastic interest, help in all aspects, and financial support of a renowned person in the business and corporate world... none other than Marjorie Kinney-- his wonderful mother!

Indeed, Kinney always endeavors to give credit where credit is due. In a nutshell, he likes to acknowledge and remember all that have helped him on his life's journey. In return, he likes to help others.

Back to his time at SDSU, five departments awarded him a total of 15 units of credits for writing the books. Those departments were: English, Sociology, Zoology, Psychology, and Multi-cultural Education.

While at SDSU, he was featured in two newspapers, the campus newspaper and the Orange County Register. He was also invited as a guest on Sun Up San Diego (TV) and won a nationwide "Search for the Adventurous Man" contest, put on by Daniel Hechter Suits (Paris).

From 1986 to 1988, Kinney accepted a full-tuition academic scholarship and attended Johns Hopkins University (JHU). He graduated with a Bachelor of Arts degree in Writing Seminars.

Kinney emphasizes that the classes were all terrific. Two memorable ones, for example, were Playwriting, taught by Pulitzer Prize winner, Edward Albee; and, Advanced Videography, where Kinney was one of two students that had access to the video editing room in the Baltimore Stadium. His final video was that of Baltimore's Inner Harbor.

In 1989, Kinney married his college sweetheart, Rosemarie. She graduated JHU in '88 as well with a Bachelor of Science degree in Nursing.

From 1989 to 2019, Kinney wrote eleven screenplays and was involved with many creative projects and outdoor activities, mostly of the adventurous varieties. During that time, they raised six children of their own--two daughters and four sons. For six and a half of those years, they lived on a two and a half acre ranch in Diamond Valley, California, and had four horses among many other animals.

While the introduction of this book mostly covers ocean-related activities...

Kinney, as a rockclimber, climbed a few routes on the 900 to 1,000-foot face of Tahquitz in Idyllwild, California. As a runner, he ran the OC Marathon in 2016. As a backpacker, he has trekked through the Sierras, hit the trails for two weeks in Glacier National Park, crossing into Canada, and summited Mt. San Jacinto, Mt. San Gorgonio, Mt. San Antonio (Baldy), and Mt. Whitney--all in California.

His oldest brother was very influential of all the above, since he had not only climbed Tahquitz regularly, but also had climbed the face of Half Dome in Yosemite and had gone on a very long backpacking trip across the Sierras. Furthermore, of recent years, he had run many marathons.

As an ice hockey player, and having been captain of several teams, Kinney has continued to enjoy winning some... and losing some. "But," he hesitates before saying, "there's nothing quite like winning the division championship when it happens."

In 2019, as mentioned in the introduction of this book, Kinney's trip on the cruise ship from San Pedro to Catalina to Ensenada, Mexico, and back, inspired him to write this book... it was the sort of book that he had looked for in libraries and bookstores, but couldn't find.

In 2020, Kinney published *The Spectacular Sea: 7 Sea Stories*.

Kinney's interests not already mentioned: drums and percussion, singing, art, music, chess, travel, horsemanship, nature, photography, camping, skiing, etc .

FOOD FOR THOUGHT BY THE AUTHOR

1. Make the best of each situation, no matter how sad, no matter how confusing, no matter how difficult, no matter how dangerous.

2. Be thankful, regularly and often, for all that is good.

3. Think of how you can give to others--gift, assistance, or encouragement.

4. There's a time for pleasure, for work, for rest, for prayer, and a whole lot of stuff in between.

5. Do all that you can to have a meaningful life, and try your best to enjoy it!

6. During your time off, relax and set your worries aside.

7. It's a daily effort to make a difference in the world that will make it a better place for all.

8. Letters... words... sentences... paragraphs... chapters... stories... other written material front and back end... makes a book. Consider writing one!

9. Have fun--whenever you can. Also have quiet and reflective times--whenever you can.

10. Go out there and make a splash--into the sea if possible!

Conclusion

Be like a lighthouse,
stand out like its height.
Be bold... be helpful...
be the light.
--G.L.K.

Please give a review! It would be greatly appreciated if you, the reader, posted a rating and perhaps even a review (that can be a few words or a detailed analysis) on a website such as any or all of the following:

1. amazon.com/books

2. www.hotsandpublishing.net

3. goodreads.com

The author sincerely thanks you in advance!

Made in the USA
Columbia, SC
21 July 2021

42106796R00200